Cowboy and the CONVICT

JANICE WHITEAKER

CHAPTER ONE
JANIE

"YOU HAVE GOT to be kidding me." Janie glared out the back door of The Baking Rack to find her newly acquired, small-town nemesis down on one knee. His current position had nothing to do with romantic inclinations—the thought of any man considering such a prospect was almost laughable—but was for a much more infuriating, and equally ridiculous, reason.

Almost as if he could sense the scowl she directed his way, Officer Peters lifted his head, squinting across the lot, hazel eyes coming to land directly on where she stood. In what was likely an effort to antagonize her even more, he had the audacity to shoot her a smile. The kind that might have gotten her heart racing a few years ago, but now only had her molars grinding together.

"Hey there." His eyes followed her as she stalked his way. "Got a call about some broken glass in this lot, and while I was checking everyone's tires, I couldn't help but notice yours are a little bald." He dusted off his hands as he stood, the act taking an asinine amount of time because of his stupidly tall height.

How did the man even find uniforms that fit? Between the length of his legs and the broadness of his shoulders, Peters probably had to have the things custom made so they didn't come halfway up his shins and cut off the circulation to his arms.

Digging the tips of her fingers into her burning eyes, Janie attempted to rub away the exhaustion that had been with her so long it was now more of a personality trait than anything. "We talked about this, Peters." She gave up trying to soothe her irritated corneas and let both arms drop. "I'm a grown woman and I don't need you lecturing me about car maintenance."

The cop who was the bane of her existence braced both hands against his hips, lifting his eyes skyward as if he was the one who should be irritated. "I'm not lecturing. I'm simply mentioning an issue you might not have noticed."

It was the same argument he tried to make every time their paths crossed. Because every time their paths crossed, he couldn't stop himself from pointing out how epically she was failing at adulthood.

Spoiler alert: she already fucking knew.

"I don't need you to *mention* shit to me, Peters." Janie crammed one hand into her purse, digging around for the keys that would save her from this situation. Standing here arguing wasn't going to do either of them any good. At this point, if anyone was going to benefit, it would've already happened. So far, the only thing it accomplished was making her dread the sight of his cruiser.

Which was a shame, because under different circumstances, she might have enjoyed watching Peters going about his business. The man could sure as hell fill out a uniform.

He could also sure as hell induce rage, which took all the fun out of admiring his physique and always managed to ruin her day.

That's why, the second her fingers closed around the fob, she whipped it out, shoving a thumb against the unlock button so she wouldn't have to wait for it to automatically engage when she reached her door.

"I'm not lecturing." Peters raked one hand through his dark, slightly graying, hair. "I'm just pointing something out to you." He swung one arm in the direction of a pickup truck a few spaces down. "The same way I'm gonna tell Brett Pace he's got an oil leak."

She snorted. "I'm sure he'll appreciate it."

If she didn't want to get away from Peters and his judgmental tone so badly, she might even stick around to see how that worked out for him. But that would leave him plenty of time to pick apart everything else she was doing wrong, and then she might have to kill him.

So she made a beeline for her car, continuing to jab the unlock button with escalating intensity. It'd been finicky lately, so she hadn't panicked when the locks didn't click right open, but now that she was closing in and the things still weren't unlatching, her stomach was starting to clench. She couldn't be stranded here in a parking lot with him. Especially not if it was due to deferred fucking maintenance. Peters would never let her hear the end of it.

She decided to switch tactics, trying to sound casual when she said, "I'm sure you have much more important things to do, so feel free to move along."

But Officer Peters didn't budge from where he stood beside her front tire. He just watched as she kept pushing that fucking button, not saying a word. His silence was almost as bad as his lectures. She might not hear him voice how disappointing he found her existence, but it was still there. Hanging in the air like smoke from a poorly lit fire. Thick and choking and determined to follow her wherever she went.

But he couldn't stay silent forever. Not when there was a lack to shine a light on. "Seems like the battery's out in your fob."

It took every ounce of willpower she possessed not to chuck the useless piece of technology at him. "Thanks, Captain Obvious." Janie spun on one heel, intending to put as much distance as she could between herself and the small-town cop who insisted on making her life more fucking frustrating than it already was.

But—in a completely unsurprising move—Peters followed her, his long legs easily catching up. "Where in the hell are you going?"

Why did *he* sound exasperated? She wasn't the one bothering him.

"None of your business." Janie picked up the pace,

knowing it was pointless, but it would cut down on the time she was forced to endure his presence.

She was just beginning to jog when Peters stepped right in her path, using his substantial size to cut her off. She tried to sidestep him, but it was no use. If she went left, so did he. And for as big as he was, the guy was fast on his feet.

Peters assumed his normal stance, bracing both hands on his hips as he stared down at her. "Have I done something to upset you?"

She laughed, because it was a ridiculous fucking question. "Are you kidding?"

Peters' brows pinched together in what seemed to be genuine confusion. "No. It just seems like you're mad at me, and I'm not sure why."

Could he really be that dense? "Everything you do pisses me off, Peters."

"I'm just trying to help." He dug back into the same excuse he used every time. Hiding his love of humiliating her behind the guise of assistance.

It was a tactic she was way too familiar with. One that had been used against her since she was born, and one she decided long ago never to tolerate again. "I don't need your fucking help."

His jaw clenched, rocking side to side as he stared her down. She lifted her chin, glaring right back as the seconds ticked past. Eventually, he stepped out of her path, holding one arm out to indicate she could go on her way.

And that was exactly what she did. Without

hesitation and without looking back, Janie went right back to her speeding steps, unable to fully breathe until she rounded the front corner of The Baking Rack, putting her out of Peters' sight.

And him out of hers.

After taking a few steadying breaths, she started walking again, stewing more with each step.

How could a man be so completely clueless about how aggravating he was? It simply wasn't possible, which meant Peters knew exactly how annoying his actions were. Knew how much his constant picking chapped her ass. He just didn't care.

Or maybe—like some other people she knew—he thrived on breaking her down. Got his kicks out of feeling superior. The possibility was a solid reason she did her best to get away from him as fast as she could whenever their paths crossed. Because at some point, she was going to snap. And snapping on him would cause a whole host of new problems in her life.

Like needing to call her bail money bitch and attending court dates.

The thought had her moving a little faster to put as much distance between them as possible. Just in case. She'd made a slew of bad decisions in her life and didn't need the temptation of adding that one to her list.

Luckily, downtown Moss Creek was quiet as she booked it down the sidewalk, aiming for the most likely place to stock a solution to her problem.

One of her problems.

Hopefully, the convenience-type store a few doors

down from the bakery carried the button-style battery her fob required. She could run in, grab what she needed, and be on her merry fucking way.

And Officer Peters could kiss her ass.

She was moving so fast—intent on staying the hell away from Peters— that when her palms hit the bar on the mini mart's door, she continued her forward momentum.

Even though the damn thing was locked.

Like a freaking idiot, she face-planted right into the glass, leaving a smudge of what was probably frosting where her forehead made aggressive contact. Stumbling back, she lifted one hand to her temple, the dull thud of the collision still ringing through her head.

Or maybe that was a concussion talking.

"Fucking ow." She gingerly felt across her skin and hairline. After pulling her palm away and not finding blood, she took a tentative step toward the glass, peering into the darkened shop. "They can't be serious." She checked her watch. *Tried* to check her watch. The face was black because she'd forgotten to set it on the charger before bed. Again.

It was yet another failure Peters would love to add to his little list. At this point that notebook he carried in his pocket was probably filled from front to back with them. It was probably what he read at night, sitting in his perfect little house, with his perfect little children, smirking smugly at his superior adulting skills.

"Motherfucker." She leaned forward, this time purposefully letting her forehead hit the glass as she closed her eyes and took a slow, deep breath. She could figure this out. No way was she going to let Peters catch her failing again.

Once the initial surge of frustration had dissipated slightly, she turned to look up and down the street, gauging who in town was most likely to have the battery she needed. And who was least likely to judge her for letting it run out in the first place.

Amelie's art studio was her top choice. While Amelie was now happily married with the cutest little baby, she had initially come to Moss Creek for a fresh start after making a few bad decisions of her own. Janie made a beeline for the storefront, hoping against hope the young mother would be there. The odds were against her, but it was worth a shot.

As she expected, the inside of the studio was dark, forcing her to take another calming breath as she regrouped. "Strike one."

Turning back to face the street, Janie went directly for option two—The Creekery. Paige, the owner and full-time bartender, would definitely be there. Whether she'd have a battery or not was anyone's guess.

Striding into the bar, Janie blinked a few times as her eyes acclimated to the dim lighting. Once she had a clear view, it was easy enough to sidle up to the bar and wait for Paige to notice her. It didn't take long. Paige shot her a grin, abandoning the old cowboy who'd likely been monopolizing her time to head Janie's way. "Hey, lady. What are you doing here?"

She and Paige were friendly. It was one of the

things that made Moss Creek so different from other places she'd lived before. Somehow, the small Montana town seemed to miraculously escape the cattiness that plagued every other part of the universe. The women around town—including the ones over eighty—were essentially one big group of friends. A girl gang of sorts.

But while they all appeared friendly and supportive and accepting on the surface, she wasn't stupid enough to believe that's how it genuinely was. Even if they didn't say it or show it, these women had to be judging each other.

Had to be judging *her*. And honestly, she couldn't blame them. She judged herself.

Daily.

"I just discovered the fob for my car is out of batteries." She lifted the offending item and gave it a wiggle. "You don't have any button batteries hanging around, do you?"

It was a stretch, but Paige was one of the most put-together women she'd ever met. The chick had the game of life down to a science. She owned a business, a house, a nice car. And didn't fuck with men.

She was brilliant.

Paige's smile fell. "I don't have anything like that here. Did you try the general store?"

She'd been around the block enough times that her hopes hadn't been up, so finding out Paige didn't have what she needed came as no surprise. "I went there first. They're already closed."

"Of course they are." Paige shook her head. "I know it sucks to stay open longer hours, but damn."

The bartender tipped her head to one side, eyes widening. "Wait a second." Her bright smile from earlier returned as she spun away and hustled down the bar. After digging around under the counter for a few seconds, she came back, a fob dangling from her hand. "I forgot I had to take one of the ranch hand's keys away last night." She went to work opening the fob. "Cross your fingers." After prying off the front, she popped the silver, circular battery free and held it up. "Is this the right size?"

"You've got to be shitting me." Janie took the battery. The thing was exactly what she needed. After switching it for the dead one in her own fob, she passed the juiceless battery to Paige. "Won't that guy be pissed when he comes back and his keys don't work?"

Paige smirked as she poked the dead battery into the ranch hand's fob. "Probably should've thought of that before he grabbed my ass."

Janie shook her head, rolling her eyes. "Those ranch hands do get a little wild, don't they?"

"You have no freaking idea." Paige carried the keys back down and tossed them where she found them. "If they keep it up, I'm going to have to hire a bouncer."

Janie leaned against the counter, wiggling her brows. "Let me know. I'd like to fill out an application." She made a show of cracking her knuckles. "I've got some rage I should probably try to get out."

Paige cackled, head tipping back. "You'd think that

would be a great stress reliever, but these idiots like it. You'll end up with three marriage proposals before the end of your first night."

Janie wrinkled her nose, disgusted. "Never mind then. I've decided I'm done fucking with men. They're way more hassle than they're worth." She shrugged. "Guess it's time for me to embrace my spinsterhood and be everyone's honorary, shit-show of an auntie." At least that was something she could excel at.

After spending a lifetime chasing down dreams only to discover she lacked the skills to catch any of them, she'd found some semblance of peace in giving up and simply accepting herself for what she was.

A fucking failure.

"A-fucking-men to that." Paige eyed her. "You want a drink before you go?"

Yes. She absolutely did. Unfortunately, it wasn't in the cards. "I have to get up early tomorrow to help Mariah set up for a big event at The Inn." She slapped the counter, backing away. "I will take a rain check, though." She grinned at Paige. "Let me know how butt-grabber likes having dead keys."

Imagining one of the fly-by-night idiot ranch hands standing there pushing the button on his fob like an ass brightened her spirits a little. Made her feel incrementally better about being that same sort of ass not so long ago.

She ducked out of the bar, eyes watering as she again had to adjust to the change in light. Her vision was clear by the time she made it to the employee parking lot behind The Baking Rack. Like the coward she was, Janie paused at the edge of the building to peek around, letting out a sigh of relief when there was no sight of Peters or his car.

Just in case he was making a lap and planning to come back, she ran across the blacktop, thumb punching the unlock button five times just to be sure her car really was accessible when she got there. But, instead of immediately jumping in and starting the engine, she stopped dead in her tracks and stared.

"Fucking asshole." She snatched the paper wedged under her wiper free, crumpling it with one hand as she yanked open the door and fell into the driver's seat. The prick really couldn't help himself. It was almost like he thought she was incapable of figuring out how to replace the tires on her own. Granted, their current condition might make him wonder, but that didn't mean he needed to leave her the name and number of his own personal tire guy on her windshield.

Tossing the paper into the passenger side floorboard, she started the engine and shoved her foot toward the floor, getting out of the area as fast as she could manage, relaxing a little more with every second she put between herself and the last spot she saw Peters. By the time she made it to her place twenty minutes later, the tension in her shoulders was all but gone.

When she first moved to Moss Creek, the lack of affordable housing was irritating as hell. Anything decently close to town was snapped up in an instant, or way above her price range, leaving her stuck at the very edge of the city's limits. Her drive to The Baking Rack wasn't terrible, but getting out to The Inn at Red Cedar Ranch was brutal. Especially at five in the morning.

But right now, the location felt fantastic. Far away from the latest reminder of just how much she sucked.

After parking in the dirt spot allocated to her, she started to get out, remembering Peters' crumpled note at the last second and leaning across the console to grab it.

Her life might be a mess figuratively, but that didn't mean she was going to let it become a literal translation.

CHAPTER TWO
DEVON

"WHERE THE FUCK is my flat iron, Olivia?" Riley stormed out of the hall bathroom all three of his girls shared right as Devon reached the top of the stairs. Her eyes went wide as she jerked to a stop. "You're home."

"I'm home." He gave her the most disapproving face he could muster up. "And you just dropped an F-bomb."

Riley scoffed, dramatically swinging one arm in the direction of the room her younger sisters shared. "We're in a hurry and Olivia stole my freaking flat iron. *Again*." She raised her voice, as if the sister in question couldn't hear her rant. "Like we don't have a whole regular iron she could be using instead."

Olivia appeared in her doorway, eyes rolling back into her skull, the hair tool in question clutched in one hand. "I took it for like, two seconds." She shoved the heated clamp at her older sister. "And there's no reason for me to go all the way to the basement to find the iron when I just needed to smooth out one of my hair ribbons."

Devon scrubbed one hand over his face, trying to ease away the exhaustion that plagued him. "I'll order another flat iron." He glanced into Olivia and Gwen's room as he passed and it was his turn to widen his eyes. "Actually, I probably shouldn't, considering the fire hazard you two live in."

He loved his daughters. Loved being a dad. Wouldn't give it up for the world. But being a single parent was the hardest thing he'd ever done in his life. Even more difficult than losing his wife, their mother, and the future he thought was in store.

Some days it felt like his time with Mags had been a fever dream. Like it hadn't really happened. Then one of his girls would start screaming at her sister, providing proof he and Mags really had made a family together. One that was currently fueled by tubes of black eyeliner and buckets of estrogen.

Raking a hand through his hair, he turned away from the avalanche of clothes and shoes piled up on the floor. "Can you please try to get it under control? Maybe just a path in case the place really does go up in flames and they need to come get us out?"

Olivia wrapped the ribbon of sisterly theft around her ponytail, tipping her head toward where the youngest of his daughters was stretched across her twin bed, a tablet clutched in one hand. "Gwen will have to do it. I'm already going to be late for the game since Riley isn't ready to go yet."

"Riley isn't ready to go yet because you stole her freaking flat iron." Riley shot her sister a glare before taking the tool and plugging it in beside the bathroom vanity. "You little klepto."

Olivia shrugged, looking unbothered by her older sister's aggravation. "Maybe if you stopped leaving your crap all over the bathroom, it wouldn't be so easy to take."

"Maybe if everyone started to clean up after themselves we wouldn't be living in squalor." Devon turned his glare onto each of the girls, rotating through them one by one. "Tomorrow we're spending the whole day cleaning. This place is a pigsty."

They had the decency to look moderately apologetic, eyes dropping to the floor. But the contrition only lasted ten seconds before each one blurted out an excuse for not being able to clean away their Saturday.

"I have to work."

"I'm supposed to help make the decorations for the Homecoming dance."

"I'm taking the practice ACT."

Looked like he was going to be handling it on his own. *Again.*

"Fine." He waved one hand toward the stairs. "Go. Do your thing."

He wasn't mad as much as he was disappointed. He'd reached the point of parenthood where getting time with his kids was next to impossible—they had their own interests, their own friends, their own schedules. Cleaning the house wasn't his number one priority—

obviously—he'd just been hoping the four of them could hang out together. Maybe order some pizza. Even if they didn't make any headway with the house, it would've been fine. Eventually the place would get cleaned.

But he would never get this time with his girls back. If there was one thing losing Maggie taught him, it was to cherish every fucking second, because you never knew when you wouldn't get another one.

The three girls swarmed him all at once, layering him in a group hug as they made apologies they probably meant alongside promises he knew they wouldn't keep. Promises they also knew he would never hold them to. Life was hard. Growing up was even harder. Especially when all you had to get you through it was a clueless father who had to Google every question they had surrounding menstruation, bras, and the best way to make glitter stick to your hair.

As quickly as they'd advanced on him, the three of them were gone, with Riley and Olivia headed out the front door and Gwen holed up in her room, consuming whatever novel she'd recently loaded onto her Kindle.

Hopefully it taught her about sex, because he really wasn't looking forward to having that conversation again.

The house was so quiet his resigned sigh seemed to echo around him as he turned and went into his bedroom, peeling away the layers of his uniform before changing into jeans and a thermal shirt. They were well into fall, and once the sun went down the air got pretty cool. He had another hour's worth of work ahead of him

—all of it spent outside— and didn't want to freeze his ass off like he had the night before.

Pausing on his way out the door, he decided to get a head start on tomorrow's tasks and spent a few minutes collecting his dirty laundry from the floor, stacking it into the already overflowing hamper. It was yet another chore that had gotten away from him as he tried to juggle everything that went with being a single parent to three busy kids. After using a previously worn T-shirt to half-assedly wipe away the layer of dust on his dresser, he gave up. His own bedroom was the least of his concerns when it came to getting the house together. And if he didn't get out to the barn soon, there would be hell to pay.

Making his way back downstairs, Devon kicked at the pile of shoes just inside the door, pretending it would look better if they took up less square footage of the un-swept hardwood. Ignoring the jackets and backpacks haphazardly discarded along the hall, he went to the kitchen to grab a snack on his way outside. The granola bar he found in a mostly empty box on the counter was fully shoved into his mouth by the time he pulled the back sliding door open and stepped out onto the deck he'd once imagined sitting on with Maggie, drinking coffee every morning as they grew old together.

But that was never in the cards for them, no matter how they fell.

Following the path from the steps and around the treeline cutting across the main yard, he pulled out his phone, the chill of the evening even cooler than he'd expected. After firing off a quick text to Olivia to make sure she had a jacket, he slid open the barn's heavy door and stepped inside. His entrance was immediately greeted with an indignant huff and a few dramatic stomps.

"You're not going to catch an attitude with me too, are you?" He moved to where Winston, the rich, chocolate brown gelding he'd owned for nearly ten years poked his head over the gate of his stall. "Looks like the girls let you in, but they didn't give you anything to eat, huh?" To be fair, he'd only asked his daughters to let the horses in, not to feed them, so maybe that was on him.

Swiping one hand along the horse's neck, he leaned closer, lowering his voice. "Next time I'll make sure they give you a little snack too, how's that sound?"

Normally Winston was a lover, but tonight the big horse yanked his head away and huffed out another loud breath, reiterating his position on not being fed at his normal time.

"Hold your horses." Devon gave Winston another neck pat before turning to collect pellets and hay. "I can't help it that I had to work late." Technically, he could have, but Winston didn't need to know that.

When the call came in about glass shattered across The Baking Rack's parking lot, he'd jumped at the opportunity a little too quickly. Quick enough dispatch might get the wrong impression he wasn't in a hurry to get home to his daughters.

And that wasn't the case.

Today, that wasn't the case. Today, he dragged his

feet for a completely different reason. A reason he didn't have the time to waste even considering. Unfortunately, his brain hadn't really gotten the message on that. Along with other parts of him.

Devon carried his load into Winston's stall, doling out feed as he brought his problems to the only available ear he had. "I think she hates my guts, buddy."

Actually, he was pretty certain of it. Janie was not one to hide her feelings, and she made hers regarding him abundantly clear. It was as if just his offers of help and advice enraged the curly-headed spitfire, bringing out every bit of bad attitude she possessed. It should have made him avoid her like the plague. Instead it sent him seeking her out. See what might happen the next time their paths crossed.

Winston nosed him, the move less of a nuzzle and more of a not-so-subtle encouragement to get the fuck out of the way and let him at his food bowl.

"I get it. You think I'm a pain in the ass too." He backed up, slapping the horse gently on the flank as the big animal moved in to start eating. "I'm not sure when everyone got so touchy about someone trying to help."

After clearing out the small amount of mess accrued in the stall, Devon moved on to the one beside it. Winnifred, the dappled mare occupying that space, was infinitely more patient than Winston. She stayed out of his way, giving him a gentle nosing as he filled her food bucket and freshened up her little slice of Moss Creek. Once she had fresh pellets and water, he offered the sweet horse a few minutes of affection—likely the only either of them would get today—before closing her in for the night, the guilt of how little time he had for the horses tugging at his gut.

He was at a point where something probably had to give, and the thing that made the most sense was to get rid of the horses. But he couldn't bring himself to do it. Not just because Mags had loved them so much, but because they were the only ones he had to talk to. His daughters didn't need to know about the gnawing loneliness slowly eating away at him, and hearing him wishing for someone at his side made his buddies on the force noticeably uncomfortable. They'd all known Mags and witnessed what she went through. Maybe on some level they felt like they'd be betraying her if they supported him moving on. Being with someone else. He got that.

But they didn't know the full story. No one did.

Deep down he knew Maggie wouldn't want him to live like this. If their roles had been reversed—if it was Mags here instead of him—he would never want her to feel the way he did now. Lonely. Isolated. Overwhelmed and under touched.

But those weren't the emotions he really struggled with. It was the cycle of anger and guilt that was hard to handle. Thankfully, he didn't have much time to dwell on the losses he'd faced and the complicated feelings that came with them.

That lack of time was also why any interest he might have in Janie—and her filterless reactions to everything he did—was futile. There simply wasn't enough time in the day for him to add another person to his life. Not when it would take away from the already limited hours he had with his girls. He was barely keeping his head above water as it was. Trying to date would send him sinking. And his daughters had already sacrificed so much. He wouldn't take more from them.

After hauling the manure he'd collected out back and sweeping the loose straw from the main floor, he paused to give each horse a treat. "You guys have a cleaner house than I do."

It wasn't true, but some days—like this one—it felt that way. He managed to keep up with the dishes and the trash, but the kitchen table was always covered in a random assortment of items and a pile of junk mail. The carpets weren't always vacuumed and the floors only got the quickest of sweeps. But there was no expired food in the fridge and the toilets got scrubbed once a week.

Would someone call CPS on him? No. But damn it would be nice to look around without seeing blatant evidence of his lacking as a parent everywhere.

He'd just made it out of the barn when a small sound slowed his steps and had him turning back. Mouth dropping open, he watched in horror as a scrawny black cat trotted up and dropped a pink, writhing kitten at his boots. She met his eyes and gave him a meow before darting off in the direction of the woods.

"No, no, no, no." He shook his head like the little cat would listen. "You can't bring your babies here." He watched in panic as she ran away, leaving him to babysit.

She raced back with a second squirming, barely

fuzzed kitten and set it on top of the first. By the time she was done, he had five squalling infants on his worn steel-toes.

"Fucking hell." Devon blew out a loud sigh. "You know a sucker when you see one, don't you, mama?" Sucking in a lungful of the chilly evening air, he crouched down to collect the newest mouths he'd have to feed.

And probably clean up after.

"Come on. Let's find you somewhere to sleep."

CHAPTER THREE
JANIE

"I CAN SEE why Paige has to throw these idiots out all the time." Janie scanned the boisterous crowd of baby cowboys packing The Creekery. "These children are out of hand."

Mariah shot her a glare across the high-top table they'd been parked at for the better part of the evening. "Stop acting like they need their diapers changed. Everyone here is over the age of twenty-one, so calm down, grandma."

She barked out a laugh. "Ninety-nine percent of the men here are practically half my age. They might as well be infants." She'd had more than her share of disappointing interactions with barely legal men when she herself was in their age group, and not a single cell in her body had any interest in circling back.

"Well they aren't half *my* age." Mariah took a drink of her vodka and cranberry juice. "So stop looking so fucking terrifying. I would like to talk to one man before the night is over."

Janie rolled her eyes, letting out an exasperated sigh. "Fine. But don't say I didn't warn you." Scooching her seat back, she slowly lowered both feet to the floor, being careful not to clench the muscles of her abdomen too tight in the process. "I probably need a bathroom break anyway." She wiggled her brows at Mariah. "I'll take my time."

Coming out tonight hadn't sounded even the smallest bit appealing when Mariah made the proposition. Way less fun than her initial plans for the evening—burrowing under a blanket on her couch while lying on a heating pad, suffering through her uterus's most recent rebellion. But Mariah didn't want to go out alone, and she didn't want to let her go out alone. The people of Moss Creek were nice enough, but there were plenty of fly-by-night ranch hands who couldn't be trusted, and Mariah was a little too innocent for her own good. So she'd popped some pain pills, put on her big girl panties—literally—and sucked it up.

A decision she was genuinely regretting.

The trek to the bathroom was a long one, primarily due to the number of loitering bodies in her path. Everyone and their brother seemed to be at The Creekery tonight, and not a single one of them had any interest in getting the fuck out of her way.

She was only about halfway to her destination when a sudden rush in her lower half had her stepping a little faster. By some miracle, there wasn't a line for the ladies' room, and she was able to dart straight into a stall and get to work on damage control. An optimistic part of her had hoped the past few months of somewhat normal cycles were an indication that the raging periods she'd suffered through most of her life were finally on the downward swing. But, as it so often did, her uterus reared its ugly head and pissed all over that parade.

After switching out her extra absorbent pad—tampons only made her gut-twisting cramps worse—she washed up and dug another pain pill from her purse, swallowing it down with nothing but spit and determination as she wove her way back to the table.

Only to find Mariah had made the most of her absence.

A strapping young guy wearing the cliched country boy uniform of Wranglers and a cowboy hat was sidled up to her friend, grinning from ear to ear in a way that made him look even younger than he likely was. Unfortunately, young or not, he was still a big guy. Definitely big enough to make him hard to bury if he hurt her friend, but that was a problem for future Janie. Current Janie's problem was that she needed another drink because the Vicodin she'd tossed back was stuck halfway down and felt like a rock in her esophagus.

She turned away from the table, leaving Mariah to flirt unhindered, and elbowed her way to the bar. Shuffling to the end of the line, she shifted from foot to foot, trying to alleviate the ache radiating through her abdomen and lower back. The line was slow-moving, and she was about to give up when Paige caught her eye over the crowd. She shot Janie a wink, and mouthed the words 'I got you'. Less than a minute later, Paige was coming to where Janie stood, passing a fresh Jack and Coke over the bar. Janie attempted to hand over her debit card, but Paige waved her off. "Don't worry about it." Her head tilted as she looked Janie over. "Are you feeling okay? You look a little peaked."

Janie snorted as she took a long drink, the cold rush of icy liquid flushing the much-needed narcotic into her belly. "Did you really just call me peaked?" She managed a smirk and a chuckle. "Don't use that word around Mariah. She'll call you a grandma too."

Paige swiped a rag across a few water rings marring the bar. "That's fine. I am happy to embrace my inner grandma." She pointed at Janie's drink as she backed away. "Text me if you need another one. I'll have someone bring it to your table."

Janie blew out a breath that fluttered her lips in a loud raspberry. "My table is currently occupied by Mariah and a random cowboy, so I'm going have to go find a new place to loiter."

Paige lifted her brows, looking pointedly around the packed bar. "Good luck with that."

"Thanks." Janie lifted her drink. "And thanks for this."

She continued swallowing down her drink as she wormed her way back through the crowd, searching for a spot to park her crampy, cranky ass. In an excellent turn of events, Mariah and her buckle baby were getting up from their seats as she closed in. Picking up the pace so she didn't lose the table, Janie shimmied in right behind them as big and brawny hauled her friend out onto the dance floor. Their absence gave her plenty of space to stretch out, so she settled into one of the bistro-height chairs before kicking both feet up onto the one across from her, leaning back against the wall as she waited for the medication—and the whiskey—to take the edge off her pain.

It was something she'd dealt with since puberty, but it still fucking sucked. Especially after a few easy months. The break was great, but the sudden reversion back to how things used to be had her a little concerned that things were getting out of control down there again. She didn't have time for that shit. Not now. Not when she was finally feeling like she was almost getting somewhere in life. Between her mornings working with Mariah at The Inn and her hours at The Baking Rack in the afternoons, she was actually making decent money. After bouncing around from job to job and career path to career path, being able to make ends meet felt really fucking good.

Was she what anyone would ever consider a success? No fucking way. But she wasn't broke. She had friends.

And she wasn't still jumping from man to man, trying to force Mr. Wrong to be something right.

Truth be told, that was probably something she would still be attempting if it hadn't been for Dianna. Her boss at The Baking Rack was one of the sweetest women she'd ever met. She was beautiful and had her life together. She was also currently happily married to

Janie's ex, Griffin, proving that chances were high Janie had been the problem in every relationship she'd ever had.

Griffin. A man Janie had been sure was the problem.

Obviously she'd been wrong, because he'd snagged someone amazing and was now fucking father of the year, walking around Moss Creek with his cute-as-a-button daughter strapped to his chest, looking like the perfect picture of domestication.

That meant, in yet another area of her life, she was a failure.

Taking another long draw of her drink, Janie watched everyone around her having a great fucking night as she started a familiar downward trajectory, sliding from feeling relatively decent about herself to crashing into the cold, hard truth. Was she better than she used to be? Maybe. But at this point, if she didn't have her life all the way together, she never would. She would never fall in love or get married. She would never be a mom. Never be more than an hourly employee helping someone else chase their own dream. It was something she would have to come to terms with at some point, and maybe tonight was that night.

If she was lucky, the combination of Vicodin and whiskey coursing through her veins would take the edge off the pain and disappointment the revelation would bring on. Might as well do something since it wasn't knocking out the anarchy happening beneath her belly button.

"Hey there, gorgeous." A broad frame suddenly blocked her view of the dance floor.

Continuing to suck down more of her barrel-aged cramp control, Janie lifted her eyes to meet the set of baby blues gazing out at her from under the brim of a cowboy hat. She angled a brow—not wanting to waste the energy on any other sort of response—hoping he'd get the message.

As her luck would have it, her new cowboy friend was either undaunted or completely clueless, because instead of tucking tail and running away, he pulled out the chair she had her feet on. Lifting them from the seat, he took their place before resting them across one of his knees. It was a ballsy move. One that should have earned him her wrath. But between the cramps and the crushing reality of her future, she wasn't feeling as bitey as normal.

"You looked kinda lonely sitting over here by yourself." He leaned back in his seat, like he had no intention of leaving. "I saw you and thought it was a shame someone so pretty would be all alone."

She probably should have taken a closer look at her face when she was in the bathroom, because it seemed like between the booze and the Vicodin, the 'fuck off' normally written across her forehead must have fallen off. Or maybe this guy wasn't much of a reader.

Either way, he was barking up the wrong tree. Even if it didn't currently feel like her insides were attempting to become her outsides, there was no way this baby boy stood a chance. There was an age limit to get on this ride, and he was nowhere near it.

"I appreciate your concern, but I'm actually fine." Janie laughed at how nice she sounded. Another thing that could likely be attributed to whiskey and pain pills. "You can find your way back to wherever you came from without worrying about me."

The cowboy across from her offered a lopsided smile that likely sent younger, less experienced, women's hearts fluttering. "Now what would be the fun in that?"

Ugh. Of course she would attract the only guy in this place who couldn't take a hint. That was fine. If he wouldn't leave, she'd do it for him.

Grabbing her drink from the table, Janie swung both feet off of his meaty thigh, happily noting the stabbing sensation that had been poking her insides was all but gone as she slid to the floor. Unfortunately, that relief came at a price, and that price was balance. As soon as she tried to step away from the table, her legs wobbled and she started careening to the side as the bar began to spin. Janie cringed, fully expecting to go down, hating that her body was about to be against the disgustingly filthy floor under her feet.

But before everything could go sideways, a pair of strong hands gripped her tight, bringing her once again perpendicular to the ground.

Great. Now this guy seriously wasn't going to leave her alone. He was going to think she owed him for not letting her fall. Shit. She was going to have to figure out how to throw up on his shoes or something, because the last thing she wanted was some strange, too-young cowboy—

Her eyes finally focused on the man holding her tight, and she realized the baby cowboy was actually the lesser of two evils.

Officer Devon Peters frowned at her, his chiseled jaw set in a disapproving line. "Are you okay?"

Scrounging up every bit of sobriety she possessed, Janie managed to lift her chin and straighten her spine. "I'm fine. I just tripped."

Devon's scowl intensified as he pulled her closer, hooking one arm behind her back as he swung his hard glare to the cowboy she was attempting to escape. "What the fuck did you put in her drink?"

The cowboy lifted his hands, eyes wide with genuine innocence. "I didn't touch her drink. I swear."

"Do you think I'm fucking stupid?" Janie poked herself in the face a few times with the straw of the drink she'd somehow managed not to drop. She finally got her lips around it and sucked loudly, the little bit of remaining liquid rattling around the ice as she swallowed down the last precious drops of whiskey. "He didn't get near my drink."

Devon's frown deepened. "It's not about being stupid. Women should be able to take their eyes off a drink without worrying what will get dropped into it."

As usual, Devon didn't miss an opportunity to chastise her. And maybe this time she deserved it.

He returned his glare to the cowboy, keeping him pinned in place a few seconds longer with nothing more than the weight of his stare, before finally jerking his chin toward the dance floor. "Go."

The cowboy didn't hesitate. He immediately jumped up and all but ran into the crowd, leaving her to deal with the man who loved nothing more than to be a pain in her ass.

"Let me go. I'm fine." Janie pushed at Devon's chest, giving it a half-assed shove before realizing this was a job for two hands. She set her empty glass on the table, not realizing she missed until it crashed against the floor. Normally, she would immediately go to work cleaning that up, but Devon's hold on her was uncompromising, barely giving her enough room to plant both palms against the front of his uniform.

To her dismay, she didn't have enough leverage to make any headway. It only got worse when he pulled her closer as he leaned into the little walkie-talkie thing on his shoulder and pressed the button. It beeped twice before he started to speak into it.

"This is Peters. I've got a patron at The Creekery who needs a ride home."

"I don't need a ride home." Even in her current state, the thought of Devon being where she lived sent panic slicing through her gut. If he saw the full reality of what her life really was, his judging eyes would never leave her. Every time they crossed paths, she'd have to hear about all the ways she needed to do better.

And then she would end up in jail for assaulting an officer.

"I have a ride home. Mariah and I came together."

She continued trying to wiggle away, but the Earth was rotating faster than she remembered, and it was difficult to keep her train of thought. "Let me go so I can find her."

"If I let you go, the only thing you're going to find is the fucking floor." Devon's voice was a low growl and it sent her chin tucking in surprise.

Usually he sounded like he was disappointed in her. Like he was dishing out the same kind of lecture he would offer to one of his kids.

Right now, he sounded... Pissed.

Thankfully, Mariah—the best friend ever—rushed up, brows pinched in concern as she took in the situation. "What happened? Is she okay?"

"I'm fine." Janie turned to her friend, knowing she was her best shot at getting the hell away from Devon. "I just forgot I took a Vicodin earlier."

Devon's brows climbed up his forehead. "You forgot?" His voice was louder now. Sharper.

Angrier.

She pressed her lips together, a little shocked by his reaction.

Without waiting for her to answer, Devon turned to where Mariah stood with the baby cowboy from earlier. He looked between them. "She needs to go home."

Mariah—the worst friend ever—hesitated. "Oh. Okay."

"I can take her." He looked the baby cowboy up and down, voice still sharp as he said, "As long as you'll be okay on your own."

She could swear her friend almost smiled at Devon's sudden grumpiness. "Of course. I'll be fine."

Devon stared the baby cowboy down a few seconds longer, expression threatening enough to make the younger man squirm in his boots. "You better be."

Janie scoffed as Devon turned toward the exit, hauling her along with him. "Why do you believe *her* when she says she's fine?"

He ignored the question as he steered her though the mass of bargoers, the weight of his well-muscled arm keeping her firmly pinned to his side. It wasn't until they reached the exit that he finally spared her a glance.

"Because she has a sense of self-preservation."

CHAPTER FOUR
DEVON

BEING THIS CLOSE to Janie was probably a bad idea. He'd always been careful to keep a safe distance between them—even while trying to look out for her. It was something she likely appreciated considering he wasn't her favorite person. Unfortunately, it wasn't an option tonight. She'd made the stupid, stupid decision to mix pain meds and whiskey, and there was no way he was leaving her with Mariah.

Not that he didn't trust Mariah, there was just no way she'd be able to handle Janie on her own. And he'd be damned if he was going to let one of the dumbass ranch hands packing The Creekery put his hands on her. Especially with the state she was in. He had to practically carry Janie out of the bar, her movements getting slower and less coordinated with each step.

Luckily, his cruiser was right outside the door, idling at the curb a few strides away. When they reached it, he supported her weight with one arm while opening the passenger's door. As he angled her into the seat, Janie's head fell back against the rest and she glared up at him as he buckled her in. "You piss me off all the time." Her words were slow and a little slurred. They were also unsurprising.

"I know." He tested the belt, making sure it was secure. "You drive me fucking crazy, so I'm gonna call us even."

"Even?" She grabbed the front of his shirt when he tried to straighten, keeping their eyes level. "We're not even close, buddy." Her nose wrinkled, lip curling in what looked like disgust. "Ugh. Are you kidding me?" She released him, pushing at the center of his chest. "You shouldn't smell so good. It's annoying." Her lips pressed into a frown. "Everything about you is annoying."

He worked hard to smother out the smile trying to work across his lips. "At least I'm consistent."

She rolled her eyes, but they only made it halfway across before her lids lowered and a long yawn dragged free. "Just take me home so I can get rid of you already."

Since her eyes were closed, he set the amused expression he'd been fighting free, softly chuckling as he closed her in and rounded the front of his cruiser. He'd never met someone like Janie. A woman ready to go toe-to-toe with anyone, anytime, anywhere. She was fearless and full of fight.

She was also full of piss and vinegar, and most of it seemed to be directed at him. If he really wanted to dig into it, there were probably a couple good reasons that appealed to him, but it was yet another thing he didn't have time for.

Blowing out a long sigh, Devon pulled away from the curb. The only light in town turned red right as he reached it, offering the opportunity to figure out where he was going. Turning to Janie, he found her slumped to one side, mouth hanging open, breaths slow with sleep.

"Janie." He reached across the console to smooth back a wayward strand of dark, curly hair. "I need your address."

She jolted when the tips of his fingers brushed against the soft skin of her cheek, her brows pinched together as she slowly blinked his direction. "I was sleeping."

"I saw that." He glanced around as the light turned green, making sure he wasn't holding anyone else up, but the street behind him was empty. "But I need your address if you want me to take you home."

"I *don't* want you to take me home." She smacked her lips and yawned again. "You just didn't leave me any choice."

"Do I need to remind you that you were falling over when I found you?" He gripped the wheel a little tighter thinking of what might have happened if he hadn't found her. If he hadn't decided to take a little stroll through The Creekery to make sure no one was giving Paige any problems.

"No. You don't." After crossing both arms over her chest she let out a long sigh. "Fine." Janie rattled off an address, her eyes sliding his way as she spelled out the street name. "W-I-L-L-O-W-D-A-L-E."

"Thank you." He didn't need to put it into the GPS. He knew exactly where they were headed. "You can go back to sleep now."

"Whatever." Janie's head rolled away from him, turning to face the side window.

He chuckled, shaking his head. The woman acted like him helping her was the worst thing she could imagine. And that only made him want to help her more. Seek her out just to watch the way she scowled at him. The way she set her emotions free—good or bad—making how she felt blatantly obvious.

To be fair, his daughters frequently acted the same way—and he usually loved it just as much when they did it. He didn't want them to spend their lives being somewhere they didn't want to be because they didn't know how to express their feelings.

That was likely another reason Janie's forthright temperament appealed to him. If he were to suddenly find time to bring a woman into his life, it would take someone like Janie to hold her own with his three hormonal teenagers.

And while his interest in the crabby, tightly wound woman snoring beside him was undeniable, so was his demanding schedule. Between the extra hours he picked up to pay for things like braces and extracurriculars, taking care of the horses, chauffeuring Olivia and Gwen around when Riley was at school or work, and all the other time sucks that came with being a single parent, this could never be more than it was.

It was nothing, and had to stay nothing.

So he kept his eyes on the road instead of where she sat beside him, even though the trip to Janie's home was a path he knew by heart. He'd driven it countless times, and every turn took him both closer to their destination and back in time. To a part of his life he could only just now think of without feeling the stabbing pain of all he'd lost.

After pulling up to the trailer Janie called home, he sat for a few minutes, taking it in. The place looked exactly the same as it did the last time he was here. The pale blue exterior was spotless and the attached deck was swept clean. Even the narrow flower beds at the front were weed free and edged. It was almost like his mother-in-law had never left.

Janie started beside him, jolting upright with a sharp inhale. After a few hard blinks she seemed to notice where they were and reached for the door handle.

"Wait for me." He automatically used his cop voice and it had her head whipping his way, eyes wide. And for once, she didn't argue.

Maybe he should have brought that out earlier.

When he reached her door, Janie had a brow cocked at him and her eyes seemed a little clearer. Reaching one hand out, he waited as she stared at it, wondering if she would finally willingly accept the assistance he offered.

But in true Janie fashion, she lifted her chin, gripped the door frame and hoisted herself upright.

Almost.

She barely had her legs under her when the effects of her cocktail of meds and alcohol tipped her sideways, sending her falling right into his ready arms. Her lean, tall body hit his as she let out a little squeak before going totally still.

Devon froze along with her. It had been years since he'd had a woman's body pressed against his, and the impact was a bigger blow than he'd been prepared for. He expected Janie to immediately pull away, and readied for the uncoordinated retreat it would no doubt be.

But she didn't budge. Her body stayed stiff against his for a few heartbeats before beginning to relax bit by bit. Slowly, her rigid stance softened. The feel of her arms wrapping around his back was shocking, but only for a second. In the next, he was pulling her closer, dropping his nose to the top of her head and breathing deep against the thick pile of her curly hair. His eyes fell closed as he took another deep breath, inhaling the faintly floral scent as he soaked up the contact.

It'd been so fucking long since he'd been touched like this. Held. Embraced. His daughters dished out grudging squeezes here and there, but each came with an eye roll. He knew they loved him, but also remembered his own teenage years. Navigating the path from child to adult and all the ways it changed not only you, but also how you interacted with the people around you.

But even if his girls still snuggled up to him the way they did when they were little, it still wouldn't be the same as the kind of touch he was receiving now. There was nothing sexual or romantic about it, but it was still different. Still something he'd been working hard to pretend he didn't desperately crave.

And it was over too soon.

Janie wiggled free, her movements jerky since she still wasn't completely steady on her feet. He released her as much as he dared, keeping one hand on her arm as they silently moved up the wooden stairs toward her front door.

She unhooked her keys from the small cross body bag strapped over her chest, blinking hard as she fumbled through the assortment until she got to the one for her home. But, while she was sober enough to be able to identify the correct key, she wasn't quite capable of getting it into the lock.

Devon gently took the keychain from her hand, slipping the key into the deadbolt and twisting the lock open before turning the knob. He braced, expecting the familiar smell of White Diamonds to hit him. Instead, his lungs filled with a rich hit of rose and plum. It was deep and a little dark. A little wild. Acutely feminine.

"Come on." He used his hold on Janie's arm to angle her through the opening. "Let's get you in bed."

Janie took one step inside, then planted her feet with a firmness that caught him off-guard. "Take your shoes off." She pointed down at his feet. "What kind of heathen are you?"

Heathen? For not taking his shoes off at the door?

Devon glanced around the dimly lit space, taking it all in under the moody glow from a lamp centered on a small table just inside the door. The trailer was tiny, only two small bedrooms with an eat-in kitchen and a living room that barely held a full-size sofa and a TV stand, but Janie had made the most of it. An overstuffed couch was fitted along the only windowless wall and an upholstered ottoman sat between it and a dresser that had been repurposed as an entertainment center. A giant arrangement of partially used candles on a wooden tray dominated the center of the ottoman. He could almost imagine how cozy the place felt when they were all lit.

Cozy and clean. The place was immaculate. Possibly even cleaner than when his mother-in-law lived there.

His eyes dropped to the laminate flooring she put in before moving to Florida. There wasn't a speck of dust or dirt anywhere to be seen. It was exactly the type of floor people were referring to when they used the line, 'so clean you could eat off it'.

Crouching down, he reached for the laces of his work boots, but had to pause midway to catch Janie as she started to tip again. After propping her up against the wall so she could kick away her pull-on Converse sneakers, he worked off his own shoes, catching her yet again as she started to sway.

"Careful." He kept his grip gentle as she wobbled her way toward the bigger of the two bedrooms, and he let out a sigh of relief that she'd chosen the room Mags's parents had used instead of the one where he'd lost his virginity over two decades ago.

"I'm being careful." Janie leaned more heavily on him as she reached her room, barely making it to the bed before collapsing face first onto the queen-sized mattress.

Like the main portion of the single-wide he'd been in countless times, this room was cozy and well-decorated. The bed took up a good amount of the square footage, but since it didn't have a large frame, the area didn't feel claustrophobic, even with a small dresser and a chair eating up more of the limited footprint. A thick comforter and mountainous pile of pillows added a softness the space didn't have when his utilitarian mother-in-law had occupied it.

Like the living area, there were candles of different colors and scents arranged on every available surface, each in varying stages of use. The room was also just as immaculate. The area rug covering most of the laminate even had vacuum lines on it, as if Janie backed out of the room to ensure not a single footprint marred the plush surface. Nothing was out of place, including the carefully organized charging cords on her nightstand.

With one exception.

A large heating pad sat in the center of her bed, sticking out like a sore thumb among the artfully draped throw and perfectly positioned pillows.

He looked from Janie to it, then back to the woman sprawled across the comforter as he put together the pieces. Pain pills and a heating pad were a combination he was becoming quite familiar with.

Facing down the realities of menstruation had been trial by fire, and after a few years of tackling the discomforts and emotional roller coasters that came with it, he'd learned enough to have a pretty good handle on navigating a safe course.

He'd also learned it was hard as hell to get bloodstains out of sheets, which was why he decided to risk waking the bear.

Moving to Janie's side, he gently rolled her toward him. "Come on, sleepy pants. If you pass out now you're going to be pissed in the morning."

Janie groaned. "For the love of God, can't you ever leave me alone?" She flung one arm over her face. "Why are you even still here?"

"I'm here because I have to make sure you're safe to be on your own." He hooked one arm behind her knees, using the hold to bring her legs over the edge of the bed. "And I'm pretty sure you want to make a trip to the bathroom before you crash. Otherwise you'll have a lot of laundry to do in the morning."

Janie stilled, her arm slowly lowering until she peeked over it. "What do you mean?"

"I mean, I have three teenage daughters, so I know when a woman's on her period she needs to wear something with a little more coverage at night."

Janie's brows slowly climbed her forehead as her arm fully slipped away. "How do you know I'm on my period?"

He pointed at the only out of place item in her home. "Between that and the pain pills you said you took, it's a pretty easy conclusion to come to." He took both her hands in his and hauled her up from the bed. "Now go get situated so you can go back to sleep."

CHAPTER FIVE
JANIE

SHE MUST HAVE consumed more whiskey than she thought. It almost seemed like Devon was talking about her period like it was no big deal, and she'd been around enough grown men to know that particular bodily function creeped them out worse than a plague would.

"Come on." Devon pulled her toward the attached bathroom. "Keep moving."

Yeah. She was either completely shitfaced or in the fucking twilight zone. Possibly dreaming, though this wasn't anything like the dreams she'd had about Devon before. Those dreams—which she did her best to forget —were no doubt conjured up by the deepest, darkest, most self-sabotaging parts of her brain. It would make sense this particular scene was being concocted by the same, fucked-up location in her cerebrum. That's why, when she woke up tomorrow, she'd pretend like this dream never happened too.

Except the weight of Devon's hand as it rested on her

still aching back felt tragically real. As did the familiar gush that came when she stood from the bed.

"I'll wait out here." Devon urged her into the small master bathroom. "Yell if you need anything."

She shot definitely-not-dream-Devon a glare. "I'm pretty sure I know how to handle this. I've been doing it since I was eleven."

He angled a thick brow, looking just as unimpressed by her snark as he always did. "Hopefully not usually while under the effects of pain pills and Jack Daniels."

She shrugged. "Whatever it takes." Before he could lecture her on the dangers of concocting codeine and alcohol, she slammed the door in his face, holding onto the vanity for balance as she made her way to the toilet. Undoing the front of her jeans took longer than normal, since it felt like every muscle in her body was moving slower than they should be. She wasn't mad about it, especially since that was likely the reason her uterus was no longer trying to claw its way up her spinal cord.

Once her pants were undone and at her knees, she dropped to the toilet and investigated the wreckage. Day two of her period had always been the worst, and this month was no exception. As much as she hated to admit it, Devon was right. If she'd gone straight to sleep, she would have woken up to not only ruined panties and jeans, but also a destroyed comforter. Even the sheets beneath it were unlikely to have escaped unscathed.

After peeling away the pad she'd put on at the bar, Janie stuck on one of the extra-long, extra absorbent versions she slept in, wrapping the wings around the crotch of her cotton, full coverage panties before standing up and pulling everything into place. She frowned down at the constricting jeans still tangled at her knees. They'd been hard enough to get on when she was dressing before Mariah picked her up, and the thought of wrestling them again held absolutely no appeal.

Under normal circumstances, she would toss them in the hamper and go retrieve a pair of pajama pants, but there was currently a frustratingly overbearing cop in her bedroom. So after wiggling the pants off her feet, she cracked the door. As promised, Devon was right there, looking a little like an eager puppy.

"Everything okay?"

"I'm on my period. Nothing's okay." She pressed her lips together, hating that she was about to ask him for something. Knowing he would hold it against her—along with everything else about tonight—forever. "Can you get in the bottom drawer of my dresser and bring me a pair of pajama pants?"

He gave her a quick nod. "Give me just a sec."

Janie pressed one hand against her lower stomach as the uterus she thought was finally calming its tits reminded her just how fucking much hell it could bring. Enough that she'd exceeded the reasonable limits of Vicodin and whiskey, and it was still marching around, banging its fucking drum.

"What about these?" Devon stepped back into view, holding up her softest, stretchiest pair of PJ bottoms.

"These seemed like they would be the most comfortable."

Janie snatched them away, just as irritated at his helpfulness as she had been at his lectures. "Thanks." Closing the door between them, she leaned against the sink base and slowly worked her legs into the supersoft jersey, sighing a little as she settled the un-restricting waistband into place.

Reaching for the doorknob, she paused. Skimming her tongue across the front of her teeth, Janie turned to the sink and grabbed her toothbrush. Once her teeth were clean, she figured she might as well spend a couple extra minutes scrubbing down her face, so after pulling back her hair, she washed away the makeup she'd put on earlier and then smoothed a layer of moisturizer over her skin. Everything took ten times longer than normal, because the Vicodin and whiskey she consumed—which were no longer doing the job she hired them for—still packed enough of a punch to have her loopy and unbalanced.

Keeping one hand on the wall just in case the world decided to tilt again, Janie opened the door and stepped into her bedroom. She blinked, taking in the scene in front of her before blinking again. Surely she wasn't seeing what she thought she was.

But when she opened her eyes again, it was all still the same. The candles on her dresser were still lit. The glass of water was still on her nightstand, placed directly on top of the coaster she kept there. The throw pillows she put into place every morning were stacked on the chair in the corner, and the duvet and sheets were pulled back.

This had to be some sort of a trick. If it wasn't a dream, and she wasn't in the twilight zone, Devon must have some sort of self-serving reason for all he was doing.

"I plugged in your heating pad and put it on the middle setting." Devon reached out to steady her as she rounded the bed. "I wasn't sure how warm you liked it, so I figured you could adjust it from there." He waited as she sat down, propping her back up against the bed pillows still in place since it felt odd to fully lay down with him here. Once she was situated, he tucked the covers around her. Then Devon held out a plate of crackers smeared with peanut butter.

She pressed the heating pad to her abdomen as she studied the offering. "What's that for?"

"You need to eat something, otherwise you're going to be sick." He settled the plate on her lap. "Crackers will help settle your stomach and the peanut butter will give you a little protein." He tipped his head, lips curving into a grin. "Plus it tastes good."

And she was back to being sure she was dreaming. It was the only reasonable explanation for why Devon Peters was standing beside her bed, all decked out in his uniform, smelling fantastic and grinning as he talked about how good something tasted. Dreaming was also the only explanation for the hard right turn her brain took at that statement, especially since not an inch of her felt sexy or desirable at the moment.

He tipped his head toward the plate. "Eat. I need you to sober up before I go."

"Fine." She picked up one of the crackers and shoveled it in, chewing through the sticky, sweet, salty goodness that checked all her mid-period boxes. After swallowing down three of the six, Devon passed over the water.

"Drink half of that."

She rolled her eyes but took a healthy swallow, washing down the tasty, but gluey, combination of cracker and peanut butter. Once she was finished drinking, he took the glass, motioning at the three remaining crackers. "Finish those up." His expression stayed serious as she worked her way through the rest. "No more pills tonight, got it?"

"Sure." She grabbed another cracker, refusing to acknowledge how oddly good they tasted. Must be the alcohol, even though its effects were rapidly diminishing, leaving her less blurry, but more uncomfortable.

"What did you take for the pain earlier?" Devon watched intently as she finished up her late-night snack.

It wasn't his business, but she found herself telling him anyway. "Vicodin."

Devon passed off the water when the crackers were gone and took her plate. "You need to get all the alcohol out of your system. They're both depressants, and mixing them was a terrible fucking idea."

She finished swallowing down the water and shoved the glass in his hands. "That's easy for you to say. You don't have to deal with cramps so bad it feels like your insides are going to explode."

"That is true." Devon walked out of her room, and she listened as he switched on the sink. A minute later, there was a jostling of dishes, then he was right back in her room, invading her personal space in a way she would likely never be able to forget. "But I have seen what happens when you start taking too many things at once, and I really don't want to wake up tomorrow and hear someone found you unresponsive and had to take you to the hospital."

"Stop being dramatic. It's really not that big of a deal, I promise." She slowly shifted her way down the mattress, wincing a little when the movement exacerbated the sympathetic tightening of the muscles in her abdomen and lower back. "If it was going to kill me, it would've done it way before now."

Devon's mouth flattened into a deep frown, moving her attention to the perfect shape of his lips. "That's not how that shit works, Janie. It just takes once. One time of underestimating how much you drank or forgetting how many pills you've taken."

"Listen, I know you think you're being helpful and that it's your job to take care of me and tell me how I should live my life, but until you've dealt with the lining of one of your organs deciding to take over your insides, you can fuck right off."

Devon's frown became deeper, his hazel eyes moving over her as she tried to find a comfortable position. "You have endometriosis?"

Her head bobbed back, eyes jumping to his. "You know what that is?"

Devon sighed, like he couldn't believe she'd even asked. "I have three daughters that I'm raising on my own. I've had to Google just about everything that has to do with the female reproductive system so I can help them deal with all the bullshit that comes with it." He stepped closer, lifting the covers. "Roll over and lay on the heating pad."

She narrowed her eyes. "Why?"

He heaved out another long sigh. "Just trust me, all right?" He held the blankets out of her way. "I know I haven't been through as many periods as you have, but I'm kind of becoming a professional at helping get rid of cramps."

His faith in his skills was amusing enough she laughed. "Sure you are." Her trust in him had nothing to do with why she rolled over and positioned her belly on the heating pad. It was desperation. The off chance that he could ease her suffering even the tiniest bit. Turning her face his way, she tried to relax. "Let's see this miracle cramp cure you've figured out."

The bed sagged as he sat down next to her, hesitating a second as his eyes lifted to her face. "Can I touch your lower back?"

Janie scoffed. "I already said you could show me whatever witchcraft you think you know."

Devon's expression remained serious. "Again, I have three daughters. I've spent a lot of time teaching them

that no one gets to touch them without clear consent."
He shook his head. "And I'm not a fucking hypocrite."

She was circling back to thinking she was in the
twilight zone. A man who not only wasn't disgusted by
menstruation, but also didn't jump at the opportunity to
get his hands on her? Definitely some sort of alternate
universe.

"Fine." Adjusting where her face rested against the
pillow, she closed her eyes, needing a little space from a
moment that wasn't going at all the way she expected.
"Yes. You can touch me."

She held her breath, expecting Devon's touch to be
hesitant and cautious, considering his concern over
touching her, but the hands that pressed into her skin
were anything but. Each move was strong and steady as
he worked his fingers into the tense muscles at the base
of her spine.

That was one of the worst parts about the kind of
cramps she got. They were all-encompassing, slowly
involving nearly every part of her, leaving her not only in
pain, but also nauseous, hunched over, and lightheaded.

"Too hard?" Devon's voice was low and deep.

And once again had parts of her that had no business
getting any ideas, perking up.

Janie shook her head. "No." She bit her lip, to the
point she could taste blood, but it was no use. At some
point she had to exhale, and when she did, a moan
slipped free.

It was probably only because it had been years since

she'd been touched this way. It was the same reason she'd accidentally hugged him earlier when he helped her out of the car. The alcohol and the pain medication had her a little out of her head, and the needy, lonely part of her took full advantage.

And as much as she hated to admit it, being held tight like that was really freaking nice. For just a moment, it felt like she wasn't alone. Like someone else had her back. Of course, she knew that wasn't the truth. Devon wasn't here because he genuinely wanted to help her. He was driven entirely by obligation and the dad code. The man was always willing to provide assistance, but would take the opportunity to tell you what you *should* be doing, or offer a lecture on why you needed to be more responsible.

He was an ass, but he could also give one hell of a backrub. And without realizing it, she was soon drifting off to sleep, dozing as he worked his way along her spine, easing the discomfort she'd tried to combat on her own.

His touch relaxed her so much, she barely noticed as his hands slid up the center of her back before dragging away. Even the press of something cool and slightly weighted against her lower back didn't fully wake her up. She was too calm. Too comfortable.

Too content.

Something she'd never, ever been.

And it would figure he'd be the one to accomplish it.

Ass.

THE SOFT LIGHT of morning filtering through the open blinds was her first reminder she hadn't put herself to sleep. The glass of water and Advil on her nightstand was the second.

Janie lifted her head, swiping at her unrestrained hair—clue number three—as she scanned the room, half expecting to see Peters glowering at her from the corner. But her room was empty.

Choosing to ignore the tug of disappointment in her gut, she slowly worked her way upright, moving carefully to avoid reinvigorating any of the muscles taking part in her body's monthly rebellion.

While day two was normally the worst, day three of her period wasn't much better, but this morning she felt shockingly decent. Her head didn't hurt. Her back and abdomen weren't tense or sore. Even her stomach didn't feel queasy in spite of how she'd spent the night before.

"Ugh." She groaned, hating the reason her body wasn't as raging as normal.

"*I've got three daughters, Janie. I know how to magically cure cramps.*" She mimicked his voice as she picked up the ibuprofen and knocked it back, swallowing both pills down in one gulp. She was about to set the glass down when she noticed a small piece of paper with shredded spiral connectors still clinging to the top.

Drink it all.

She rolled her eyes but downed the rest of the water before picking up the note, giving it a second read.

'Huh." Apparently that little book Peters carried

wasn't completely filled with all the ways she'd fucked up her life after all.

CHAPTER SIX
DEVON

THE BELL ON The Baking Rack's door jingled softly as Devon tugged it open and stepped inside. The place was quiet in the afternoons—a stark contrast to how it looked in the mornings when all of Moss Creek fought over the cinnamon rolls and pastries crafted and baked in-house. By this time of day, the display cases were empty with only a few crumbs and empty trays behind the glass, leaving anyone who might stop in with no solution to their sugar cravings.

That wasn't a problem for him. He wasn't there for anything Dianna offered.

"I'll be out in just a sec." Janie's voice sounded pleasant, but a little strained, as she called out from the back room.

He waited at the counter, ignoring the anticipation curling through his stomach. He was just there to make sure she was feeling better. That was all. Once he knew she was fine, he'd put any thoughts of tucking Janie into bed—and the way she moaned when his hands were on her—out of his mind forever.

Or at least until his girls were older and didn't need him the way they did now.

Janie rushed out of the back room, wiping her hands on a towel. Her steps slowed when she saw it was him waiting for her and a flicker of uncertainty crossed her face. "Hey."

"Hey." He took in her appearance, looking for any sign of how she was recovering from the night before. She was dressed in jeans and a T-shirt with an apron tied across her front. The long length of her curly dark hair was piled on top of her head, giving him a look at the tiny butterfly tattooed just behind one ear.

He'd never really noticed tattoos before, but right now he was wondering what other hidden designs Janie might have inked into her skin.

Clearing his throat like it would also clear his mind, Devon dropped his eyes to the empty display cases. "Looks like you guys sold out."

"We always sell out." Janie's steps were slow but steady as they continued carrying her closer. "Was there something specific you were hoping to get?"

"Actually..." He scratched at the rasp of hair growing along his jaw. He hadn't had time to shave before beginning his shift thanks to Olivia's urgent need to be dropped off at her friend's house so they could practice homecoming hairstyles for the upcoming dance. "I came to see how you were feeling."

Over the past few years, he'd witnessed just how

fucking awful periods could be. It had given him a whole new respect for the women of the world. Especially when he knew they still had to go to work or school, powering through the pain and discomfort.

Over and over and over again.

Janie shrugged. "I've been worse."

As she reached the other side of the counter, he could see the slight pinch of her expression. The lack of color in her cheeks. The barely hunched way she stood. It had him gritting his teeth to hold in the suggestion that she should have called in sick. Not just because he knew that wasn't an option—calling in sick every month would likely make it hard to keep a job—but also because he knew she fucking hated it when he offered suggestions. No matter how well-intentioned.

For whatever reason, Janie didn't understand he was just trying to help and she took his recommendations and advice as a personal offense.

But it wasn't in his nature to walk away from someone who needed help, regardless of the feelings they had—or didn't have—for him. Never had been. That's how his life turned out the way it did. "Is there anything I can do to help?"

Janie let out a huff of a laugh. "I'm pretty sure you've got way more important things to do than help me assemble cinnamon rolls."

A smile worked across his lips. He couldn't help it. "You might be surprised." He'd expected a snarky response and was prepared to go toe-to-toe with her, so this milder reaction had him relaxing a little. "I don't know if you've noticed this, but Moss Creek isn't exactly a crime hot spot. Most of my job entails helping people stranded on the side of the road and running interference when a cow gets loose." He motioned to the white cotton wrapped around her midsection. "You got another one of those? Probably wouldn't be a good look if I walked back into the station covered in white powder. Everyone would think my shift was way more exciting than it really was."

This time Janie's laugh was a little louder. "That actually makes me want to give you an apron even less." Her eyes stayed on him for a few seconds as she pinched her lower lip between her teeth. Finally, she sighed, rolling her eyes. "Fine. But only because I feel like fucking shit and I don't want to stay here any longer than I have to."

He followed Janie into the back room of The Baking Rack, getting his first look at the behind-the-scenes area of one of Moss Creek's favorite establishments. Like Janie's home, the place was fucking immaculate, and he wondered who was responsible for that. Dianna was a great businesswoman, and definitely not afraid of hard work, but the perfectly aligned bins and gleaming floors would take something more neurotic than simple business sense.

Something that might border on OCD.

"This place is spotless, isn't it?" He scanned the large central island, taking in the perfectly organized system covering its surface, as Janie grabbed an apron from one of the hooks lining the wall. "It looks like you have this down to a science."

She handed him the crisp white cotton, a smile teasing her mouth. "Nobody wants to eat somewhere dirty." She waited as he tied on the covering, her eyes barely narrowing. "And I don't have a lot of time. Doing it in an assembly line style is what goes the fastest." There was a hint of her usual sharpness edging into her tone. Like she was just waiting for him to piss her off.

He held both hands up, hoping he wasn't already fucking up this truce they'd found their way into. "I wasn't passing judgment. I was just making an observation."

"Yeah? Well," Janie pointed at a large rectangle of dough spread across the counter, "observe less and spread filling more." Her admonishment lacked the snark she usually directed his way.

Not hiding his smile, Devon tipped his head. "Yes, ma'am."

He took his spot at the stainless-steel counter, listening carefully as Janie gave him directions. Once she'd shown him how much of the filling to scoop out, and where to stop the spread so the seam would close properly, she left him to his task and went to work rolling out the next rectangle.

His job was relatively simple and required only the most basic amount of focus, so he was able to watch her as she worked, taking in the skilled, precise movements she used to work the next lump of dough into a perfectly formed rectangle.

"Looks like you've done that a time or two." Devon scooped out the next portion of buttery, sugary filling, dropping it into the center of one rectangle as Janie moved down the row. "How many of these do you make every day?"

Janie didn't slow her motions as she continued squaring off another plot of pastry. "We usually sell about a dozen trays' worth from the cases, and a dozen more full trays from the back. Each of these rectangles makes a dozen, which is one tray, so in total I make two hundred eighty-eight rolls." She finished up her current rectangle then grabbed another plastic-wrapped piece of dough from the giant bucket in the center of the counter and slapped it into the next available space. "I can fit six on the island at a time, so I do them in half-dozen groups, rolling all the dough out, then adding the filling, then rolling each one into a tube, then cutting." She adjusted the edges of the rectangle in front of her before continuing. "Then I do it twenty-three more times."

He stared at her for a second, stunned by the numbers. It was easy to see that The Baking Rack sold a shit-ton every day. The line was always out the door, even in the coldest and hottest weather. The few times he'd had enough wiggle room in his morning to sneak in for a treat before his shift, the special orders had been stacked high. "And that's just the cinnamon rolls?"

Janie finished up her current rectangle and glanced at where he stood, looking pointedly from the un-spread ball of filling to him. She angled a brow. "You know you actually have to do something to help, right?"

He shot her a wink, undaunted now that he was starting to figure out a little more about the woman beside him. "Not all of us are as used to being as efficient as you are."

The more time he spent with Janie, the more he understood that her personality—and the abrasiveness it could bring—stemmed mainly from the fact that she didn't have time for bullshit. She said what she meant and she meant what she said because there was no time to clarify. No time to beat around the bush or soften any blows. She didn't hide or hold back her feelings. No matter how ugly they might be.

And it was starting to make his undeniable interest in her make a little more sense.

Devon redoubled his efforts, following behind her with his spatula and managing to catch up, so that by the time she was finishing the last wad of dough that would fit on the counter, he was stepping in to fill it.

Janie looked down the line of rectangles, lifting her brows. "You're actually not doing too bad." She circled the island, going to the other end where the first plot of pastry sat. "Have you ever made cinnamon rolls before?"

"I have not." He carefully worked the sugary sweet paste to the edges. "But I can butter a mean piece of toast, and this is sort of in that same scope."

Janie laughed, the sound amused and lighter than he was used to hearing from her. "Not much of a cook?"

Devon finished up his task and followed the same path Janie had, taking his spot behind her and waiting for direction. "I do okay with the basics, but between work and running my daughters all over town, I have to keep things simple, so from-scratch breakfast pastries aren't really in my rotation."

Janie paused what she was doing, glancing at the rectangle of dough in front of her. "We should probably switch spots." She stepped behind him, grabbing his hips and urging him into her spot. "You roll. I'll slice."

Giving her a little bow he shot her a wink. "I am at your service, milady."

Janie rolled her eyes. "You're such a dork."

He gently worked the growing tube of dough into a tight roll. "That is actually not the first time I've heard that today."

"Not surprising." Janie reached in front of him, demonstrating how to pinch the seam down the log closed. "But to be fair, I'm guessing most kids think their parents are dorks, so mine is the first one that counts."

Devon finished watching her demonstration before moving to the next rectangle and beginning to roll. "How did you guess it was one of my daughters?"

Janie picked up a very long, very thin knife and a clean kitchen towel. "You have three teenage girls. It wasn't rocket science." She slid the knife down the center of the log, cutting it in half before wiping the blade clean and cutting each half into quarters. "Legally, teenagers are required to think their parents are dorks."

Devon finished rolling and went to work pinching. "That makes me feel a little better I guess."

Janie finished slicing her log and they each moved down a spot. "I didn't say they weren't right." She peeked his way, the corners of her mouth twitching. "I've seen you in your dad jeans."

"Ouch." Devon carefully pinched his way down the roll in front of him. "I didn't know you were so vicious."

Janie worked her way through the second cinnamon roll log. "Liar. You know exactly how vicious I am, and yet you still keep crossing my path."

He shrugged, finishing up and moving to the next rectangle. "I guess I'm just a glutton for punishment."

Or, maybe he found her authenticity refreshing. The more he thought about it, the more likely that was the case. Janie didn't hold back, not to spare her feelings, and not to spare anyone else's.

Could it be a little abrasive? Sure. But it was better to know how someone felt rather than discovering years down the road things weren't what you thought they were.

After finishing another roll, he was starting to get the hang of things, and the rest went together easily. Once they were all sliced, Janie showed him how to line them into a pan, and he did that while she topped them with a layer of sliced peaches. The last thing they did was sprinkle on a crumbly concoction of what appeared to be brown sugar, cinnamon, and oats. She did that, while he covered each in a sheet of foil.

Then they started the whole process all over again.

"You do this every day?" He worked on spreading the filling over the dough. "By yourself?"

Janie lifted one shoulder and let it drop. "It's not bad. I get into a groove and it goes pretty quickly." She finished rolling out a rectangle and moved to the next. "I don't get many people stopping in to buy anything, since everyone knows we're all sold out. So I only have to pass out the special orders and other than that, I just stay back here and crank these out."

"But still. This is a lot to do in an afternoon." He understood hard work. His job wasn't always as calm as he'd claimed and the hours were long. Then he still had to go home and manage an entire household. "Plus you work at The Inn in the mornings. That's a lot to do every day."

Janie finished up the last of the dough and circled the island. "It's not every day." She gave him a little grin. "I'm off on Sundays."

"Ohhh." He nodded in mock understanding. "You get a whole day off every week. That's fine then." He circled the island and went to work rolling the first rectangle. "I was being sarcastic, in case you didn't catch that. One day off every week isn't normal."

"I know, but you do what you have to do, right?" Janie went to work slicing through the log as soon as he finished. "And technically, you don't get *any* days off. So don't give me shit."

Devon worked down the line, thinking about what she said. Not about him not getting any days off—it was true—but about how you do what you have to do. "Why do you have to work six days a week?"

Janie was quiet for a minute, slicing as her jaw clenched. "Not all of us found our way into happy little marriages and happy little lives."

Her assumption chafed a wound he still carried. One he couldn't even begin to know how to heal. It almost felt selfish to try. What right did he have to be upset over the way things had gone? Probably none.

"And what else do I have to do?" She sliced through another roll, continuing to work at his side. "You've seen what happens when I try to go out."

"I've seen what happens when you try to go out under less than ideal circumstances." He corrected. "I would assume, under normal circumstances, you end up being the life of the party."

Janie laughed and it was just as genuine as the one she offered earlier. "If you think I am ever the life of a party, then you clearly have *not* been paying attention."

Now was his turn to laugh. "I don't know. I can imagine you're pretty entertaining when you want to be." He finished up the last square of dough and circled the island again. "And I bet it's funny as hell to watch those ranch hands try to hit on you."

Janie groaned. "Oh God." She shook her head. "They're all like, twenty-two, and they don't understand why I'm not flattered they want to crawl into my pants." She finished slicing the last roll and leaned against the counter, shooting him a look of disbelief. "Do you have any idea how bad most twenty-two-year-old guys are in bed?"

"I do not, and I don't know that I want to hear about it, because I feel like I'm going to retroactively get my feelings hurt." He started lining cinnamon rolls into a pan. "But I'll take your word for it."

Janie studied him a second before circling the island to begin adding peaches. "You know, you're really starting to kind of annoy me."

He scoffed, adding more cinnamon rolls to a pan. "I'm glad to hear you're so grateful for my help."

Janie shot him a scowl. "Don't get your panties in a bunch." She added a layer of peaches to the next pan. "You're just turning out to not be as big of an asshole as I initially thought."

Devon snorted. "And you find that annoying?"

"Very." Janie's tone was dry, but her lips hinted at a smile.

He stared at the side of her face, taking in the delicate slope of her nose and the fullness of her mouth as she refused to look his way. "I'm going to take that as a compliment."

One of her dark brows angled as she continued dropping slices of peach into place, that twitch of a smile still teasing her lips. "You shouldn't." Her eyes finally came his way. "You were a pretty big asshole to me the first few times we met, so it didn't take a lot to slightly redeem yourself."

CHAPTER SEVEN
JANIE

"YOU LOOK WAY too fucking happy for this early in the morning." Janie took in Mariah's bright smile and sparkling eyes. "You got laid last night, didn't you?"

Mariah scoffed. "I can be happy for reasons besides sex." She turned her attention to the long line of vegetables in front of her. "But in this particular situation, yes. I did get laid last night."

Janie finished tying on her apron before going to the pile of potatoes that needed to be peeled, chopped, boiled, and mashed for an event taking place later at The Inn where Mariah was the head chef. "I want to be happy for you, but first I need to know whether or not you got off."

Mariah's smile dimmed a little, and she didn't look up as she hacked the end off a carrot. "That isn't the only thing that matters."

Janie's head dropped back and she groaned. "Are you fucking kidding me?" She slammed one of the potatoes onto the towel lined down the counter before flinging both arms out. "It might not be the only thing that matters, but why are you acting like it's an irrelevant part of the fucking process? Do you think he would feel the same way if he didn't get off?" She pointed a finger at Mariah's face, before her friend could answer. "Because I can tell you, he would absolutely not."

She'd been around the block a time or two. She was over forty and had never been married, but she had a string of failed relationships behind her. And if there was one thing she'd learned the hard way, it was that any man who didn't put effort into getting you off, wasn't worth shit.

Half the ones who did still weren't worth shit.

"I think he was just caught up in the moment." Mariah offered an excuse Janie had used too many times herself. "I'm sure it will be better next time."

"For your sake, I hope you're right, but I've never been right when I made that same assumption." She scrubbed the next potato so aggressively part of the skin wore away. "Please tell me he knows where the clit is."

Mariah was quiet beside her.

Janie's head spun her way. "Seriously?"

Mariah blew out a long sigh and had the audacity to act aggravated. "It's not like there's a neon arrow pointing to it."

Janie stared at her friend, eyes getting wider by the second until they burned from her lids stretching so far. "It is literally front and center."

Mariah's earlier smile was completely gone now,

replaced by a frown. "I knew I shouldn't have told you. You're still fucking bitter over Griffin falling in love with Dianna."

Janie's head bounced back like Mariah had slapped her. "Are you kidding me right now?" Sure, she hadn't initially been happy about Dianna and Griffin's relationship, but it had nothing to do with her history with Griffin. The reason she'd been unhappy was because Dianna's amazing—beautiful and smart and successful and sweet and kind. And, up until recently, Janie's opinion was that Griffin was a piece of shit. But, in the time her boss and ex had been together, she'd seen him be everything she'd wanted. A good and communicative partner who supported Dianna at every turn.

It was the kind of thing that might send her spiraling if she thought on it too long. But thanks to the steady stream of bills and debt she'd racked up while chasing down more unfinished dreams than she could count, sitting and stewing in her own shortcomings wasn't something she had much time for.

"I'm sorry." Mariah's shoulders slumped as she leaned against the counter. "I shouldn't have said that. I know you don't have any sort of feelings for Griffin anymore." She lifted one arm to swipe at a bit of her hair. "I just really like this guy, and you're kind of shitting on my parade."

Janie sighed. Bitterness was an emotion that always came easily. One she spoke just as fluently as bitchiness and sarcasm. It made her the kind of person you wanted to have your back when shit went down. But it also occasionally made her a shitty friend, too jaded and cynical to simply be happy for someone she loved.

Forcing her tone to soften, she twisted on a smile. "I'm sorry. I just worry about you and don't ever want you to waste time on someone who doesn't deserve you." It was the same sort of conclusion she'd jumped to with Dianna, and it nearly led to the loss of their friendship. She didn't want to make the same mistake with Mariah. "I really genuinely want him to be as great as you think he is, because you're awesome and deserve someone fucking amazing."

A little of Mariah's smile came back. "Thank you."

Janie stepped away from the sink, coming to rest her hands on Mariah's shoulders. "But, fair warning, if he ends up hurting you, I might make him dead."

Mariah rolled her eyes on a laugh. "I would say you can't go around killing men who are mean to your friends, but I feel like you'd do well in prison. You'd probably end up running the place."

That was honestly a really nice compliment. Janie grinned at her friend. "Believe it or not, I don't plan on finding out. I've gone this long without getting arrested, and it's a life goal of mine to keep that streak going." Not that goals were her strong suit. Or streaks. Or consistency. Or follow through. That's why she latched onto any sort of achievement and held tight with both hands. "So, unless they can start arresting people for outstanding debts, I think I'll be able to remain on this side of the bars."

Mariah's expression fell a little. "I thought you were starting to get caught up."

Janie sighed again, dropping her hands and turning back to the potatoes. "Caught up is relative. I've made a lot of dumb mistakes over the years. It was going to catch up with me sooner or later."

She'd hiked halfway down lots of career paths in her lifetime. That was how she found Mariah. They met during her stint in culinary school. But while Mariah finished and went on to have a great career, she dropped out part way through, realizing running a kitchen wasn't how she wanted to spend her life.

Unfortunately, just because you didn't get a degree, didn't mean you weren't still responsible for your student loan debt, so her history of quitting cost her dearly. Not only did she still owe money on her time in culinary school, she still owed for the two thirds of a cosmetology degree she had, the time she spent in massage school, and the community college where she took a stab at accounting.

Mariah leaned in to give her a tight hug. "You'll get it all straightened out." She pulled back, meeting her gaze. "And you might even meet a nice guy while you're at it."

Janie snorted. "I'm pretty sure a nice guy will see me and run in the opposite direction." She wouldn't blame him either. Chances were good she'd chew him up and spit him out anyway.

Mariah wiggled her brows. "Doesn't seem like Officer Peters runs when you cross his path."

She'd been waiting for her friend to bring that up.

They hadn't had much time to chat since the run-in she'd had with Devon in the bar a few nights ago, and it was only a matter of time before her friend wanted all the details. "That's because Officer Peters isn't a nice guy."

Even as she said it, the words felt less right. Maybe not wrong, but also not entirely correct. Any man who spent two full hours in both police gear and an apron assembling cinnamon rolls, couldn't be all bad. But any man who took every opportunity to point out shortcomings the way Devon Peters did, couldn't be all good either. Regardless, he was pretty fucking good at getting rid of screaming menstrual cramps, so there was a place for him in this world.

"Cut him some slack. He's a widower with three teenage daughters." Mariah went back to their morning task. "He's got a lot going on."

"We all have a lot going on." Janie looked her friend over. "Except for you. You've only got a ranch hand who definitely won't be able to find your G-spot going on."

They'd been friends long enough that Mariah recognized her sarcasm, and instead of being offended, she laughed. "Whatever, bitch. At least I've seen a dick in the past five years."

"I've seen one." Janie dug back into her stack of potatoes. "I just didn't have any interest in touching it." She'd been in enough tumultuous relationships to experience some pretty good sex in her day, but the fallout wasn't worth it. Especially when she learned the better a guy was in bed, the more problematic he was outside of it.

Maybe it was actually great that Mariah's little ranch hand was terrible in the sack. He'd probably treat her like a fucking queen. As long as she invested in a good vibrator, she might just live happily ever after.

The rest of the morning flew by in a blur of food preparation and idle chatter. Like her relationship history, her job history was all over the place, so she'd worked a decent number of jobs over the years. Enough to know that she was lucky to find the two she had now. Working at The Inn and The Baking Rack with people she liked, doing things she didn't hate, was more than she'd had up to this point. Add in her little trailer on the outskirts of town, and she had it pretty good in Moss Creek.

For the first time in her life, things were looking up and—outside of her run-ins with Officer Peters—she was almost feeling pretty good about where she was in life.

For the most part. There was still no forgetting all the ways she'd fucked up to this point—especially as she watched every penny she made disappear from her bank account—but she wasn't making shit worse. No more pretending she could follow through on a career path. No more dreaming she'd find a man to whisk her off her feet.

The revelation was surprisingly freeing. Depressing, but freeing.

When her shift was over at The Inn, Janie packed up and headed home, tidying up and grabbing a quick lunch before going into town for her solitary afternoon at The Baking Rack.

Dianna had hired a few more employees, but they all worked the morning shift since that was the wild one. For now, she was still able to handle the afternoons herself, and today was no different. Her period was finally finishing up, so she wasn't struggling with bloating or cramps or any of the litany of other things that came with it, and getting through the bucket of dough waiting for her was a breeze.

Even without a maybe-nice, but also occasionally dickish, small-town cop to help.

Her eyes slid to the large apron hanging on the wall. She gritted her teeth, hating herself for almost wishing he'd stop in again. Only for the extra set of hands, of course.

Possibly also for the conversation. Talking to him hadn't been hateful, and had given her something to do besides mental math as she worked. Normally calculating how close she was to being caught up on her student loans and credit card bills was what got her through the silent afternoons of repetitive work, but having Devon to entertain her made the time fly by.

When he wasn't lecturing her on the baldness of her tires or her decisions about pain management, the man was actually pretty nice to talk to.

And even nicer to smell.

She had a thing for good scents—that's why there were a million candles around her home—and whatever Devon sprayed on in the morning was like freaking catnip. It was rich and masculine and carried an oaky hint that made her think of the outdoors. There was also another note to it. One she hadn't been able to identify yet.

Her eyes drifted back to the apron she'd been working hard to avoid all afternoon. Even with the heavy scent of cinnamon and buttercream hanging in the air, she kept getting a rogue whiff of Devon's cologne.

What in the hell was that last scent? Not leather. Not coffee. Not spice.

"Fuck." Janie dropped what she was doing and marched over. Grabbing the apron off its hook, she smashed it against her face and inhaled, pulling the too-familiar smell into her lungs. Her eyes slipped closed, and for a split second she let herself remember what it felt like when he held her close the night he took her home.

It was an indulgence she couldn't allow again, but there was no one here to witness this particular moment of weakness. Or insanity, depending on how you looked at things.

Pushing the Devon-scented air from her lungs, she dumped the apron into the hamper to be washed and went back to her prep work, still fighting to figure out what that last hint of an undernote was.

An hour later, all the cinnamon rolls were assembled and stacked in the refrigerators, the doors were locked and the lights were off, but she was still no damn closer to figuring out that fucking note of his cologne. It was driving her crazy enough she considered pulling the apron from the hamper for one more smell, but that felt like taking things a step too far.

She was *not* going to give a shit about Devon Peters or how he smelled or whether he was a nice guy or an asshole. It didn't matter. It's not like she was interested in him—or any man—taking up space in her life. She learned a long time ago they were all more hassle than they were worth.

After switching on the security system, she ducked out the back door, determined to go home and hit the reset button on whatever part of her brain was shorting out thanks to Devon and his confusing, conflicting ways. But she only made it three steps toward her car when she looked up and stopped so short her runners skidded across the blacktop.

"Shit." The word came out under her breath as she stared at the exact same man she'd decided to forget existed no more than two seconds before.

Devon was leaned back against his cruiser, well-defined arms folded over his broad chest, an odd look on his face.

She lifted her chin, sucking in a steadying breath as she marched toward him, doing her best to look unaffected by his unexpected appearance. Stopping in front of him, she gave him her best glare, trying hard to fall back into old ways. "You here to lecture me about my tires again?"

Devon studied her for a minute, his expression strangely unreadable. Finally he shook his head. "No."

Janie swallowed hard, because if he was there for

something else—something that might result in more of his taunting scent permeating her brain—she might just be stupid enough to forget how to tell him to fuck off.

And the realization was terrifying.

But then Devon said something that ensured her ability to keep hating him was alive and well.

"I'm here to arrest you."

CHAPTER EIGHT

DEVON

IT'D BARELY BEEN a half-hour since he found out about the warrant another jurisdiction put out for Janie's arrest, but it was more than enough time for him to come up with a few different scenarios for how this might play out. Not a single one of them involved her laughing in his face.

But here she was, standing in the middle of the employee parking lot at The Baking Rack, head thrown back, laughing so loudly it echoed off the building behind them.

It wasn't a great start.

Straightening off his cruiser, Devon walked her way, doing his best to keep his tone calm even though he was already struggling. "I'm being serious. We got a call this afternoon from Tukwila. They issued a bench warrant over unpaid parking tickets."

Janie sobered almost immediately, her eyes

widening. "They can put a warrant out on me over unpaid parking tickets?"

He scrubbed one hand over his face, exhausted from spending his morning doing laundry instead of sleeping. "Technically, they can. They just don't normally work so hard to get an arrest." It didn't happen often, but he'd come across a few warrants for unpaid parking tickets in his career. Never before had a municipality called them to have someone brought in, though. The warrants were usually only discovered during a traffic stop or other interaction.

Which made this especially strange.

Janie's jaw went slack, and her complexion paled. "Are you serious?" There was a hint of desperation in her voice. Like she was hoping he was the kind of asshole who would joke about something like this.

And that didn't sit great. Made him wonder kind of men she was used to dealing with.

"Unfortunately." Devon tipped his head toward his cruiser. "They sent me to bring you in." It was an approximation of what happened. He *was* there to bring her in, but only because he made it clear no one else would be handling this situation but him. They didn't understand her like he did. Wouldn't be patient and give her time to wrap her brain around what was happening. Wouldn't stay calm when she reacted.

Not that he was doing a great job of it either. Right now he was calculating just how long it would take him to get to Tukwila and back again, because whoever was behind this was doing it simply to be a prick.

Janie stared at him a second longer before finally straightening. She lifted her chin and shot him a glare. "Fine." After adjusting the purse she had slung over one shoulder, she held both hands out. "Might as well cuff me then."

"I'm not going to cuff you." He moved in a little more, hands itching to reach for her. Wanting to provide comfort she would not appreciate. "We just have to go in, do some paperwork, and then you can go home."

Janie's eyes moved over his face. "That's it? I don't have to stay?"

Devon shook his head. "You don't have to stay. I made some phone calls, so you just have to get a court date, and then you can leave." He'd had to work fast to get it all done before five, but keeping her overnight wasn't an option. Even though he was pretty sure that's why the call came so late in the day. Janie had pissed someone in Tukwila off, and they were hellbent on making her pay for whatever she'd done.

Luckily, he had a few friends in high places and was able to sort the situation out in a way that would keep it under the radar. He wanted to keep this as easy and as quiet as possible. If it made it back to his mother-in-law that her renter had been arrested, there was a good chance she might try to find a way to get out of the lease agreement, and that would leave Janie scrambling for not only whatever money it was going to take to make this fiasco go away, but also a new deposit and first month's rent.

Doing it this way, no one had to know what happened.

Janie's jaw clenched, but a flicker of something he'd never seen before flashed across her eyes as she stared him down. "Fine. Let's go."

She aimed for the back door of his cruiser but he redirected her trajectory, resting one palm against her back and urging her around the vehicle. "I don't know what's going on, but someone in Tukwila is pretty pissed off at you." He opened the passenger's door and urged her inside. "You have any idea who that might be?"

Janie plopped into the seat, eyes going straight ahead to stare out the windshield, her expression flat. "I don't really want to talk about it."

He crouched down beside her. "I can imagine, but I can't help you if I don't know what's going on."

Janie's head snapped his way. "I didn't ask you to help me."

"No." He shook his head. "You didn't." He held her gaze. "I'm still going to."

He'd never been one to fight. For most of his marriage, he assumed there was nothing to fight about. That things were exactly the way they seemed.

He'd been wrong.

So while he preferred to go with the flow, he was starting to realize sometimes he had to put his foot down to get his point across with Janie. And this was one of those times. "Now tell me who in the hell is so pissed off at you they called in a warrant just to fuck you over."

Janie closed her eyes, head falling back against the rest. "I swear to God, if you try to lecture me—"

"No lectures. I promise." He hadn't considered the way he was coming across. Didn't have a clue Janie would look at it that way. If he had, he would've shut his mouth about it a long time ago. Found a different way to approach things.

Taking a deep breath, he did just that. "Just tell me whose ass I have to kick."

A bark of laughter jumped from her mouth as her eyes flew open and fixed on his face. "I'm pretty sure they frown on cops threatening to assault government officials."

"Good point." He reached inside to grab the seat belt, pulling it free to wrap it across her chest. "Tell me who's ass you're going to kick then."

Janie groaned, head dropping back against the seat again. "He's not even worth the effort." She sighed, shoulders slumping. "Sometimes even I'm shocked at how dumb I am." Pursing her lips, she twisted them from side to side before meeting his eyes. "Before I tell you, I need you to understand I have terrible fucking taste in men."

He straightened, leaning one arm against the frame as he continued studying her. "I sorta gathered that already."

Her brows jumped up. "Was that a dig at Griffin?"

He'd almost forgotten about Janie dating Griffin, but now that she mentioned it, an ugly emotion threatened to rear its head. "No." He watched her face. "But now that you mention it, I'm judging him a little for walking away from you."

Her lips curved before pressing flat. "Technically, I threw him out." Janie's eyes left his, moving back to the windshield. "He was a different person back when I knew him. Super closed off and unemotional." Her expression turned almost sad. "Apparently, yelling and screaming for him to open up to me wasn't the best way to accomplish the sort of intimacy I wanted from him."

It wasn't hard to imagine Janie getting frustrated and losing her shit. He'd actually seen it happen. More than once. It was exactly what was drawing him to her. Janie didn't stuff anything down. She didn't hide how she felt. She didn't ignore it thinking it would go away or change. She put it out there to be dealt with. Good or bad.

And he'd rather face yelling and conflict than silence and distance.

"Don't take the blame for his fucking issues." Devon paused, trying to soften the sharpness of his tone. "If Griffin couldn't give you what you needed, he should have told you." He hesitated, but couldn't stop himself from adding on, "It's not your fault you were more than he knew how to handle."

He liked Griffin. Thought Dianna's husband was a decent guy. But seeing the way his behavior still affected Janie had him itching to throw a punch.

"It's kinda hard not to take it personally." Janie sighed, her eyes dropping to her lap. "He's happily married and I'm sitting in a squad car because I broke up with a guy who didn't like taking no for an answer."

"Neither of those things says anything about you." He was slipping dangerously close to lecturing territory, but didn't care. Janie fucking needed to hear this. "Griffin just lucked into finding somebody who suited him. And any asshole who tries to fuck up someone else's life just because they didn't want him, deserves whatever you said to him." He rocked his jaw from side to side, trying to unclench his teeth. "And probably a little more."

This conversation was frustrating him on so many different levels. Not just for Janie and all she'd gone through, but for what awaited his daughters. There wasn't a doubt in his mind they weren't going to be the type of women who kept their mouths shut and took what came their way. They would be like Janie. They would be fighters. They would stand up for themselves at every turn. And while he knew that would serve them well in many ways, it was clear it wasn't any easier—or more likely to lead to happiness—than the path their mother chose.

"Now." He reached in to push back a curled lock of hair, curving it behind one ear. "Let's go to the station and figure out what the fuck is going on, okay?"

Janie's wide eyes moved over his face, and for a second he saw another hint of the vulnerability he caught earlier. It cut into him deeply, making him even more determined to fix this.

She offered a small nod. "Okay."

Janie was silent on their way in, sitting stiffly in the seat beside him. The urge to reach across and squeeze her hand was strong. He wanted to reassure her. Wanted her to know this would all be okay. He would make sure of it. Unfortunately, they weren't in that sort of a spot.

Yet.

But the more he was around her, the more he thought eventually they could be. That maybe she would finally start to understand him the way he was beginning to understand her. And if he was lucky, that understanding might be enough. Might offer him a little of what he was craving as his daughters got older. He couldn't dedicate the kind of time a relationship would require, but maybe they could form something else. A friendship of sorts. Something that might one day turn into more.

Until then, he would do whatever he could to help Janie find the happiness she seemed reluctant to admit wanting.

Yet another thing he understood well.

After pulling into his designated spot, he parked his squad car and helped Janie out, using one palm against her back to lead her to the door. Once they were inside, he ushered her into an interrogation room. Not because he wanted to question her, but because he wanted to offer privacy. For both of them.

He'd just gotten her situated with something to drink when Josh came in carrying her paperwork. The attorney sat down across from Janie and started to flip through it. The only remaining chair in the room was next to Josh, but it didn't feel right to sit there. Instead, Devon grabbed it and dragged it around the table, taking his place at Janie's side. He'd promised to help her through this, and leaving her alone on one side of the table would make her feel like they were fighting for different causes.

Josh glanced up, lifting a brow as he looked between them. Like the smart man he was, he kept his mouth shut and went back to the paperwork, flipping through the pages before turning his attention to Janie. "This is a pretty simple thing. The city of Tukwila wants its money. All you have to do is send them a check and it'll be done. They can't come after you for anything else."

Janie's skin paled and she seemed to shrink back in her seat. The reaction surprised him, because, in the scheme of things, this was a pretty simple fix. Devon leaned forward. "How much does she owe?"

Josh flipped back through the pages, pausing. "$4372.64."

The number had Janie's spine snapping straight. "No way. That's wrong." She gripped the edge of the table, leaning to squint at the number typed out in the paperwork. "I owe a third of that."

Josh shook his head, looking over the numbers. "Technically, they can charge interest, and it looks like they did. Combined with fees and penalties, the number looks accurate."

Janie's tone turned pleading. "They can't do that. He said they would settle with me. That I could pay them eight hundred dollars and be done with it."

Josh opened his mouth, but Devon held up one hand. "Give us a minute."

His buddy shot him another look that said he was

going to pay for every second he spent here, before pushing back his chair and walking out the door.

Once Josh was gone, Devon turned to Janie. "How long ago did you make that deal?"

She rocked a little in her seat, hands twisted together in her lap. "Before I moved here."

"And did you pay that amount?" He was pretty sure he already knew the answer to that, but wanted all the information before he decided how pissed off he was about to be.

Janie wiped at the corner of one eye. "Half of it." She hesitated. "When I had the money to pay the other half, the terms of the deal had suddenly changed."

Seemed like he was going to be fucking irate. "So you didn't pay the other half, whatever city official you were dealing with got pissed off, and you left town."

Janie shot him a glare, a little flash of her normal attitude flaring to life. "If you're going to—"

"I'm not going to lecture." He cut her off before she could finish. "I'm just trying to understand. That's all."

Janie slumped back in her seat, arms crossing tight around her middle. "We'd been going out for about six months when he saw the letter I got from the city about my parking tickets." Her posture tightened even more, shoulders climbing higher. "He said he could help me, and at first he did, but after that he started acting like a dick. Treating me like I should be eternally grateful that he saved me some money." She lifted one shoulder and let it drop. "I told him to go pound sand."

That made him feel a little better even though he knew how it worked out. "Sure he loved that."

Janie's lips softened into a hint of a smile. "The look on his face was pretty priceless." She shook her head. "But I was dumb enough to assume we had an official deal. I didn't find out it was an under the table sort of thing until I tried to pay off the rest and they told me I owed sixteen hundred dollars instead of four." She tipped her head to one side. "Mariah called the next day and told me about this job she knew of, and I figured I'd just move away and he could go fuck himself."

"He can still go fuck himself." Devon met her gaze as an idea formed. One that would help them both. "Because I've got a proposition for you."

CHAPTER NINE
JANIE

THIS WAS PROBABLY a bad idea, but what in hell else was she going to do? The desire to put yet another of her past bad decisions behind her had been so strong she hadn't really thought the whole thing through when Devon made his offer.

So here she was, holding the key to a man's house in her hands for the first time in her life. She didn't like being indebted to anyone, but maybe this wouldn't be so bad. She'd clean Devon's house once every two weeks for the next six months, and then they'd be even.

Sure, this whittled her days off down to one Sunday every two weeks, but it would be worth it. She could check off one more bad mistake rectified and one more debt paid, bringing her closer to finally having her shit together. Would it prove her mother wrong? No, but at this point that was never going to happen. But she *would* be one step closer to proving herself wrong, which was better than nothing.

Shuffling around the caddy full of cleaning products she brought along just in case Devon used crappy shit, she slid the key into the deadbolt and twisted it open. After turning the knob, Janie stepped inside, getting her first look at Devon Peters' private world.

And dropped her caddy of tools to the floor.

"What the fuck?" She couldn't believe what she was seeing. "He's got to be kidding." No way did Devon think an every-other-week cleaning was all he required.

The place was a wreck. Not filthy per se, but certainly not clean. The primary issue with the interior of the mid-seventies tri-level was the chaos. There was shit everywhere. Bags were piled on the floor. Clothes were on the couch. Personal items were stacked on end tables and entertainment centers. The front living room alone would take her all day to clean.

Her stomach dropped. What the fuck was the kitchen going to look like?

Walking slowly so she could take it all in, Janie made her way down the hall leading to the back of the tri-level. Two sets of stairs sat on her left, one leading to the upper floor and one going to the lower level. Past them, a kitchen with an attached dining room took up the entire back end of the ground level. Both rooms were just as bad as the formal living room. The large dining table was covered with mail and the most random assortment of items she'd ever seen. Everything from pencils and pens to makeup and... Was that cat food?

She snapped her head around, but there was no sign

of a cat. She wasn't sure if that made things better or worse.

There were no dirty dishes in the sink, but that was about the only redeeming quality the joined rooms had. The windows were smudged. The stove needed scrubbing. It looked like someone just piled the groceries onto the counters instead of trying to put the items away.

And then there was the floor. The tile itself was pretty enough, but she had a sneaking suspicion the grout lines were not intended to be dark brown.

No wonder Devon was so eager to make this deal. The asshole knew he'd be getting the better end of the bargain. "Motherfucker." She was pissed. Seriously considering marching her ass to the station so she could lay into him.

But she was also a little excited. It was nothing she would ever admit to him, but the opportunity to whip a place this chaotic into shape had her itching to get started. Of all the dumb things, cleaning had always been oddly soothing to her. She'd failed at just about everything else she'd ever attempted but had always been able to keep her home spotless.

It was an odd thing to be proud of—much like her former pride at never being arrested—but she was. Even though every other aspect of her life was a total shit show, knowing her home was organized and tidy made her feel like she wasn't a complete failure.

And right now, seeing that while Devon seemed to have it all together, his house was a shit show? That sort of made her feel better too. Like she wasn't the only one dropping the ball. And since he'd helped her juggle one of her proverbial balls, she could probably help him out too.

But she was still going to lecture the fuck out of him over it.

Going back to the front door to collect her caddy, she carried it into the kitchen, deciding the heart of the home made the most sense to start with. She pulled back her hair and got to work.

It took over two hours to go through all the food on the counters, sorting it by type and size and then doing the same with the food in the cabinets. After clearing out anything that was expired or almost used up, she put every item in place, doing her best to come up with an organizational system that made sense and would be easy for a single man and three teenage girls to be consistent with. Or, at the very least, easy for her to keep up with every two weeks.

Now that the counters were clean, she went to work scrubbing them down, wiping both the surface and the tiled wall behind it. Next were the cabinets. After filling the sink with hot water and a splash of dish liquid, she dipped in a sponge, kicking herself for not bringing a bottle of wood degreaser. If she'd known how the place looked, her car likely would've been packed to the gills with every cleaning product she owned, making the mess a little easier to tackle. But it was probably better she didn't know what was in store, because she might not have made this deal.

Or maybe she would've made it faster. She'd barely made a dent in the kitchen, and already felt real fucking good over how much better it looked. Not much she'd done in her life made her feel good about herself, but right now she was genuinely accomplishing something. And once the counters and cabinets were done, she stood back and looked it all over, a little smile curving her lips at the difference she'd made.

An unexpected sound put a little damper on her happiness, and had her spinning toward the side door, sucking in a surprised breath as it swung open. Three young girls tumbled into the kitchen, stopping short when they saw her standing there. For a few long seconds, everyone stared at each other in silence, equally shocked at seeing someone else in the kitchen.

Finally, the oldest of the girls stepped forward, brows pinching together as her blue eyes snapped from the newly scrubbed cabinets and counters to where Janie stood. "I'm not complaining, but who are you and why are you cleaning our kitchen?"

Janie shifted on her feet, not quite sure how to respond. "Did your dad not tell you I was coming today?" Devon told her the girls would be gone for the afternoon, assuring her she would have the house to herself, but she'd assumed he'd let his daughters know someone was coming to clean their house.

The older girl shook her head. "No. He told us he was going to do some cleaning before he went to work today." She propped both hands on her hips. "That jerk was going to pretend like he'd been the one cleaning the house."

Janie checked her watch—pleasantly surprised to discover she'd remembered to charge it the night before. Somehow she'd accidentally worked an hour longer than she'd intended. "That is actually kind of hilarious." She shrugged. "And a little brilliant, honestly." She'd intended to lecture Devon over the state of his home when she saw him, but might as well get warmed up now. "Because this place was ridiculous. You three girls are old enough to clean up after yourselves." She crossed both arms over her chest. "Do you just drop things wherever you're at and then forget they exist forever and ever?"

She wasn't their parent, but for the love of God. The least they could do was pick up their own fucking tissues after they blew their noses. Devon worked hard. It seemed like he was always working. And on the few days he wasn't, she'd seen him driving these girls all over town. The man did everything he could to make sure they were loved and taken care of. The least they could do was—

She nearly stumbled back.

Holy fuck. She was defending Devon.

The middle daughter lifted her brows, and for a second, Janie thought she was going to argue back. Finally the girl gave her a sheepish grin. "It is pretty bad, huh?"

Janie threw her hands up. "It's fucking awful." She motioned at the bags each girl carried. "Go put those where they belong and come back here. There's no way I can clean this place on my own." She probably shouldn't be bossing his kids around, but it seemed like Devon might need a little help with that too.

And she was hella good at bossing people around.

Janie made a shooing motion with her hands. "Go. I don't have all night."

The girls glanced at each other a second before filing down the main hall. They paused at the closet just inside the door, glancing back her way before opening it. A rush of items rolled forward, piling onto the floor at their feet.

Janie's jaw dropped, but her next reaction came completely out of the blue. She threw her head back and started to laugh, feeling lighter than she had in—ever.

Because Devon Peters—lecturer of lecturers—was just as big of a fucking mess as she was. Only in the literal sense.

The youngest of his daughters leaned closer to her older sister, eyes wide. "I think she's lost it."

Janie wiped at the corner of one eye, pulling in air as she tried to get herself back under control. "Honey, I don't think I ever had it."

She snapped off her rubber gloves and moved to where they stood, shaking her head at the stack of crap they'd been piling up pretending it would never form an avalanche. "I guess I know what you girls are going to be doing tonight." She turned back toward the kitchen. "I'll get you some trash bags."

Collecting a bag from the kitchen, she shook it out as she walked down the hall, intending to pass the task of organizing the closet off to Devon's daughters, but it became clear this wasn't the kind of project they'd tackled before. So she stayed beside them, helping sort through the mess, separating everything out into manageable piles before deciding what needed to stay, and what needed to go. By the time they were hanging winter coats and backpacks into place, someone's stomach growled. Loudly.

Checking her watch again, Janie was shocked to see it was well after seven o'clock. "Are you girls hungry?"

"Starving." The youngest turned to her older sisters. "Can we order pizza?"

"Nope." Janie answered for her. "I just spent three hours going through all the food in your kitchen, so I know there's plenty here to eat."

The youngest pushed out her lower lip in a pout. "You sound like our dad."

Janie curled her lip. "That was mean." She pointed at the remaining items left to be dealt with. "Why don't you three finish up here, and I'll make some dinner."

She was sort of taking over, but Devon knew what he was getting himself into when he asked her to come here. At least he should have. If he hadn't already guessed she was the kind of woman who made shit happen, then that was his own stupid fault.

Carrying the three garbage bags worth of trash they pulled from the closet out to the deck, she left them there for Devon to deal with when he got home. Going into the somewhat cleaned kitchen, Janie went through the cabinets, pulling out two packages of macaroni and cheese, two cans of tuna, and then went to the freezer, fingers crossed she would find the last item she was looking for.

Devon had plenty of food, but most of it was snack items or ingredients. She could have gone through all of it and come up with something a little fancier than what she had in mind, but there was way more to do than worry about impressing these girls with her culinary skills. She decided to whip up one of her childhood favorites, hoping these kids would enjoy it too. As luck would have it, there was a bag of frozen peas on the top shelf, so she added it to her pile, carrying everything to the stove where she started a pot of water boiling.

As it heated, she grabbed a broom and swept the floor, dumping the collected pile into the trash just as the water bubbled. After adding the noodles, she started on the mail in the center of the table, separating out the junk and dropping it into the trash before draining the noodles and mixing all her items together. As she was stirring, all three girls filtered in, expressions curious as they peeked into the pot.

The middle daughter leaned over her shoulder. "What's that?"

"It doesn't really have a name, but it's something I ate a lot when I was young." She pointed at the cabinet to her right. "Grab some bowls so we can eat and get back to work."

The older daughter lined four flower printed bowls down the counter and Janie scooped some of her doctored-up macaroni and cheese into each one. Once dinner was all dished out, she picked up her bowl and turned to the still overflowing table. "Where do you guys usually eat?"

The oldest daughter gave her a sheepish smile. "On the couch while we watch television."

Janie opened the silverware drawer and fished out spoons, adding one to each bowl. "Not judging. That's where I usually have dinner too." She carried her bowl toward the hallway. "Come on. Let's go eat." She situated herself on the overstuffed loveseat, waiting until all three girls were seated on the couch before saying, "We didn't really get to introductions. I'm Janie. You probably already figured out your dad hired me to come clean your house on Sundays."

The oldest daughter gave her a little smile. "I'm Riley," she thumbed at the middle daughter beside her, "this is Olivia," then she pointed to their youngest sister, "and that's Gwen."

Janie studied Devon's daughters for a minute. "I'm sorry I was a little hard on you girls. I was just really surprised when I got here. This place is pretty—"

"Disgusting." Olivia finished for her. She grinned, looking unoffended. "We know. Our dad tells us all the time."

Janie leaned forward, meeting their gazes. "If you know, then why don't you help him? He's got a lot on his plate. I know you guys are kids, but—" She stopped short.

What the fuck was she doing? She was lecturing

these girls the same way Devon had lectured her countless times.

But it was kind of for their own good. And fuck if she didn't hate that, because now it had her looking at Devon's lectures a little differently.

Janie groaned, flopping back as she shoved a spoonful of macaroni and cheese into her mouth. "Being an adult is stupid."

CHAPTER TEN
DEVON

JANIE'S CAR STILL being parked in front of his house offered some warning about what he was about to find, but it didn't come close to preparing him for the full reality of what was happening in his house right now.

He'd managed to get through the front door, past the entryway, and now was standing in the doorway, without a single one of them noticing. "What's going on here?"

Four heads swiveled his way and three sets of eyes widened. The last pair narrowed.

Riley was the first to speak up. She gave him a tentative smile from where she sat behind Gwen, fingers twisted in her younger sister's hair. "You're home early."

Devon shook his head, hooking his keys beside the door as he continued trying to make sense of what he was seeing. "Nope. Right on time."

Olivia, who was currently standing in the middle of

the rearranged living room with both hands over her head, grinned. "Guess we just lost track of time."

He took a few more steps into the house, looking over a living room that looked quite different than it had when he left. "Looks like you've been busy." His eyes found Janie. "I didn't expect you to rearrange the whole house."

She angled a brow at him, lifting her chin. "Oh, you mean the house that would have taken me an *entire month* to clean?" She walked around where Olivia stood. "The house that you told me I could spend *just a few hours* on every other Sunday?"

She did have him there. He hadn't been entirely forthcoming with the condition of his home when he told Janie she could even out the payment he'd sent to Tukwila by doing a little housework every couple of weeks. It wasn't that he didn't think she should know, it was just embarrassing. It was the same reason he made sure not to be there when she came over. He didn't want to see the look on her face when she saw just how bad he'd allowed it to get.

"Don't yell at Janie." Gwen winced as Riley continued twisting her hair. "She's awesome."

He turned back to where Janie stood next to Olivia, looking her over. "Is she?"

Olivia tightened her ponytail and straightened her shoulders. "She's helping me with my backflips." His middle daughter pointed at where the furniture was shoved against one wall. "That's why we had to move everything out of the way."

Gwen piped up. "She's teaching Riley how to braid my hair so it won't get in my face when I'm studying."

Janie stepped a little closer, smirking at him. "And, for the record, not only did I clean your kitchen, but your daughters also cleaned out the front closet."

He'd been surprised to see Janie was still at his house. Even more so to discover what was happening inside. But finding out his daughters helped clean? That shocked the shit out of him.

"Really?"

He looked between his daughters before turning to the closet in question and yanking open the door, half expecting a ton of shit to come tumbling out on top of him. They were notorious for saying they'd cleaned something, when in reality they hadn't done shit. To his continuing shock, the closet was perfectly organized. All their coats were hung in an orderly fashion. Their boots and the rest of the shoes that had been piled up were now lined in neat rows. Backpacks and purses were hooked on the door. They'd even vacuumed out the debris covering the floor and crusted into the corners.

"Told you." Janie stood right next to him, still smirking his way. "So, do I lecture you about the state of your house now, or later?"

He chuckled. "So now you're all about lectures?"

Janie shrugged. "Turns out they're more fun when they're not directed at me."

Devon glanced into the living room where his daughters were back to being focused on the tasks they'd been doing when he walked in. "I don't know how people keep up with everything." He raked one hand through his hair. "I feel like I'm barely treading water. It's exhausting."

"Ugh." Janie rolled her eyes. "If you can't handle being lectured, just say it. You don't have to guilt trip me." She looked over the entryway and the mess it still contained. "I know our initial agreement was every other Sunday, but honestly I don't know that I'm gonna be able to make a dent in this place if I'm only here every two weeks."

It made him feel slightly better to see she was just as overwhelmed by the place as he had been. "I know it's a shitshow, I just didn't know where to start."

"I can imagine." Janie let out a quiet laugh. "I wasn't really sure where to start either." She turned to where Olivia was making serious progress on her backflips and Riley was nearing the ends of Gwen's light brown hair. "The girls and I had a talk though, and right now they're saying they'll clean their rooms, so hopefully they follow through."

Devon snorted. "I'll believe it when I see it."

He'd tried a million times, and a million times they'd picked up a few things then flaked out. He couldn't even be mad at them because he did the same thing. There were only so many hours in the day, and between work and school and activities, the ones they had left to clean were few and far between.

"Might as well get them started now." Janie stepped forward, clapping her hands. "Let's put the furniture back, and then you girls can go work on your rooms."

All three girls groaned, but didn't complain. The five of them pushed all the furniture back into place, and his daughters went upstairs, grumbling a little, but not acting too put-out over Janie stepping in.

When they were all out of sight, Janie gave him a little smile. "You'll have to let me know how they do." She turned away, going to collect the plastic caddy filled with cleaning products by the door. "If nothing else, you'll get a little peace and quiet tonight."

"Not really." He blew out a breath at the reminder of all that still had to be done. "I've still gotta take care of the horses and make sure everyone's ready for school tomorrow."

Janie stilled, abandoning the caddy to face him. "Horses?"

Her tone was a little strange. Higher pitched, like it would be if she was excited, which didn't make sense considering she worked at a whole-ass ranch every morning. "That's right. Horses." He tipped his head toward the back of the house. "You want to go see them?"

Janie rocked on her feet for a second, chewing her lip before finally offering a small shrug. "Might as well. Since I'm here."

He studied her for a second, trying to read her odd reaction but coming up empty. "Give me a few minutes to change, and then we can go out."

"That's fine." She crossed both arms over her chest for a second, but then ended up dropping them to her sides. "I'll be here when you're ready."

She was definitely acting strange. Oddly excited

when he mentioned his horses and now awkwardly dismissive.

Leaving her in the entryway, he hurried upstairs, taking them two at a time. With no small amount of shock, he glanced in his daughters' rooms to discover they were, in fact, cleaning. He shook his head as he went into his own room and closed the door. "Figures."

If he'd known all it would take was Janie putting the smack down, he'd have figured out a way to get her over here months ago. On their own, his eyes drifted to his bed, his neglected libido immediately imagining the other things he could invite Janie to his house for.

If only he had the time.

Speaking of time. He changed quickly, shucking his uniform before pulling on jeans and a long-sleeved Henley. After stuffing both feet into his boots, he hustled back downstairs to find Janie frowning at him disapprovingly.

"You seriously wear those all through the house?" She pressed one hand to her temple, eyes snapping from his feet to his face. "Those are your barn shoes."

He looked her over, noticing for the first time she was in her socks. He should have expected it given her reaction when he tried to walk into her home. "Are you gonna start making us take our shoes off at the door?"

She grabbed her discarded sneakers from beside the front door. "I should. It will make my job a hell of a lot easier." She hooked them over her fingers and followed him down the hall into the kitchen. He stopped a few steps in, looking over the space like he'd never seen it before.

He had, but it'd been years since he'd seen it like this. "Holy shit. I can't believe you got so much done."

Again, Janie shrugged. "It still needs a lot of work, but all your food is put away and I got rid of everything that was expired."

"You did way more than that." He opened the back door and stepped out onto the deck, coming face-to-face with a pile of the consequences of his non-actions.

"Oh yeah. I'm not taking those out." She toed the mountain of trash bags with one of the sneakers she'd pulled on. "Those are your problem." Janie poked him in the shoulder as she passed. "Mister Messy Pants."

The nickname didn't bother him. It was the truth. "Funny." He pulled the door closed, leading her across the deck and down the stairs. "If I'm Mister Messy Pants, does that make you Little Miss Immaculate?"

Janie grinned up at him from where she walked at his side. "I feel like you're getting dangerously close to dad joke territory."

He scoffed. "You started that."

She tipped her head. "Come on. I bet you have a whole list of them, just waiting for the perfect opportunity to whip one out."

"No." He paused, trying like hell not to prove her right. "I'm not Indiana Jones." He risked a peek Janie's way and found her watching him with a raised brow. "Whip one out? Indiana Jones has a whip?"

"Oh, I got it." She pursed her lips, but he could swear

it looked like she was about to smile. "I think I liked it better when you were lecturing me."

"Well that's just mean." He bumped her shoulder with his so she would know he was teasing. "See if I ever tell you a joke again."

"I'll mourn the loss." Janie peeked up at him from under her lashes, unsuccessfully smothering out a smile as she returned his shoulder bump.

Following the path he'd taken twice a day for the past ten years, he headed for the barn. Since his daughters didn't come out here much, it was the first time he'd had anyone with him in longer than he could remember, and it was a little strange. In a good way.

Moving past the line of trees taking up the back of the main yard, he glanced at Janie when the barn came into view, trying to gauge her reaction.

While she didn't say anything, her eyes were bright as they locked onto the John Deere green structure, and a small smile played on her lips. Her steps were quick beside him, giving away her eagerness as they crossed the last remaining bit of grass. She rocked up onto her toes as he pulled the door to one side, standing back so she could be the first one inside. Janie didn't hesitate. She went straight for Winston's stall, fearlessly going right up to his horse.

Devon lingered behind her, watching as she made long strokes down the gelding's neck. "I didn't know you were a horse girl."

Janie didn't turn his way, keeping all her attention on the animal in front of her. "This is actually the first horse

I've ever met." She leaned back, looking over Winston's face. "He's beautiful."

Devon stood there for a second, trying to make sense of what she'd just told him. "You've never been around a horse before?"

Janie shook her head. "No, but I've always wanted to. They're just so pretty."

He was listening to her, but it still wasn't quite connecting. "But you work at a ranch. How have you not been around a horse before?"

Janie finally glanced his way, her expression slightly irritated. "I work in the kitchen of an inn on a ranch." She turned back to Winston. "As soon as I finish there, I have to leave to go to The Baking Rack. I don't exactly have a ton of time to spend in their barn."

It was a stark reminder that he was taking up even more of her time. He should probably feel guilty for it. For monopolizing Janie's only day off. But he didn't. Maybe that made him an asshole. Maybe it made him selfish. But it was easy to see Janie got along with his girls. And it was easier to admit than it should have been that he liked having her there with him now. Having someone to keep him company. Someone to joke with. Someone to talk to.

They were only one day into their agreement, and shelling out the money she owed Tukwila already felt like a small price to pay for all Janie brought to the table.

But there was no avoiding that his end of the table was a little lacking. Good thing he had an idea that might level the scales. "What time are you done at The Baking Rack tomorrow?"

Janie continued petting Winston. "Same time I'm always done. Pretty sure you're familiar with it since you were waiting to arrest me after work the other day."

She didn't sound upset, which was a relief. He was a little worried she'd hold that against him. He expected to hold it against himself. But so far, that arrest might be the best thing that ever happened to him.

Devon leaned against the stall. "You want to come here when you're done? We can go out for a ride."

Janie's head snapped his way. "On the horse?"

Devon stepped to the stall next to Winston's, slapping the door and waiting until Winnifred poked her head over the edge. "Horses."

Janie's eyes went even wider. "Oh my gosh. That one's beautiful too." She abandoned Winston and went straight for Winnifred, smoothing down her dappled coat. "What are their names?"

"That one's Winston, and she's Winnifred."

He went to collect Winston's feed while Janie continued dishing out attention. She was still dishing out affection when he returned. "I think you're their new favorite person." He carried a bucket of pellets into Winston's stall, switching it out for the empty one. "Just a heads-up, they're going to expect the same kind of treatment the next time they see you."

"Then they're going to be extra sad when I have to spend all my time cleaning the house instead of out here petting them." Janie smoothed down the center of

Winnifred's nose, directing her next question to the mare. "Aren't you?"

Devon collected a pile of hay, adding it to Winston's stall. "Not if you come over tomorrow for a ride." He watched as Janie continued loving on Winnifred, the joy she found in being so close to a horse written all over her face. "I don't get to ride them as much as I used to, so I'm sure they'd love to be taken out."

Janie chewed her lower lip, eyes sliding from Winnifred to him. "The girls don't like to ride?"

"The girls don't have time to ride."

He gathered Winnifred's food, carrying the bucket back to where Janie stood. "Even if they did, they're teenagers. They've got a million other things they'd rather be doing then hanging out with their dad."

A smile teased Janie's lips. "And you think I don't have a million things I'd rather do than hang out with their dad?"

"You don't have to pretend." He leaned against the section of wall between the stalls, propping one arm on the wood surface. "I know you'd only be coming to hang out with Winnifred."

Janie pushed up on her toes, peeking over the gate into Winnifred's stall. "She does keep a better house than you do."

"That's because she doesn't have three messy teenage tornadoes tearing everything up all day." He swung open Winnifred's gate, sending Janie stepping back. Tipping his chin toward the stall, he stepped inside. "Come on. Might as well get real close. Make sure you'll feel comfortable going for a ride tomorrow."

It didn't matter whether she was going to be comfortable or not. Janie was already decided, he could see it all over her face. Hell, she'd probably go out tonight if he offered.

Unfortunately, he'd had a long day, and there were still three girls who'd be fighting and bickering as they got ready for bed. They could handle the actual task themselves—and did on the nights he had to work late —but when he was home, he tried to run interference.

Janie cautiously followed him inside, sticking closer than he expected as she sidestepped around Winnifred. "She seems a lot bigger without the gate between us."

"Winnie's not a small horse, but she's sweet as pie." He gave the mare a gentle slap on her flank, collecting her empty bucket as she shifted out of his path.

"Was she your wife's horse?" Janie's question was soft. Hesitant.

They'd never discussed Mags, but he didn't discuss her with most people. Because—like most people—Janie appeared hesitant to bring her up. Worried he might not want to talk about his dead wife.

It was always an uncomfortable spot to be in. Not for the reasons most people assumed either. He'd loved Maggie. She was a great woman. She'd given him three amazing daughters and shown a strength unlike anything he'd ever seen as she fought to stay here with her girls. But the last two years of their marriage hadn't been what most people thought. Hell, the five before that hadn't been what *he* thought. It was only when Maggie found out she was sick that he learned the truth.

That she wasn't happy, and hadn't been for a long time.

"She was my wife's horse." He gave Winnifred her food and hay, watching as Janie continued smoothing one hand down the horse's side. "She used to love riding. After she died, I couldn't bring myself to get rid of them even though I can't give them the time they deserve."

The horses were one of the few memories he had that Maggie's admission hadn't tainted. So much of his life had turned out to be nothing like he thought it was, but there wasn't a doubt in his mind Maggie was happy when they went riding, and it felt wrong to let that go. To give up the only bit of what they'd had that still felt real.

Janie turned to him and he braced himself for the sympathy that always came his way during discussions of Maggie, but—as if she was determined to remind him of how different she was—Janie rolled her eyes on a groan. "Fine. I'll come over and go for a ride." She poked him in the stomach as she moved out of the stall. "But if you keep trying to guilt trip me, I'm going to hide your daughters' flat irons and tell the girls you threw them away."

CHAPTER ELEVEN

JANIE

JANIE WAS JUST reaching the porch of Devon's house when a car pulled into the driveway. She stopped, turning to find Riley pulling up to the two-car garage in her secondhand sedan. She gave Janie a smile and a wave as the door lifted, then pulled inside, barely managing to squeeze her car into the small amount of space available.

"For the love of..."

She'd thought it was strange when Devon came in through the front door but his girls came in through the garage. Now she knew why.

And damned if it didn't melt a little more of the ice she packed around her heart. Her mother would never have given Janie the one spot in the garage. Karen Kendrick wouldn't inconvenience herself for anyone, and that included her children. No matter how great Janie's grades were, how perfect she looked and acted, her mother never saw her as anything more than an accessory. Something that existed only to make her look better.

"Fucking hell." Janie mumbled the words under her breath as she turned from the porch, heading for the open double bay. She walked into the cluttered space just as Devon's oldest daughter got out of her car. The teenager let out a long sigh, shoulders slumping as she groaned. "I'm so happy to be home."

"Long day?" Janie stood back, eyeing all the crap occupying the other side as the girl opened the back door and pulled out an overloaded backpack.

She should be irritated by all the random piles stacked onto the floor around her—it was yet another mess Devon neglected to tell her about— but instead she was itching to get her hands on it. Eager to chase the same sort of high that carried her home last night after making a surprisingly big difference in Devon's kitchen.

"Mondays are freaking crazy." Riley slammed the back door and slung the bag over one shoulder. "I leave at six in the morning and don't get home until six at night." Her steps were slow as she headed for the door leading inside. "It seemed like a great idea to schedule as many classes as I could together, so I wouldn't be driving back and forth all the time, but it's so much."

"That is a lot." Janie followed behind her. "The longest day I had when I was in college was six hours, and by the end my brain was fried. I can't imagine how you feel after twelve."

Riley paused on the single step leading inside, turning to face her. "You went to college?"

Janie laughed. "I went to a lot of different schools, but I started with community college." She rolled her eyes. "I thought I wanted to be an accountant." She laughed again, because, looking back, that was probably the most ridiculous of her aspirations.

Riley's eyes narrowed, not in suspicion, but in curiosity. "You didn't?"

Janie considered before answering. "Technically, I did, but accounting didn't want me. I was fucking terrible at it." She tipped her head from side to side. "And, honestly, if I hadn't been terrible at it, I still probably would've hated it. Sitting behind a desk crunching numbers is not something I can see myself enjoying."

As tiring as it was, she much preferred the physical requirements of the jobs she did now. Were they careers that would impress anyone? Hell no. But she never dreaded working, and she never came home miserable, so that had to count for something.

"So you're glad you didn't become an accountant?" Riley continued to study her, expression open and curious and carrying zero judgment.

It was refreshing, and made her feel more comfortable continuing to talk about what most people saw as failures.

"I am now. My mom gave me a hard time about quitting, but by that point I'd already figured out nothing I did would ever impress her, so..." She shrugged again, unsure how to finish that sentence.

Because it wasn't actually true. That was the point she *should* have figured out she'd never be able to make her mother happy, but it took a long time for the reality of it to really sink in. Even now, it was still difficult to come to terms with. Maybe it wouldn't be so difficult if she was able to feel proud of herself, but she was turning out to be just as tough to impress as her mother was.

Riley opened her mouth, likely to ask another question, but the door behind her flung open. Devon lifted his brows, eyes moving between them. "Are we hanging out in the garage now?"

"Yeah. All the cool kids are doing it." Riley shot him a grin and an eye roll. "But you can't come because you wear dad jeans."

Devon stepped back, giving them room to come inside. "Why are you always giving me hell about my jeans? You're the one who picked them out."

"What did you want me to pick out?" Riley started to drop her backpack on the table but stopped, her eyes moving to Janie before she hauled it back on her shoulder. "You would look stupid in anything else."

"So the jeans I'm wearing are uncool, but I would look stupid in anything else." Devon shook his head. "I feel like I can't win here."

Riley widened her eyes, giving him a pointed look. "You're not supposed to win. You're a dad." She gave Janie a quick smile as she moved for the hallway. "Can you do something with him so he stops giving me shit?"

The request was surprising. Part of her expected

Devon's daughters to be weirded out by her showing up at their house tonight. She assumed they'd get the wrong idea—that she and their dad were something more than just acquaintances. But it didn't seem like Riley was bothered to see her again. The teenager seemed just as unbothered by the idea of her father spending time with a woman who wasn't their mother.

Devon turned to her as Riley's heavy steps went up the stairs. "See? You're not the only one I annoy."

"Yeah, but I think it's your job to annoy them." She poked his middle. "You just annoy me for fun."

"Right. Because your reactions are always so fun." He gave a strand of her hair a little tug. "We need to get moving. Otherwise it's going to get dark on us."

Janie followed him out the back door, the same way she had the night before. All day, she'd been anticipating this. Both excited, and a little apprehensive. After loving horses from afar for so long, what if she was terrible at riding them? What if her ass fell right over the side and broke a leg?

"Relax. It's easy." Devon slung one arm around her shoulders, tucking her into his side.

The move didn't feel romantic, only friendly, and she leaned into him despite her better judgment. Being single was lonely. Being single and not close with your family was even lonelier. She went weeks sometimes without really touching another person in any sort of way, and the weight and warmth of him felt really freaking good. As good as it did the night he brought her home and they 'accidentally' hugged.

He pulled her closer as they ducked around the treeline. "We'll just do a short ride tonight. Get you used to everything. Then if you want to do it again, we can plan for something a little longer."

Janie lifted her brows. "You mean in all that free time we have?"

Devon groaned. "Don't remind me. I don't know where the days go." He dropped his arm from her shoulders to slide open the barn door, leaving her feeling too light. "They all just blur together. Before I know it, all three girls are going to be grown and gone and I'm gonna be sitting there wondering how in the hell it happened."

She didn't know much about having kids, but she did know about time getting away from you. For years, she'd just been taking life one day at a time, and now the only thing she could do was wait for the days to pass, each one bringing her closer to paying off the significant debt she'd accrued being young and stupid.

And then not young, but still stupid.

It hadn't even crossed her mind to consider what would happen after that. Would she be left sitting there —just like Devon—wondering where all the time went? Probably. And it was kinda depressing. Because none of her time had gone to anything that mattered.

"Don't you think everyone feels that way though?" Janie followed him into the barn, hoping he might tell her that it wasn't just them. That it wasn't one more way she was fucking her whole life up.

"Probably. I think a lot of people, anyway." He opened up Winnifred's gate and led her out into the main area of the barn. "At least I hope so, because if I find out everybody else is out there enjoying every day and living without regret, then I'm gonna be real depressed."

She couldn't even imagine what that would be like—to live without regrets. Regrets felt like all she had sometimes. They said hindsight was twenty-twenty, but even looking back she couldn't see a way to make things better. Just a different kind of mess.

Devon disappeared into a side room and came out hauling a saddle and a mat looking thing printed in a southwest design. "Want me to show you how to do this?"

"Now you want me to clean your house and saddle your horses?" She tried not to smile, but failed. "You're turning out to be pretty fucking needy."

"I wouldn't be so needy if you weren't so capable." Devon tipped his head toward the mare. "Come closer. She's not gonna bite." He grinned. "I promise I won't either."

Janie swallowed hard. It wasn't so much Winnifred she was worried about. It was the man wearing decidedly not dad jeans and a deep green, long-sleeved shirt that hugged him in all the right places. The man who parked in the driveway and didn't bat an eye at shelling out thousands of dollars to make her problem go away.

The man who also called her capable.

Devon might not bite her, but that didn't mean she would come out unscathed if she let herself get too close.

Pressing her lips together, she took a few tentative steps his way, trying to ignore how good he smelled as he first layered on what turned out to be called a saddle pad. Then he lifted the saddle onto Winnifred's back and went to work tightening it in place, explaining every step as he did it. Once that was finished, he repeated the process with the bridle and reins, the smooth, deep timbre of his voice in her ear almost as distracting as his closeness, his body brushing hers with every movement.

"She's all ready for you." Devon stepped back, finally giving her a little space. "You want to try to get up?"

She'd been so focused on his directions—and his proximity—that she almost forgot what was coming next. Her stomach tightened a little as she faced down the prospect of getting her whole self up and over the back of this gigantic animal. "Sure." She didn't want him to think she was nervous, and it was an action she'd seen done countless times in her life. It couldn't be that hard, right?"

Lifting her left foot, she hooked it into the stirrup, bracing as she grabbed the horn thing on the saddle. Gripping tight, she held her breath and shifted her weight, swinging her right leg up and over.

Well, almost over.

Winnifred was fucking tall as shit, and her estimations were just a bit off. Instead of making it onto the horse's back, she ended up clinging to her side, heel barely hooked over her rump, flailing around as she attempted to get a little more purchase.

And Devon—asshole that he was—fucking laughed. Hard.

The prick was still laughing when he planted both hands on her ass and pushed, giving her the extra oomph she needed to get where she wanted to go.

Once her butt was planted in the seat, she shot him a glare. "I was serious about that flat iron threat."

Devon held up both hands in surrender, but kept laughing, like a man with zero respect for his own well-being. "I'm sorry. You just should have seen the way you looked hanging off the side of her." He bent at the waist, hands on his knees as he started to laugh harder. "Like a fucking spider monkey."

It took everything she had to keep frowning at him. "You're just lucky I'm all the way up here and you're all the way down there." Winnifred shifted on her feet and Janie yelped, gripping the reins tight. "Now you're making Winnie mad too." She managed a glare. "One of us is going to kick you soon, and it's not the horse."

Sucking in a shaky breath, Devon straightened. "Not a surprise." He stroked one big hand down the horse's neck. "Winnie's a sweetheart. She'd never get mad at me."

It was impossible not to connect the comment back to his wife. The woman was probably a freaking saint who never lost her temper and farted sunshine and rainbows. No doubt the exact opposite of the one currently situated on her horse's back.

And that sent an ugly stab of jealousy slicing through her insides. It might not be so bad if that jealousy was only brought on by knowing his wife had a family and a house and a horse—all measures of success she'd never attained—but a big part of the envy trying to ruin her mood had to do with the man mounting the horse next to her.

Devon was an ass—she still firmly believed that—but he was lots of other things too. Things she could become partial to if she let herself. And that would be a terrible idea, because she'd learned the hard way she was not cut out for relationships. Definitely not with a single dad who carried almost as much baggage as she did.

Urging Winston with a gentle nudge of his heels, the man she would *not* be jealous over shot her a grin, wiggling his brows as he passed. "Hold on tight."

The warning barely registered before Winnifred started to move, her steps heavy as she hurried to keep up with Winston. Each one slapped her ass against the leather, rattling what was left of her brain cells around her head.

They could use it. Dumb things were trying to notice how good Devon looked in those dad jeans his daughter hated so much.

Luckily, once Winnifred caught up to Winston, the mare slowed down and settled into an easy pace as they followed the path of a worn trail through the trees surrounding the pasture attached to the barn. She hadn't initially realized Devon's property was so big, but as they wove their way along the trail, she was starting to wonder just how much of this he owned. "Are we still on your land?"

"Not anymore." Devon took a deep breath of the cool fall air, blowing it out as his shoulders relaxed. "This belongs to my neighbors, but they're nice enough to let me use it whenever I want." His eyes roamed the changing colors around them. "I really wish I had time to do it more often. The horses love being out here."

Janie relaxed a little herself as she acclimated to Winnifred movements. "It looks like you enjoy being out here too."

Devon took another deep breath, his eyes lifting to the trees overhead. "I do." A flicker of something she couldn't identify flashed across his features. "Not as much as my wife did, but enough that I wish I could do it more often."

The reminder of his lovely, perfect wife—and realizing Devon was likely thinking of her at this moment—dampened her spirits yet again, and Janie fell silent, doing her best to simply enjoy the ride. It wasn't difficult to do. Between the scenery and the steady pace Winnifred and Winston kept, the experience was soothing and almost hypnotic.

By the time Devon slowed, her lids were heavy and all her muscles were feeling a little like Jell-O. He dismounted, reaching one hand up for her. "Come on. I want to show you something."

Taking his offered hand just in case she struggled as much to get off as she had to get on, Janie slid down to the ground. Devon's hand was warm and strong in hers, and even once she was steady, he didn't let go, giving her palm a squeeze as he led her through the trees.

The ground started to angle, and her feet skidded a little, making her yelp. He glanced down at her sneakers. "We might have to get you some boots if we decide to make a habit of this."

Was that what he was planning? To make a habit of taking evening horseback rides together? She'd certainly spent her evenings in worse ways, but the constant reminder of the kind of woman she would never be—and things she would never have—had her feeling hesitant.

Right up until she saw what Devon was so excited about.

The trees in front of them opened up to reveal the rushing waters of a creek. Directly in front of them was a wide shelf of flat rock that dropped off to create a waterfall that was almost three feet high. It wasn't majestic or awe inspiring, but it was prettier than anything she'd ever had in her own backyard. Coupled with the horseback ride to get here, the little natural wonder felt a little magical.

"Holy crap. This is beautiful." Janie moved closer to the edge, crouching down to let her hands trail in the current. "It's also fucking cold."

Devon chuckled, lowering beside her. "It's not too bad in the summer. Still cold, but it feels refreshing then."

"I can imagine." She let her fingers drag through the water a few more seconds before flicking it away and wiping her skin dry on her jeans. "Thank you for bringing me here. It really is beautiful." She turned toward him and their eyes locked, the intensity in his gaze making her breath seize in her lungs.

She should put some distance between them. Hell, she should run her ass all the way back to her car and drive away. Get as far from Devon and his horses and his waterfall and his butt-showcasing dad jeans as possible.

But no one had ever looked at her the way he was now. Like she wasn't a failure with a bad attitude and a terrible track record.

His eyes moved over her face as he reached up to smooth back that damn piece of hair she'd cut as punishment for not staying where she put it, curving it behind one ear before tracing his fingers down the line of her jaw. "You're really beautiful."

It was a corny line, one she'd heard countless times before, but it hit differently coming from him. And without thinking, she leaned in and pressed her lips to his.

His mouth was firm and full, and before she could fully process what she'd done, Devon was pulling her close. One strong hand curved against the back of her neck as the other dragged her body to his. Dropping to his ass in the dirt, he hauled her across his lap, never once breaking the kiss she'd accidentally started.

The scent of his skin was amplified this close. It swarmed her senses, permeating every inch of her as he nipped at her lower lip, sucking gently before slicking his tongue along the seam of her mouth. She gasped at the sensation, the realization it brought, and Devon took full advantage, breaching her parted lips like he'd kissed her a thousand times before. No hesitation. No uncertainty. Nothing about his kiss was questioning or cautious, but it also wasn't demanding or possessive.

Devon Peters kissed like he knew exactly how much he was fucking her life up, and made no apologies for it.

Which is why she pulled her mouth from his and ran as fast as her fucking legs could move.

CHAPTER TWELVE
DEVON

HE WAS NOT expecting to see Janie's car sitting outside his house when he got home. Not that he thought she'd go back on their deal. He just assumed she'd get the job done and get out of Dodge as fast as possible to avoid crossing his path since she'd spent the past week ducking under the counter at The Baking Rack every time he passed.

Taking her out riding had been a mistake. Almost as big of a mistake as kissing her.

But damned if he still wasn't disappointed in the way she left.

He thought Janie was the kind of person who stayed in your face until shit was handled, not someone who ran the second things went sideways. It had been a big part of what drew him in.

So maybe it was better she ran, because he didn't have time to be drawn anywhere but to his daughters.

Last Sunday had left him a little more prepared for

what he was about to see as he opened the front door and made his way into the kitchen. Last time she was there, Janie had made a pretty big dent in the room, but today she'd taken no prisoners, and it was spotless.

The table they hadn't eaten on in months was completely cleared and scrubbed clean. The tile floor was gleaming and the grout was a color he hadn't seen in years. But not only did it look good, the place smelled good. Walking into a clean home hit different. It felt a little like someone pressed the reset button on his life.

He'd told Janie things went downhill after his wife died, but honestly it happened long before that. The two years Maggie was sick were hellish. Both because he had to watch her suffer, and because he was suffering himself. Struggling to come to terms with not just one, but two new realities, each bringing their own unique hell.

Going to the fridge, he pulled a bottle of beer from the newly organized shelves and headed toward the sound of laughing. Once again, Janie and his daughters were in the living room, but this time the furniture was where he'd left it. Instead of pushing it aside and practicing gymnastics indoors, Janie and Riley were situated on the couch with Olivia and Gwen on the floor in front of them.

"Now you fluff everything out." Janie worked on Gwen's hair, pulling at some sort of a multilayered ponytail spanning the back of her head. Riley watched closely, repeating the actions on Olivia's blonde hair.

"You guys know Janie's not here to be your personal hair instructor, right?"

Riley didn't look up from what she was doing, all her attention staying on the task in front of her. "She offered, so calm your tits."

He rubbed a hand across his chest, smoothing over the thickness of his vest. "I don't have tits." Sure, he was getting older, but he wasn't letting himself go. He managed to hit the gym for an hour every other day, both for his sanity and to maintain the level of fitness his job required. Did he have the time to work out the way he'd like? Of course not. He didn't have time to do half the shit he wanted to do.

"Give your dad a break. He just spent the day dealing with Moss Creek's most annoying residents." She gave him a little smile. "Except for me. I behaved myself today."

Her teasing caught him by surprise. He was fully prepared for awkwardness after she literally ran from him, but Janie seemed relaxed and at ease.

It was weird.

"I'm going to change." He waited for someone to acknowledge his words, but the four of them were back at work, oblivious to his presence.

Shaking his head, Devon made his way up the stairs, drinking down some of his beer as he stripped off his uniform, deciding to take a quick shower before changing into jeans and a long sleeved shirt. By the time he got back downstairs, Janie and Riley were finished doing Gwen and Olivia's hair, and they were milling around the kitchen as a bag of popcorn rattled around the microwave.

"I'm going to go take care of the horses." He watched Janie, hoping she might be as eager to help as she had been last week—having someone to keep him company was nice—but Janie wasn't the one who responded.

"We already took care of them." Riley leaned down to peer in at the cooking snack. "Janie wanted to see the horses and said we might as well take care of them while we were out there."

"Did she?" He turned to where Janie was collecting her cleaning supplies. "Interesting."

Gwen came in from the garage juggling an armful of the sodas he stocked in the spare fridge. Her eyes landed on where Janie was slinging her purse over one shoulder. "Where are you going?"

Janie's eyes widened and moved from side to side as if the question caught her off-guard. "Home, so you guys can watch your movie?"

"We wanted you to watch it with us." Gwen's tone was pleading as she batted her eyes. "Please?"

Janie appeared unmoved by his youngest daughter's antics. "I'm sure your dad is ready to spend some time with you guys." She lifted her brows, expression stern. "That's why we took care of the horses, remember? So he could hang out with you?"

"He doesn't mind." Olivia had her arms full of pillows and blankets as she entered the kitchen to join the attack. Her eyes swung his way. "Do you?"

Did he mind if Janie spent the evening here? In his

home. With him? "I don't mind." He met Janie's surprised gaze. "As long as she doesn't mind you girls asking five hundred questions while she's trying to enjoy a movie."

Riley opened the microwave as it started to beep, shaking the bag of popcorn as she gave him an unamused scowl. "Don't act like you don't do the same thing."

He snagged the bag away. "You got it from somewhere."

Riley reclaimed the steaming stack. "Make your own." She turned to her sisters. "Come on. Let's go pick a movie."

Janie lingered as his daughters left. Once they were out of sight she cleared her throat, avoiding his gaze. "About Monday..."

He pulled a second bag of popcorn from the pantry, finding it easily thanks to the woman wiping both palms down her jeans, and popped it into the microwave. "You mean when you kissed me and then ran like hell?"

Her jaw dropped open. "I didn't kiss you." Her cheeks flushed a little when he cocked an eyebrow. Blowing out a sharp breath, she amended, "I didn't kiss you the way you kissed me."

And thank god for that, otherwise he might have ended up doing some pretty questionable things in the middle of the woods.

"Anyway." She took another breath. "I shouldn't have run off like that. I don't know why I did it." She crossed both arms over her chest. "I should have stayed and told you to keep your fucking lips to yourself because I'm not interested in a relationship."

"That would have been a great plan, except you were the one not keeping your lips to yourself." He smiled. "I was just following your lead." Ignoring his relief at her confession, he continued. "And I understand. I'm in no position to start any kind of a relationship either."

Janie seemed to relax, giving him a sharp nod. "Good."

He nodded back. "Good."

She wiped both palms down her jeans again. "I guess we should go watch the movie then."

He pulled his popcorn from the microwave, tearing the top open. "Guess so." He held the bag her way. "I'll still share my popcorn with you."

She gave him a smile that was almost sheepish as she picked a few kernels free. "So generous of you."

"What can I say? I'm a generous guy." That was exactly why he would have ended up making some very bad decisions if Janie hadn't taken off the way she did. The temptation to show her just how generous he could be would have been hard to resist.

Finding out Maggie wasn't happy with what they had was a huge blow to his confidence. Left him feeling unwanted and undesired. When Janie kissed him, it stoked a fire he hadn't tended in years. If things had continued the way they were going, he would have likely kept her there until she couldn't walk straight just to feed his own ego. To prove he was worth wanting. And whether she wanted to admit it or not, Janie wanted him. Just as much as he wanted her.

Not that it did either of them any good. He didn't have time and she didn't have the inclination to see where this might go. So they would just have to keep things friendly. Casual.

But as they entered the living room, it became clear that was going to be easier said than done, because they were about to be sharing much more than popcorn.

"We saved you seats." Gwen motioned to the empty loveseat. All three of his daughters had monopolized the couch, leaving him and Janie no choice but to sit together.

Which was fine. They'd talked things out and come to an understanding that suited both of them. They were adults. They could spend an evening in close proximity. No problem.

It would be fine.

"Great." Devon plopped down, making sure he was firmly planted within his half. "What are we watching?"

"Blended." Riley gave him a bright smile. "It's an Adam Sandler movie, so you'll love it."

Janie's eyes slid his way as she settled into the spot next to him. "Big Adam Sandler fan, are you?"

"Don't act like you weren't around the same time I was." He relaxed a little, stretching his legs out as he shifted lower in the seat. "You know damn well he was everywhere when we were young."

"When we *were* young?" She scoffed. "Are you trying to get me arrested for assaulting a police officer?"

He grinned and popped another handful of the salty snack into his mouth. "I'd have to handcuff you this time."

Gwen leaned forward, her brows pinched together as she watched their interaction. "Are you flirting with her?"

"What?" He straightened in his seat, posture going stiff. "No. We're just friends." It didn't sound right coming out of his mouth, but that was what it had to be.

Even though the few seconds he'd had her close Monday were some of the most heated he'd ever experienced.

"Good." Olivia shoved in a handful of popcorn, her eyes glued to the screen as Drew Barrymore chugged a bowl of French onion soup. "You need some friends. Your social life is mournful."

"Mournful?" Of all the words she could have picked in the English language, she chose that one? "I have a social life."

"Right." His middle daughter snorted. "And I'm passing Algebra."

"You aren't passing algebra?" His voice was louder than he intended, but the immediate reaction only sent his daughter into a fit of laughter.

"Didn't expect you to admit the truth so easily." She blew out a long breath. "But I should actually go upstairs to study so I continue passing algebra." Turning toward the stairs, she waved one hand over her head. "Enjoy the movie."

"Now she's making me feel bad about not studying."

Riley groaned. "I've got a test tomorrow and I'm not even close to being ready for it." She stood, passing the bag of popcorn off to Gwen. "You guys have fun. Hopefully I can watch it with you next time." She offered Janie a smile. "I'll see you next week. Maybe you can show me how to do a messy bun that doesn't make me look like the principal on Matilda."

Janie grinned. "You got it."

Riley was barely gone five minutes before Gwen jumped up from her spot on the couch. "This movie is stupid." She wrapped the blanket she'd brought down around her shoulders. "I'm gonna go read my book."

Janie watched his daughter go, her brows pinched together in confusion. Once Gwen was out of sight, she turned to him. "They ditched us."

"Welcome to the world of living with teenagers." He stretched one arm across the back of the sofa. "This is a pretty regular occurrence around here." He and his daughters had made plans to spend time together more times than he could count. And—also more times than he could count—those plans never ended up fully fleshing out. One of them always had to back out because of school or cheerleading or work or any other number of things, and he ended up doing whatever they'd planned on his own.

But not tonight. Tonight he had company.

Janie tipped her head to one side, eyes going back to the television. "At least they want to spend time with you enough to make plans." She snorted, shaking her head. "I'm pretty sure I stopped wanting to hang out with my mom well before my teenage years."

"I guess your mom's just not as cool as I am."

"That might be the understatement of the century." Janie's mouth flattened.

Devon studied her face, looking over the suddenly hard lines of her expression. "That bad, huh?"

"She's a bitch." Her eyes jumped to his face. "And I know I shouldn't say that about my mother, but it's true." She swiped at that little, rogue piece of hair always falling into her face. "Nothing I've done has ever been, or will ever be, good enough for her, and she never misses the opportunity to remind me of it."

The information was a kick in the pants. One he deserved. He'd figured out Janie didn't appreciate his assistance, but still wasn't one hundred percent sure why. Now he knew, and it explained why she got so pissed off every time he tried to offer advice. To her it was just more of the same shit she'd been dealing with her whole life. Yet another person pointing out flaws and shortcomings. That wasn't what he was doing, but he could see how she might see it that way.

"So you see her much?" He wasn't paying any attention to the movie now. Not when the woman beside him was opening up. It was the kind of closeness he and Maggie never had, and he was only just beginning to see how much he craved it.

How unfulfilled he might have also been in their marriage.

"I haven't talked to her much since I moved out here, so that's been kinda nice." She gave him a weak smile. "She's got a new husband whose daughter is married to a doctor, so I'm sure what I'm up to is less than interesting to her. My life isn't the kind she can go bragging to her friends about."

He knew not everyone had great parents, but had been lucky not to experience it firsthand. It was hard to imagine what a life without someone backing you up would be like. It was unlikely he would have made it through Maggie's death as well as he did without his parents supporting him. "Were you and your mother ever close?"

Janie's lips curved in a sad smile. "No. Never." Her head dropped back, resting against his arm instead of the cushion. "When my dad died five years ago, the gap between us only widened. And honestly, that was the best thing that could've happened to me." She pinched her lower lip between her teeth, eyes far away as she continued. "For the first time in my life I wasn't chasing her approval anymore, and it was pretty fucking fantastic."

He twisted to face her, reaching for that wayward bit of hair that always taunted him. "You'll have to forgive me for saying this, but it sounds like she's not just a bitch, but a stupid bitch." He squinted, thinking his words over. "I don't think I've ever called a woman a bitch before."

Janie's smile lifted a little, the weight of her head settling heavier against his arm as she seemed to relax.

"Well, I appreciate that you used your bitch cherry to defend me."

She was so close. Smelled so fucking good. Now that he knew she tasted even better, the temptation to pull her against him was almost overwhelming.

But it couldn't happen.

Pulling his hand from her hair, Devon straightened away, giving her a wink. "That's what friends are for."

CHAPTER THIRTEEN
JANIE

THIS PLACE WAS insane. It had been years since she'd been to a high school football game, and holy hell were they different when you were over forty and not looking to socialize.

Janie dodged a group of teenage boys paying zero attention to where they were going, shooting them a glare not a single one of them noticed, as she shoved her freezing hands into the pockets of her fall jacket. It was way colder than she thought and the chill in the air was already starting to sink through the fleece lining, making her regret not digging her down coat out of the closet.

If she hadn't promised to be here, her ass would be turning around and heading back to her car. The last thing she wanted to do on a Friday night was sit in a packed football stadium, freezing her tits off, watching a bunch of high schoolers scramble their gray matter.

Thankfully, it was the last game of the season, so she couldn't be talked into coming to another one.

Stopping at the concession stand, she ordered the biggest hot chocolate they offered and a soft pretzel. She was just digging through the small purse strapped across her chest in search of her wallet when a deep voice made her fumble the leather pouch.

"Make that two hot chocolates and two pretzels." Devon dropped a twenty onto the counter and tucked another into the donation jar dedicated to whatever sports team was slinging hot dogs and popcorn tonight.

Janie dropped her wallet back into place, ignoring the flip of her stomach, as she tipped her head in a nod and offered a little smile. "Thanks."

"Don't thank me." He leaned close, bringing that scent she was becoming way too familiar with into her personal space. "I may have used you to skip the line."

Janie scoffed, faking outrage. "You are a man of the law."

Devon collected the first of the hot chocolates and passed it to her. "That makes it even more impressive when I break the rules."

He took their pretzels and his hot chocolate before leading her away from the cinderblock building situated next to the home stands. Shooting her a sexy grin that pulled all her focus to his lips, he winked. "Don't pretend you aren't in awe of my rebellion."

"Ugh." She rolled her eyes. This guy was really starting to become a problem. All the shit-eating grins and corny jokes and overused winks should be reminding her he was a dad, but the more she was around him, the more impossible it was to think of

Devon as anything other than a man. One who was frustratingly charming.

"I'll be in awe when you clean out your garage so you can park your car in it."

It was impossible to resist giving him a hard time. Lecturing him the way he used to lecture her. But somehow it always came out as teasing. Possibly flirting.

"Always bringing up the mess in the garage." He shook his head but didn't look put out. "Even though the house looks a thousand times better."

"The house does look a lot better." She could give him that. "You and the girls have done a good job of keeping it up." She gave him a sidelong glance. "But you'll thank me for giving you shit about the garage when it starts to snow."

Devon glanced up at the night sky as they continued walking toward the bleachers. "It's feeling like that won't be very long, so I guess I should get on it."

Janie adjusted her grip on the hot chocolate cupped in her hands, moving her bare fingers around to warm as many spots as possible. "It is pretty freaking cold, isn't it?"

"The last game of the season is usually the toughest one to sit through." Devon led her up the bleachers, still carrying her pretzel in his hands. Leaving her no choice but to follow. "I'm surprised you decided to come out for it."

Janie continued trailing him as he chose a row and moved down the line of corrugated aluminum serving as seats. Devon stopped and sat, choosing a location that gave them a great view of where the large group of cheerleaders stood at the edge of the field.

"It wasn't so much that I *decided* to come out." Janie lowered to the spot beside him, scanning all the girls bouncing around the sidelines. "Olivia asked me to come so I could see her cheer. She said the last game of the season they let the JV girls cheer for the varsity team, and she wanted me to see how well she's doing with her backflip."

She continued looking for Devon's middle daughter, so immersed in the task that it took her a few seconds to notice he was staring at her intently. Dragging her eyes away from the field, she looked his way, tucking her chin at the thoughtful look on his face.

"What?"

He shook his head, eyes moving over her face. "Nothing." He finally turned toward the field, tipping his head toward her cup as he did. "Might want to drink that before it gets cold and doesn't do you any good."

Janie lifted her brows. "Now you're going to lecture me about how to properly drink hot chocolate?"

"Seems like I have to since you haven't taken the first sip." His focus came back her way, eyes drifting over her. "I should probably also lecture you on the proper attire for the last game of the season."

She tried to fight the smile working across her face and failed. "That was a lecture I could have used an hour ago, so you can save it and stuff it."

Devon chuckled, taking a big bite of his pretzel while

also handing hers off. "Eat up. You're going to need as much sustenance as possible to keep your body heat up."

"I'm sure I'll be fine." She bit into the warm, slightly chewy snack. "It's only a couple hours."

"A couple hours can feel real long when you're freezing your ass off." Devon's eyes moved past her to fix on something farther down the row. "It's a good thing someone I know likes to be prepared for anything."

Janie turned, following his line of sight to find an older couple shimmying their way down the same row. There was no reason to wonder why Devon had noticed their arrival, because he was the spitting image of the woman offering her a wide smile.

"There you are." The older woman reached Janie's side and dropped the giant canvas tote she was carrying onto the metal next to her. "I was starting to think we would never find you." She dug into her giant bag and pulled out a seat cushion. Shoving her bag to the side, she set the cushion in its place and plopped down. "Have you been here long?"

"Just a few minutes." Devon polished off the pretzel he'd practically inhaled and leaned close, tipping his head her way. "This is Janie." He motioned to the older woman at her other side. "Janie, this is my mother, Alice, and my dad, Frank."

Devon's mother continued smiling, not batting an eye at Devon's very lacking explanation. "It's lovely to meet you." Her smile slipped as she looked Janie over. "But it looks like my son could have helped you pick out something warmer to wear."

"Actually," Janie started to explain what Devon had not—that they weren't here together—but Alice had already turned back to her bag and was pulling out a thick, plush blanket.

"Here. Use this. It will help keep the chill off you." She went to work draping the covering around Janie. "Next time you should wear your heavy coat when you come to a game this late in the season." Alice finished wrapping her up and gently worked her hair free. "And probably some long-johns." She finished up and went back to her bag. "No sense in freezing to death."

Janie almost laughed out loud as Alice pulled out a set of instant hand warmers and started to shake them, continuing with her lecture. "I know it's not the most comfortable to layer up in all that, but you don't have enough body fat to keep you warm in this weather." She handed over the activated warmers. "Here."

Janie worked her hand out from under the blanket she'd been burritoed into. "Thank you."

Alice brightened, her smile flaring back to life. "Of course, honey." She looked over to Devon. "What about you? Are you warm enough?"

"I'm fine." He took a sip of his hot chocolate. "You worry about her."

Janie shot him a glare as Alice went back to her bag, but Devon no longer seemed fazed by her scathing looks. In fact, he appeared to be having a hell of a time watching his mom fuss over her like a mother hen.

It was an odd situation. One she'd never come close to being a part of. Her own mother was emotionally distant at best, emotionally abusive at worst. Never once had she worried over Janie's well-being. The only thing that mattered to her was that her daughter excelled. That everyone they met was impressed by her manners and her appearance and her achievements.

For a while, she'd bought into it. Busting her little kid ass to be the smartest. The prettiest. The best.

But eventually, she fell short, and that's when it all went downhill.

"You should be the one worrying about her. You're the one who brought her here." Alice gave Devon a not-so-gentle admonishment. "The least you could have done was packed a blanket."

Normally she enjoyed when Devon was being lectured—she did it frequently. But he didn't deserve this particular talking to. "We didn't come together." Janie paused when Alice's eyes lifted. "We just ran into each other at the concession stand." Devon's mother was misreading the situation—and judging him because of it —and letting it go on any longer didn't feel right.

But neither did her attempt to explain their accidental run-in. They could have parted ways at any time. She could have grabbed her pretzel and gone on her merry little way to freeze her tits off alone.

But she hadn't.

Alice looked between them before finally settling on Devon. "Still. You need to be more prepared."

Devon chuckled at his mother's gentle reprimand. "Yes, ma'am."

"I mean it." She finally settled into her seat, tucking

her Mary Poppins bag into the enclosed area at her feet. "Maybe if you got that front closet a little more organized, you'd be able to find all your stadium blankets."

"Actually," Devon's face split into a smug grin, "the front closet is very organized."

Janie found herself smiling along with him. He looked proud of the fact his closet was back in shape, and it made her a little proud since she was the one who facilitated it.

Alice's brows lifted. "Really." She dragged the word out as her eyes slid Janie's way. "You wouldn't have anything to do with that, would you?"

Janie shook her head, deciding to pass the credit off. "Not me. I think the girls did it."

She knew for a fact the girls did it because she's the one who told them to, but that could be their little secret. Devon's daughters had been working hard to help get their house back in order and they deserved recognition for it.

Alice's expression warmed. "They are such good girls." She turned to where the cheerleaders were still stretching and warming up. "They all work so hard."

"That they do." Devon shifted in his seat, bringing the bulk of his body closer to hers. "Riley's working and going to school and Gwen is pushing to graduate a year early. She's already thinking about the ACT and researching scholarships."

Devon's mother clasped her gloved hands in front of

her chest. "We're so proud of them." She turned to where her husband sat beside her. "Aren't we, Frank?"

Frank's thick brows pinched together. "What?"

Alice patted his knee. "Never mind, dear." She turned to Janie, animatedly mouthing the words, *he can't hear a thing*.

The speakers above and behind them crackled to life and the announcer's booming voice filled the stadium, cutting off any further conversation as he introduced the players. Once everyone was on the field, the teams wasted no time getting to the line of scrimmage. She kept track of what was going on, but mostly kept her eyes on Olivia, not wanting to miss her backflip.

"Does this take you back?" Devon's voice was low in her ear. His breath warm against her skin. The combination sent a shiver racing down her spine.

His full lips pressed into the frown he'd inherited from his mother. The one she initially read as disapproving, but now knew was concern. "Are you cold?"

She pushed on a smile, a little too affected by the way his question rumbled through her insides. "I'm fine."

"Liar." Devon straightened, shucking off his coat. "Here." He draped it across her legs, the heat of his body sinking straight through her jeans, soothing the goosebumps across her skin.

"Now you're going to be cold." She moved to give him his coat back, but he shook his head.

"You need it more than I do." His lips twitched. "What with your freakishly low body fat and all."

Janie let her jaw fall open in false outrage. "She didn't say *freakishly*. You just added that on yourself." She wiggled one finger out from under the warmth of the blanket keeping her upper half toasty warm and poked it against his pec. "Not all of us have the time to grow a layer of freakishly big muscles."

Devon angled a brow at her. "It sounds like you've been looking at me a little more than I realized."

Her face heated in spite of the chilly air. "What? No."

The denial was weak at best. Especially since her eyes accidentally dipped down his coatless frame, pausing a little too long on the way his henley clung to the width of his shoulders and chest. Her only hope was to redirect. "And stop acting like you're not cold. I can see your nipples trying to stab through your shirt. They look ready to cut glass." She loosened her hold on the blanket Alice gave her, stretching it out so she could sling one end across Devon's shoulders. "Here."

Devon was still for a minute as she fed him more of the blanket. Then he slowly worked it around his big body. "Thank you."

She tried to cuddle back into the warmth, but there wasn't quite enough fleece to go around. Not with the way they were sitting now. Her eyes dipped to the slight gap between them. If she scooted closer, not only could they share the blanket better, they could also share body heat. They'd been that close on Devon's couch the other night, and that was with no one else around. Here they were surrounded by people. If anything, it would be less weird.

"This will probably work better if we're a little closer." Janie scooted her butt toward him, bringing her body right to his.

But there still wasn't quite enough blanket to make it work. She huffed out a frustrated breath, the air fogging around her.

"Here." Devon shifted, angling his body toward her in a move that brought her right against his side. The weight of his arm curled around her back, tugging her so close she was plastered against him. "How's that?"

That was a really good question.

On one hand, the blanket was now wrapped around them both and she was once again toasty warm. On the other, she was enveloped in Devon's heat and that mysterious scent she still couldn't put her finger on, being held close by a man she disliked less and less every damn day.

It made her want to wonder what would happen if she hadn't decided to swear off relationships. If she wasn't sure they would all take the same path to destruction. If she let herself hope, for just a second, things might finally start to be different.

If *she* might finally start to be different.

CHAPTER FOURTEEN
DEVON

"LAST ONE." JANIE passed up the final sparkling clean glass shade, watching as he went to work putting it back into place on the kitchen ceiling fan. "Don't screw it too tight. It might crack the glass."

He shot her a scathing look. "This is the five hundredth time I've done this today. I think I've got it figured out."

Janie matched his expression as she passed up the lightbulb. "Don't get snippy. You offered to help, sir." She propped both hands on her hips. "And for the record, you only have four ceiling fans in your house."

He carefully twisted the final bulb into place, giving her a wink. "I'm pretty sure that math checks out."

"Speaking of math..."

He and Janie both turned to the doorway where Riley stood, a scowl on her face.

His oldest daughter held up her computer. "I have a question."

Devon stepped down from the ladder, taking a deep breath. "I'm not sure I'll be much help, but I'll give it my best shot."

Riley's brows pinched together. "I wasn't talking to you." She turned to the woman at his side. "I was talking to Janie. She's done this before."

Janie's eyes widened and she began to shake her head. "It's been over twenty years. I don't know that I remember any of it."

Riley's shoulders slumped. "Crap."

Janie groaned, dragging out one of the chairs. "Bring it over here. Let's take a look at it." She lifted one finger. "But no guarantees."

Riley perked up a little, giving Janie a smile. "Got it." She settled into the seat Janie pulled out and waited as Janie sat beside her. They both hunched over the laptop as Riley explained her question, taking all of Janie's attention.

And it was fine. He didn't mind at all.

Technically.

He understood why his daughters liked Janie so much. She was fun to talk to and hang out with. Plus she had a skill set that was turning out to be pretty damn useful. She'd been a cheerleader in high school just like Olivia. Considered being a hairdresser and knew all sorts of styles. She'd even put her culinary skills to good use by teaching his daughters a handful of simple recipes they could whip up on their own so dinner wasn't all on him every night.

And, it would seem she had another skill set he hadn't yet learned about. One that involved math?

Leaving Janie and Riley at the table, he ventured out the back door. It was probably time to get a fire going.

Now that their house wasn't an embarrassment, the girls had started inviting friends over, and tonight—since they had tomorrow off for some sort of teacher workday—he would be hosting a house full of teenagers. They'd requested a fire, and since the sun would soon be setting, now was a good time to make that happen.

It was yet another thing that wouldn't have been possible without the woman inside. With Janie coming every Sunday to help with the house—and the not-so-subtle encouragement she'd given his girls to start pulling their own weight—he'd managed to eke out enough time to clean up the backyard a bit. The fire pit they hadn't used since before Maggie died was now freshened up and ready to go.

After setting up a few logs and sprinkling on some charcoal to even out the heat, he squirted on some lighter fluid and got a pretty decent blaze going. Once it was burning, he went to work setting up their collection of collapsible chairs. He'd picked up a few more in preparation for tonight, and tore away their tags, adding them to the fire. By the time he was finished, there were nearly a dozen single chairs and two loveseat versions surrounding the fire.

When he went back into the house, Riley and Janie were still at the table, his daughter looking half ready to throw her laptop across the room.

To be fair, so did Janie.

"How's it going?" He was pretty sure he knew, but felt obligated to ask.

"Awful." Riley slammed the computer closed. "I can't stare at this anymore." She stood. "I'll work on it again later." She collected the laptop and left, her steps heavy as she went upstairs.

"On that note," Janie stood, pushing her chair and Riley's in, "I'm going to head out."

"You have somewhere exciting to be?" He tried to sound casual. Like this was nothing more than small talk. It was just that Janie wasn't normally in a hurry to leave on Sundays. She usually lingered, staying later than they'd agreed on every single time.

But today she was packing up right on time. Like maybe she had somewhere else to be.

Someone else to meet.

"Yeah." Janie rolled her eyes as she added her cleaning supplies to the caddy she always brought. "I've got a ball to attend and I need to go put on my hoop skirt and wait for my fairy godmother." She straightened. "I just know you have people coming over and I don't want to be in the way."

"You won't be in the way." He said it too fast, but there was no way to undo it, so he forced his next words to come slower. "Unless free pizza and a night surrounded by giggling teenage girls isn't your idea of a good time."

"That does sound tempting." Janie looked him over. "Where's the pizza from?"

"Is that a trick question? There's only one pizza place in town." He wiggled his brows at her. "I might even let you pick the toppings on one."

Janie's eyes narrowed, but the expression on her face remained playful. "What if I like pineapple on my pizza?"

"Then I guess you'll have an entire pizza all to yourself." He narrowed his own eyes. "*Do* you like pineapple on your pizza?"

Janie didn't react for a second, but eventually her nose wrinkled. "Only psychopaths like pineapple on their pizza."

"So that's a yes then?"

He loved the way she teased him. The way he could tease her back. Throwing good-natured jobs at each other was something he and Maggie had never done. Looking back, he could see the signs that things weren't all they should have been, but at the time, she was all he knew.

They were all he knew.

Janie scoffed, eyes widening as her mouth dropped open. "I'm gonna tell your mom on you." She whipped her phone out, keeping eye contact as she swiped one thumb across the screen.

He watched her digit move, and it sure looked like she was pulling up a number. "My mom gave you her phone number?"

"Sure did. Told her I'd call her the next time Dianna put blackberry cinnamon rolls on the menu." Her smile turned devilish. "Now I'm realizing I can get plenty of use out of it."

"You better not. You'll be opening a whole can of worms you won't be able to close." He took a step toward her. "Don't make me confiscate your phone, tattletale."

Janie started backing away, but her smile—and the sparkle of mischief in her eye—held. "Now you're really making me want to text her."

He didn't really care if Janie texted his mom. She's the one who would have to deal with his mother sending her weather warnings and calling every time she heard something interesting on the news. It was more the light and easy playfulness of the interaction that had him continuing to prowl closer. It was the kind of fun he'd never had with a woman, and he wasn't quite ready for it to end.

He lunged for the phone, sending Janie jumping back on a squeal just as the doorbell rang. They both froze in place—his hand wrapped around hers, the lean line of her body so close he could almost feel it—as footsteps thundered down the stairs and his daughters' excited voices filled the entry.

"*I got it.*" Olivia's voice was the loudest, but immediately cut off by Gwen.

"No, *I* got it. It's Isabella."

Devon winced a little at the announcement, all the lighthearted fun he'd been having with Janie dissipating in a flash. He hadn't asked who his daughters invited over, and the last he heard, Gwen and Isabella weren't on the best terms. That must have changed.

Unfortunately.

The sound of the front door opening accompanied

new voices joining his daughters'. One of them hit him like nails on a chalkboard and had him spinning toward the doorway, bracing for impact.

"Hi, Gwen. How are you, honey?" Isabella's mother's tone was saccharine sweet. She didn't wait for Gwen to answer before asking, "Where's your dad?" Again, she didn't wait for Gwen to answer, her footsteps getting louder as she strolled right through their house, coming straight into the kitchen. A smile curved her lips the second her eyes landed on him. "There you are. I was wondering where you were hiding."

"Here I am." He couldn't muster up any sort of enthusiasm or even politeness, making his words flat and a little sharp. He never knew what to say to this woman. She'd been blatantly hitting on him for the better part of two years, and if there was a way to get her to understand he wasn't interested, he hadn't figured it out yet. She was determined, he'd give her that.

But that was all he'd give her.

Undeterred—as usual—Isabella's mother kept coming his way, hips swaying suggestively as she looked him up and down. His skin crawled at the thought of her touching him. She took every opportunity to do it, and it sent him stepping back.

But then she froze, the suggestive smile on her lips twisting into a scowl. Her nostrils flared as if she'd smelled something putrid

"Did you want me to go ahead and order the pizza since the girls' friends are starting to arrive?" Janie's voice was close. Close and missing the sharp edge he was so fond of. She almost sounded... Sweet?

He turned to find her eyes on his face as she reached up to smooth down the button placket of his henley.

The tightness in his muscles—brought on by the thought of Isabella's mother's hands on him—eased a little as Janie stepped closer to his side, her hand sliding down his chest.

"Let's give it a few more minutes in case some of them run late." He wrapped one arm around Janie's back, spreading his hand across the curve of her hip the way he had at the football game Friday night. After holding her gaze a second longer, he turned to the woman gaping at them with an icy glare. "Have you met Isabella's mom?"

Janie finally acknowledged the woman's presence, giving her the biggest, fakest smile he'd ever seen. "I don't think I have."

Janie shoved one hand out, continuing to beam at the scowling woman in his kitchen. "It's nice to meet you. I'm Janie."

Isabella's mother looked at Janie's outstretched hand. After a few long seconds, she took it, limply shaking it before pulling away and wiping her palm down the front of her black stretchy pants. She faced him, working her jaw from side to side. "I didn't know you were seeing anyone. "

"You didn't?" He used his hold on her to pull Janie a little closer, almost using her as a shield. "That's weird."

He wasn't going to deny her assumption, because that would only make her think he wanted her to know he was single. And even though that felt equally wrong, he also wasn't going to confirm it. He and Janie weren't seeing each other. Not in an official sense. But he talked to her more, touched her more, and thought about her more than any other woman he'd crossed paths with in recent years.

And that included Maggie.

Isabella's mother stood a little taller, lifting her chin. "Well, congratulations I guess." She shot Janie a dirty look, before turning and marching back down the hallway, the front door slamming harder than necessary when she left.

Janie turned to him, widening her eyes. "Yikes."

He huffed out a laugh. "Yeah."

"That happen to you a lot?" There was something off in her voice but he couldn't quite put his finger on it.

"Not a lot." He shot her a grin, relaxing a little more. "I rode the sad widower wave for a while."

"Seems like that only works for so long."

She hadn't moved away from him and didn't seem bothered that his arm was still around her. He understood why she'd moved in close, and appreciated it. But he appreciated the feel of her against him even more now that they were alone.

"Seems like." He reached out to catch one of the springy dark curls framing her face. "Good thing you were here. Otherwise she might have tried to invite herself to stay."

"Oh, she was definitely planning to bark her way up to the top of your tree." Janie lifted her brows. "And seeing as how she was wearing leggings, she expected you to take her up on it."

That last part threw him for a bit of a loop. "What does her wearing leggings have to do with anything?"

"Wow. You really are out of the loop, aren't you?" Janie lowered her voice, leaning in like his daughters hadn't all run straight back upstairs after letting Isabella in. "Easy access."

It still took his brain a second to pick up what she was putting down, but the second it caught on, the damn thing took off running. And connecting a few dots that would have him distracted all night. "You're wearing leggings."

Janie's eyes widened and her cheeks flushed. "Because I came to clean and wanted to be comfortable."

"Likely story."

He'd never taken their teasing quite this far. Up until now they'd all but ignored any physical closeness they'd shared, including that kiss by the river. But with her this close, skin flushed and eyes a little glazed, the way she felt against him was all he could think about.

Releasing the curl he'd been toying with, Devon trailed the tips of his fingers along the line of her jaw. "Is it bad if I say I wouldn't mind if you wore them for other reasons?"

He'd been pretending they could just be friends. That he could keep this growing connection they had on ice until his daughters were older. That he could have Janie in his life without wanting her in his bed.

He was wrong. Real wrong.

"But..." Janie's lips parted and he traced the softness of them with the pad of his thumb.

"But, what?"

Her lids drooped as one hand came to rest against the center of his chest. "I don't remember."

"Good." He caught the point of her chin with his thumb and finger, opening her mouth a little more as he leaned in, sealing his lips over hers.

The air rushed from her lungs, the warmth of her breath heating his skin as she sagged into him. It was all the encouragement he needed, and in the next second he lifted her up onto the clutter-free counter, her legs around his waist as he claimed her mouth for himself.

Janie whimpered, her hands fisting in his shirt as he gripped her thighs to pull her closer, rocking the hard length of his cock against the seam of her leggings. He knew she looked great in them, but never would have guessed just how fucking great those pants were. They were so thin he could feel the heat coming off her body, and the next flex of his hips had him groaning into her mouth.

Right as the fucking doorbell rang.

CHAPTER FIFTEEN
JANIE

SHE WAS OUT of her mind.

At least her libido was.

That was the only explanation for how she ended up wrapped around Devon, letting him tongue fuck her mouth while strongly considering letting him regular fuck other parts of her. Probably would have if the doorbell hadn't interrupted, sending each of them jumping different directions as his daughters raced down the stairs.

Now she was standing in a kitchen full of teenage girls, trying to act casual and pretending to eat the pizza she picked, filled with panic.

And horniness.

She was attracted to Devon—there was no denying it. But who wouldn't be? Obviously not Isabella's mother. Maybe that was why she ended up dry fucking him on the kitchen counter. Jealousy had her all riled up.

But if that was true, then she had to face the reasons

she would be jealous, and having an existential crisis surrounded by a gaggle of giggling girls wasn't the way tonight was going to play out.

So she shoved a bite of pizza into her face and started to chew, looking everywhere but at the man watching her with the most intense stare she'd ever witnessed. When people called a gaze devouring, this must be what they meant, because Devon looked like he wanted to consume her inch by inch.

And she might let him.

"Why is it so hot in here?" Janie grabbed a paper plate from the stack on the counter and started to fan herself, abandoning the slice of green pepper, onion, and mushroom so she could flap the front of her top around to get more air moving. "You girls need to start taking turns breathing. You're going to turn this place into a freaking sauna." She made a beeline for the back door, needing some fresh air and some space from whatever in the hell just happened in that kitchen, ignoring the odd looks everyone was shooting her way.

Ducking out onto the deck, she sucked in a deep breath, pulling the cold, crisp night air into her lungs. The chill felt good for about two seconds, but then it started to sink through her long-sleeved T-shirt and leggings. She shivered, weighing her options. She could go back inside and try not to combust over the heated looks Devon was casting her way. Or, she could brave the cold, hoping it would numb the part of her brain that kept wondering what was going to happen the next time she and Devon were alone.

And the part of her body trying to convince her to find out.

"Shit." She paced across the deck and down the stairs, going straight for the flickering fire. Dropping down into one of the double-seat chairs, she let her head fall into her hands, and groaned.

Because she knew exactly what was going to happen the next time she was alone with Devon.

"You're going to freeze your ass off out here."

Her head snapped up as her whole body—but especially her nethers—clenched tight at the sound of Devon's voice. She swallowed hard at the sight of him. After working for so long to ignore how devastatingly handsome he was, her brain decided it had a lot of catching up to do. And it sent her eyeballs dragging down his long frame, past the armful of fleece he was carrying, to linger on the part of him she now knew was just as long as everything else.

"What are you doing out here?"

"There's nowhere else to go. The girls have taken the place over." He settled into the seat next to her, dropping the load of blankets he carried into her lap. "Plus, you looked cold. And I don't want you calling my mother to tell her I let you freeze." His lips twitched as he went to work wrapping the first of the blankets around her back. "Tattletale."

"You would probably never hear the end of it." She sat still, watching as he continued tucking the blanket around her body. "It does seem like you get your love of lecturing from her."

One corner of his mouth tipped up. "What you call lecturing, I call guidance." His eyes came to hers. "I wasn't ever trying to make you feel bad. I was just trying to look out for you."

She bit her lower lip in an attempt to keep the question burning her insides contained. It didn't work. "Why?"

"I didn't see anyone else stepping up to do it." His warm hands worked alongside her neck, carefully easing her hair from the wrap of the blanket. "That includes you."

Janie swallowed hard around the lump in her throat. "I had other things to worry about."

"I know." Devon's touch lingered even when her hair was free, the raspy brush of his calloused hands along her skin sending shivers down her spine. "But you've still got to take care of yourself."

"Do you take care of *yourself*?" The accusation jumped out. An automatic defense she'd lost control of long ago.

"I try." The mouth she was a little too focused on lifted into a smirk. "Those muscles you mentioned Friday don't come out of nowhere." His thumbs brushed along her cheeks. "And yes, I know I could have spent the time I put in at the gym cleaning my house, but if there's nothing left of me, what in the hell am I supposed to give my girls?"

A wry smile worked onto her mouth. "There's the difference between us. I don't have anyone wanting a piece of me."

Devon's gaze heated, eyes dropping to her mouth. "That's not true and you know it."

Every nerve ending in her body went haywire, sending her heart racing and her pussy throbbing. This was why she'd tried to escape him. Many times. From the very beginning, she knew Devon Peters was dangerous. A hazard to be avoided at all costs. But his kind of threat was so different from all the ones she'd faced before.

With him she wouldn't lose money or sanity. She wouldn't risk her safety or her well-being. Only her heart. Maybe her soul. The only two things she'd managed to hang onto all these years.

And she couldn't do it. Couldn't go down that road knowing it might be the path to ruin.

"I can't..." She swallowed hard, the words bitter and wrong even though she knew they had to be said. "I can't be what you need. What your daughters need." She hesitated before adding on the last bit. The part that was maybe the most important. "What you had before."

She'd done her best not to think of Devon's wife. Being jealous of someone who'd lost everything felt wrong. Ugly. But that didn't mean there weren't moments that guilty emotion didn't slip through the cracks to remind her he'd had it all. A perfect life with a perfect wife.

That was how she imagined the woman she never knew. Perfect. It's what he deserved.

And what she wasn't.

Devon's expression turned sad, a punch to the gut

knowing she'd brought it on. She'd reminded him of his wife and how he would never get that back. Especially not with her.

But then he said something that stunned her.

"Maggie was planning to divorce me before she found out she was sick." He took a deep breath, one she felt in her own chest. "I found out the day we got her diagnosis. She confessed everything. That she hadn't been happy in years." One hand moved to her hair, slowly coiling a curl around his finger. "That she'd never loved me the way she should have."

Janie stared at him, unable to fully process what he was telling her, which was probably why she asked, "Was she an idiot?"

Devon's eyes widened in surprise the same time hers did. Clamping one hand over her mouth, Janie shook her head. "I'm so sorry. I didn't mean—"

Devon caught her hand, pulling it away. "Don't apologize. That's part of why I like you. You say exactly what you're thinking." His thumb stroked the center of her palm. "You don't hold it in." He lifted her arm, brushing his lips against the pulse point at the inside of her wrist, revealing how surprisingly sensitive the spot was. "I don't have to wonder what's going on in your head." Another pass of his lips. "How you feel."

She couldn't look away from where his mouth teased the bit of skin peeking out the bottom of her sleeve. "Most people don't like that about me."

"Most people don't find out their wife hadn't loved them for years and just didn't want to tell them." Devon released her hand, letting it fall to the blanket. "Right before she died."

The full impact of what happened to Devon hit her like a ton of bricks. "Oh shit." It was an impossible scenario to imagine. One she wouldn't begin to know how to come to terms with. "But... Wait..." The timeline he'd laid out started to sink in, bringing her to another painful realization. "You stayed with her even after you found out she didn't want to be married to you anymore."

"Of course I did." He said it like he'd never considered anything else. "She needed me. Needed my insurance and my help while she went through chemo."

This time it was Janie reaching for his hand, lacing their fingers. Offering support she didn't really know how to give. "I'm sure she appreciated it."

"She did." His grip tightened around hers. "It was difficult at the beginning, coming to terms with all the changes." Devon's thumb stroked across her skin. "But then it started to become clear she wasn't going to get better." His eyes dropped. "And it got even worse."

Her throat tightened and she scooted closer, spreading the second blanket Devon brought out over their laps, covering as much of him as she could as the night grew colder. "Because you were going to lose her?"

"That's a complicated answer." He took a deep breath. "I think it would have been easier if I could have just been sad over losing her." Devon's words were soft. Like he'd never said them out loud before tonight. "But I was also angry. Mad she hadn't told me sooner. Mad she held something like that back for so long." He swallowed, Adam's apple bobbing with the act. "It made our whole marriage feel like a lie."

She'd been through her fair share of relationships with an emotionally closed off partner. But this was different.

They'd been married. They had children. A life. A partnership. She couldn't imagine how betrayed Devon felt by his wife's admission.

"I know this is going to surprise you, but I don't know what to say."

Devon's eyes lifted to her face again as a hint of a smile eased across his lips. "There's that complete honesty I love." He studied her for a few seconds. "I didn't know how much I needed it until I met you."

She stared back at him, at a loss in more ways than she could count. While she didn't hold back, no one had ever been so open and honest with her. After a lifetime of chasing this kind of connection, finding it was overwhelming. So intense it was difficult to breathe.

"I didn't know how much I needed a lot of things until I met you." He lifted their joined hands, lacing her arm around his neck. "It was easy to ignore how lonely I was. How long it had been since I'd touched someone who wanted to touch me back." Devon leaned close, the tip of his nose teasing hers. "And now I'm having a hell of a time being the friend I said I would be."

As her fingers found their way into the hair at his nape, her body leaned into his all on its own. "How do you know I want to touch you back?"

"I mean," his lips curved into a sexy smirk, "you don't exactly keep your hands to yourself when we're together." His eyes dropped to where her other hand was gripping the front of his shirt, holding tight.

She started to let go, but he caught her before she could, the width of his palm wrapping around her fist. "Don't do that. Don't overthink it." He brushed his lips against hers. "Just let it be what it wants to be."

The thought made her gut clench in fear.

"That's not something I do."

She'd fought for every relationship she'd been in. Sure, she'd sent a few men packing over the years—like the one who brought her to Devon's literal doorstep—but the men she'd genuinely liked and wanted to keep around were always the same ones who left her feeling insecure. Left her holding on so tight she didn't notice she was gripping something she needed to let go of.

And it was easy to see herself doing that with Devon. Clinging to him at all costs.

Devon continued teasing his lips over hers. "Why doesn't that surprise me?" His breath was warm as it fanned over her face. "You're the kind of woman who makes shit happen." He nipped at her lower lip. "Another thing I love about you."

Had anyone ever loved anything about her? Not her mother, that's for sure. Not any of the men in her past. It led her to the conclusion there wasn't much appealing about her. Not in the ways that mattered.

But hearing Devon liked—loved—the parts of her personality most people found abrasive, prodded at an ache she'd carried forever. Since that first moment her mother made it clear she wasn't good enough the way she was.

"I..."

Was she ready to make a similar confession? To finally admit there were things she loved about him too? Like how hard he worked to be a good dad. The way he took care of the people around him. Even those damn lectures he gave were appealing now that she knew what they really were.

Devon shook his head. "You never have to feel like you need to give me something back, J. Never." The warmth of his fingers brushed over her cheek. "I just thought you should know how I felt. Why I can't stay away from you even though I said I would." His lips left hers, tracing a path along the line of her jaw to pause just below her ear. "And why I'm going to do my damndest to convince you we should be more than friends." His teeth raked across yet another spot on her body that was way more sensitive than she realized. "That we probably already are."

"Are you saying that because we cuddled at the football game?" She sucked in a breath as the heat of his mouth worked down the column of her neck.

"No."

Devon's lips lifted, claiming hers in a kiss that stole all the breath from her body after setting every nerve ending on fire, leaving her aching and filled with an amount of need she'd never experienced.

It wasn't just physical. Her desire for more of Devon

wasn't only confined to her body. It had settled into those two things she'd held so close for so long, guarding them at all costs.

"I'm saying that because I'm about to give you a reason to believe me." His eyes held hers as his hand slid under the blanket, the warmth of his touch skimming over the skin of her belly. "And to test that legging theory of yours."

CHAPTER SIXTEEN
DEVON

HE WATCHED HER face for any sign of uncertainty. Any hint Janie wanted to hit the brakes on what was happening between them. And something was definitely happening between them. Not just in this moment, but in a much more general sense.

Like it or not—time for it or not—he could no longer deny she should be in his life and he should be in hers.

"What do you think, J? Can I touch you?" He harped on his daughters all the time about consent and its importance. The respect it showed. At the river, Janie had made the first move, but this time it was all him, and he wanted to be sure she was right there with him. It sure looked like she was, but looks could be deceiving.

Her eyes were wide on his, skin flushed, chest lifting in short, choppy breaths. "You want to do that? *Here*?" She glanced toward the house. "But the girls—"

"The girls are all wrapped up in their friends." He stroked across the soft skin of her stomach, giving her plenty of time to tell him to go pound sand. "They decided it was too cold to come outside."

And the second they had, he'd grabbed an armful of blankets and rushed out to where Janie was, knowing they would be alone. That he could carve out a little more time with her. Have her to himself for a while. Never did he expect the turn it would take. The truth he would share for the first time. The confession he would finally make.

No one knew what Maggie told him when she got sick. Not her mother. Not his parents. No one. They'd decided together it was something they'd tackle when she got better. But that never happened, and he didn't want to change everyone else's perception of what they'd had. It didn't seem right to put his own pain on someone else.

But with Janie, it was different. She felt so deeply. Carried her emotions front and center for everyone to see. She wouldn't see his feelings as a burden. She would see them as a connection. The kind of intimacy he believed they both craved.

"What do you think, J?" Devon teased one finger along the waistband of those damn leggings he would never be able to look at the same way, hinting at another kind of intimacy he was eager to offer. "Is it too cold to come outside?"

The air rushed out of her lungs in a sharp exhale. "I can't believe you just asked me that."

"Why?" He dipped one finger under the stretchy

fabric. "Did the dad jeans make you think I didn't have any game?"

Janie huffed out a little laugh, relaxing just the tiniest bit. "It was more the dad jokes than anything."

"If you think you're going to hurt my feelings, you're wrong." He continued stroking her stomach, fingers barely breaching the waistband of her pants. "I know what I am and I've embraced it." He met her gaze. "Just like you."

It was another reason he knew they'd be good together. Neither of them was trying to be something they weren't. He could take her at face value and she could do the same.

"I didn't really embrace it. I was just too over everything to care what people thought of me anymore." Her voice was soft. "It's exhausting to live your whole life trying to meet someone else's expectations." The vulnerability in her eyes cut into him.

But it also soothed the parts of him that were still raw from Maggie's confession years ago. Knowing the honesty and openness Janie possessed wasn't just limited to certain feelings only made him more positive there could be something there.

Something big. As long as he could get her over this hump.

And showing Janie what all was in it for her would be a great first step.

"Then it's good I don't have any." He'd learned long ago what could happen when you lived in your expectations. You missed signs you should have seen. Signs that could have pointed you in a different direction —possibly a better one—before it was too late. "We can just take this one step at a time and see where it takes us."

Janie snorted. "Again, I'm not really great at that kind of thing."

He smiled, pulling her closer with the arm around her back, dragging her up onto his lap so he could feel her body against his the way he wanted to.

"Then I'll go with the flow and you can make the waves. How's that sound?"

She curled closer, melting into him the same way she had at the football game. "You make it sound so easy."

"I'm pretty sure it doesn't have to be hard." It could be, he knew that. His parents had one of the best marriages he'd ever seen and they still had their fights. Their disagreements. But all in all, the love they had for each other was easy. Natural. Honest and real.

That's what he wanted. Something real. Something he didn't have to question.

Janie studied him. "Was your marriage hard?"

"It was." He pulled the blankets closer, tucking them tighter around her body. "I just didn't know it."

Janie worked one hand free from the blankets he'd just carefully put in place, bringing the tips of her fingers to move along his face in a touch unlike any she'd offered before. Usually she just held on tight. Gripped him like any second he might run away. Leave her behind.

"I'm sorry."

The words were simple, but they lifted a weight he'd

been carrying for a long time. She wasn't sharing his burden, he wouldn't put that on her. But she understood it. Empathized with his pain and anger.

"I'm not. Not anymore." Not now that he saw what was on the other side of all of it.

Would he give anything for Maggie to still be here, loving on their girls, living a life that would make her happy? Of course. But that wasn't an option he had. So all he could do was keep moving forward. Learn from the pain and heartache.

And appreciate his second chance. Be grateful he got one.

Not everyone did.

"*Dad.*"

Riley's voice cut through the night, sending Janie scrambling off his lap so fast she tipped straight toward the dirt. He managed to grab her, depositing the ass that was just warming his lap into the seat next to him, right as his daughters and their friends filed down the deck carrying a bag of marshmallows and the roasting sticks he'd laid out on the counter, but assumed would remain untouched.

"Is the fire still hot enough to make s'mores on?"

If he could have lied, he would have, but the flickering flames and hot coals filling the pit would have given him away. "It's probably perfect for roasting marshmallows." There was no keeping the disappointment out of his answer.

And that disappointment only grew when Janie jumped up, a smile frozen on her face. "I should probably get going." She gave his daughters and their friends a wave as she booked it to the deck. "See you girls next week. Have fun. Give your dad hell."

"Wait." Riley chased after her as he attempted the same. "Could you show me again how to do that braid before you go? I promised Olivia I'd do her hair before school Tuesday."

Olivia's eyes widened for a split second, but then she was nodding along. "She did. She promised."

"It's late and Janie's been here all day." Devon kept moving, following the path Janie cut up the steps and across the deck. "She'll have to show you again the next time she's here." He didn't narrow that date down to the following Sunday. He had every intention of figuring out how to get Janie back before then.

As long as he could catch her.

The woman in front of him barely slowed down as she rushed into the house, collected her caddy of cleaning supplies and yanked her coat from the closet, then she was out the front door.

But by then he'd closed the gap between them, staying right at her side as she all but ran down the steps and along the sidewalk. "You're running again, J."

"I'm not running. I just don't like the idea of your daughters catching you," she paused, head snapping back toward the house as she lowered her voice to a harsh whisper, *"with your hand down my pants."*

"That wasn't going to happen." His confidence was way higher than it should have been considering how out of practice he was, but he wasn't lying earlier when

206

he said he wanted to take care of her. He meant it. In every imaginable way. Except the more he learned about Janie's life, the more he realized how disinclined she was to believe it.

And the more determined he was to show her how very serious he was.

Janie finally stopped at the driver's side of her car, eyes flashing to his face. "What? Were you just fucking with me?"

Christ this woman was prickly. But he'd take it over the alternative any day.

"I'm not talking about the me having my hand in your pants part." He moved closer, crowding her. "I'm talking about the getting caught part." He continued closing in. "I've been a cop for a long time, J. I think I can get away with a little necking in my own backyard."

Her lips rolled inward, the expression on her face turning serious. "Did you really just say necking?" She set her caddy on the roof of her car. "Because I can handle you being a dad, but if you're going to start acting like a grandpa—"

Her words cut off as his body met hers, pressing her back against the side of her car as his lips coasted up the side of her neck. "If I start acting like a grandpa, you'll like it because you like me." He caught the lobe of her ear between his teeth, giving it a little nip, eliciting the same gasp the move earned him earlier. He was pushing his luck in lots of ways, but couldn't stop himself from trying to pin her down on one important fact. "Isn't that right?"

Janie's hands came to his shirt, fisting in the front as

her coat fell to the ground at their feet. "I shouldn't like you."

"Probably not, but you do anyway." He palmed her hip as he took a long breath against her skin. "Why don't you let me give you a reason to like me even more." His hand slid under the hem of her T-shirt to toy with the waistband of her leggings, making sure she'd know exactly what he was getting at.

Her eyes darted around. "But—"

"No one can see anything from here. Even if it wasn't dark, they can't see through your car, J." If he was going to pursue this—and he was—privacy would always be an issue. One they'd have to learn to work around. "And, as long as you can be quiet, no one will suspect a thing." He paused, hand going still. "But if you don't want me to touch you—"

"I want you to touch me." The words rushed out of her mouth as Janie's eyes met his, her expression filled with conflicting emotions. "I'm just scared of what will happen if I do."

Hearing she wanted his touch boosted his ego, but her admission of fear knocked everything else down a peg. "All that happens is you get to drive home with a smile on your face." He rested his forehead against hers. "That's it."

Her eyes moved over his face, lower lip pinched between her teeth. "What about you?"

She probably had no idea what her question did to him. The satisfaction it brought. "Don't worry about me."

"But—"

He shook his head at her again. "I've been alone a long time, J. I know how to take care of myself."

She sucked in a breath, lips parting as her eyes glazed. "You do?"

He nodded. "I do and I will." The thought that she might be picturing it now had his dick flexing against the confines of his jeans. "Does that mean I can touch you?"

Janie offered a jerky nod. "Are you sure you don't mind... I can—"

Holy hell. She really was testing him right now, and likely had no idea. No clue how desperate he was to feel her hands on him. To be with someone feeling the same kind of need that was coursing through his own veins.

"I will be just fine, J."

Tucking his hand into the front of her leggings, he slid his fingers into the elastic of her panties, the movement easy to do thanks to the forgiving stretch of her pants. Pushing deeper, he groaned when they slicked along her drenched flesh. "This is what I'm going to think of when I fuck my fist later. How wet you are for me." Her pussy was hot and swollen, her clit a hard nub as he gently stroked alongside it, watching her reaction. "You were going to go home like this? Suffering?"

She shuddered, legs parting a little more as he eased a finger into her body. "Oh my God."

Continuing to watch her face, he pressed deeper. "Tell me if I hurt you."

He'd done a little more research on endometriosis since that night at her trailer, and discovered it could lead to pain during penetration. The last thing he wanted was to cause her pain because the first thing he wanted was the opportunity to do this again. "Not too much?"

"No." She whimpered as he slowly worked his finger in and out, thumb settled onto the bead of her clit. "Not too much."

He groaned again as she clenched around him, the front of his boxers clinging to the head of his leaking dick as he soaked up every sound, every expression, every sensation.

"Is this how you like to be fucked, J? Slow and steady?"

"Yes." The answer came immediately. Short and sharp and punctuated by another whimper, this one louder than the ones before.

Devon leaned close, resting his forehead against hers again. "Shhh. You've got to be quiet, remember?" He pulled his finger from her body, curling it as he went to stroke against the spot just inside her, smirking as she twitched. "I want to come to your house this week, J." He flattened his fingers between the lips of her pussy, working it with a circular motion. "I want to hear what happens when you don't have to be quiet." He trailed his lips to her ear, keeping his voice low. "I want to hear what happens when it's my mouth making you come instead of my fingers."

Janie's thighs clenched around his palm as something akin to a wail built in her throat, forcing him to seal his lips over hers so he could swallow it down as she came, muscles twitching, body sagging. He braced one arm around her back, supporting her weight as he teased out the last bit of her climax, only pulling his fingers free when she gasped, pulling away from the contact. He lifted his fingers to his mouth without hesitation, sliding the taste of her across his tongue, cock twitching at the thought of consuming it at its source.

Janie's eyes fixed on the movement, following along as he pulled his fingers free. "I can't believe you just did that."

It was the second time she'd said that tonight and it was starting to make him wonder just how low her expectations were. And hoping he'd be able to blow them out of the water.

"Why not?" He leaned into her ear, carefully pulling the hem of her T-shirt back into place. "Dads can be dirty too, J."

CHAPTER SEVENTEEN
JANIE

THE LAST THING she expected to see when pulling up in front of her trailer was an unfamiliar car sporting a rental sticker parked in the spot she normally used. "Seriously?"

Changing her trajectory, Janie redirected her small sedan, bringing it up alongside the other car. There was only one person it could belong to, and their arrival had her stomach clenching.

What in the hell was she doing here? Had Sharon decided Florida was too hot? Too lonely? Too far from her family? Was she planning to move back and reclaim Janie's home as her own?

She had time left on her lease, but finding a new place in her price range would be near impossible no matter how many months she had to search. She'd barely managed to find this place, no way would she find another needle in the Moss Creek haystack.

The panic circling her insides ramped up when

Sharon came out of her neighbor's house, laughing and smiling with the woman who lived next door. From what she understood, they'd been friends forever. Sharon was probably over there telling her the good news. Assuring her that they'd be together again soon.

After giving her friend a hug, Sharon turned Janie's way. Her lined face split into a wide grin as she waved.

Janie fought to smile back, struggling against the upset wanting her to do the exact opposite. As Sharon came down the steps, Janie reached for the door handle. As tempting as it was, she couldn't just sit in the car and hide out, hoping her landlord would teleport back to Florida.

Unfortunately.

After collecting her purse and the tray of overflow cinnamon rolls from the seat beside her, Janie climbed out, straightening just as Sharon rounded her bumper.

"There you are. I was just asking Brenda what time you got home and she said there was no telling." Sharon grabbed her in a hug, offering a quick squeeze before leaning back. "How's everything going?"

Boy was that a loaded question. Up until she saw Sharon's car parked at her home, she would have told her everything was fine. Possibly better than fine if she wanted to tempt fate. "Not bad." As much as she didn't want the answer, Janie found herself asking, "What brings you to town?"

Sharon perked up even more. "I came to visit my granddaughters before the weather gets too cold."

A little of the air frozen in Janie's lungs funneled free,

the tightness in her shoulders relaxing a little. "That's nice." Her eyes lifted to the overcast sky. "I think you came just in time."

Sharon snorted. "I think I came a couple months too late." She rubbed her arms. "The weather down south has me spoiled. I can't take the chill like I used to."

Janie relaxed a little more. Sharon didn't sound like a woman who was planning to move back to Montana. "You want to come inside? It's warmer there."

Sharon was already turning toward her trailer. "That sounds great. We can talk things over in there."

There was something ominous about her words. *Talk things over.* It had her anxiety ratcheting back up as she led Sharon inside.

Her landlady stood just inside the door as Janie put her purse and coat away. The older woman propped both hands on her hips, looking around the small living room and kitchen with an approving gaze. "You sure have taken good care of this place." She turned to Janie with a big smile. "That's why I wanted to give you the first go at buying it from me."

Janie nearly dropped the tray of cinnamon rolls in her hand. "You're going to sell it?"

It hadn't occurred to her that Sharon might get rid of the place. Maybe it should have, but her landlord had owned the place long enough it was free and clear. Janie paid her rent early every month, kept the place up, and only called in the most dire of circumstances—like when the fridge went out. She'd assumed there was no reason for Sharon to sell it. Not when she was likely making money from the deal.

"When I first moved to Florida, I wasn't sure I was going to stay. I was mostly just looking for a little break from everything here." The sadness that flickered across her face was replaced with another smile. "But I love it down there. The weather's good, and I've made plenty of friends." She wiggled her brows. "Some friendlier than others, if you know what I mean."

She did, and didn't want to dwell on it even though imagining her landlady tangled with another retiree would probably be one hell of a distraction from the worst-case scenario playing out in front of her. "But I thought you had family here."

"I do." Sharon sighed. "But as they get older, my granddaughters get busier and busier with their own lives." She lifted a finger and her brows. "Which isn't a bad thing, but I can't make my life all about them."

Of course she couldn't make her life all about them, but didn't she want to make it a little about them?

"I figure I can come up a couple times a year and visit." She shrugged. "Hell, they can come visit me at the beach whenever they want."

Setting the cinnamon rolls onto the counter so they didn't end up on the floor, Janie brought one hand up to rub her aching head. "When are you planning to sell?"

"If you buy it, as soon as possible." Sharon hesitated. "If you don't, then I'll put it on the market when your lease is up."

It was a lot to take in. More than she could wrap her

brain around with Sharon staring at her expectantly. She needed time. Room to come to terms with what was happening before having this conversation. "Can I have a few days to think about it?"

Sharon held up both hands. "Of course. I wouldn't want you to make any snap decisions."

It wasn't that. There was no decision to make, really. She couldn't afford to buy the place. Was even less likely to get a loan. Janie smiled anyway. "Thanks. I'll get back with you in a couple days."

"I'll be in town the rest of the week, so take your time." She opened the door. "I'm off to surprise my granddaughters."

At least Janie wouldn't be the only one shocked to see her. "I bet they'll be super excited you're here."

Sharon snorted. "They'll be excited about getting their Christmas money early."

She turned toward the porch, jumping back in surprise. "*Oh.*" She let out a breath, sagging forward. "You scared the hell out of me."

Janie moved in behind her, concerned about what had Sharon clutching her chest the way she was, only to discover she had another visitor. Devon stood on her welcome mat, still decked out in his uniform, looking shocked to see a strange woman at her door. Janie stepped closer, intending to introduce them, but stopped short when Devon greeted her landlord.

"I didn't know you were in town, Sharon."

Of course he knew her. She forgot most of Moss

Creek's residents had lived there forever. And with his job, he likely knew more of the residents than most.

"I was just about to come see you and the girls." She poked her head out the door. "Is everything all right?" She lowered her voice as she stepped outside, eyes swinging around the park. "Did someone do something illegal?"

Janie ignored the hint of excitement in Sharon's voice. She also ignored the way her landlady kept babbling on about who could be the most likely culprit behind Devon's arrival.

Because the only thing she could focus on was that Sharon said she was just about to go see Devon and his girls.

Devon's eyes met hers as Sharon hustled down the stairs. If she was like the rest of the town's population, she was likely already deciding how to spread the fire of gossip that didn't exist on her way to Devon's house.

The shock of discovery was quickly turning to anger. Betrayal. Hurt. And she wasn't known to make her best decisions when she was hurt. So she did the smartest thing she could and slammed the door in his face, spinning away to march straight into her bedroom so she could fall onto her bed and cry like a teenage girl.

Only the door didn't slam behind her.

By the time the lack of sound registered, turning her back toward the door, Devon was inside, shutting it behind him, eyes still locked on her. "Take a breath."

"Don't fucking tell me what to do." She sucked in air anyway, but it wasn't to calm down, it was to fill her lungs so she could unleash everything boiling over. "You're a fucking hypocrite. You want me to be an open book but won't give me the same." She laughed, the sound bitter and broken. "It's the same fucking thing that always happens. I knew I should have—"

"Janie." Devon's tone was calm and cool, which only pissed her off more.

"—told you to fuck all the way off." She pointed an accusing finger at his face. "I knew you were too good to be true. I knew—"

"Janie." He kept coming closer. Kept saying her name in that calm way that sent her already explosive rage into spontaneous combustion.

"—this is what would happen, and you made me think—" Her voice broke and she looked around for something to throw. Wanting to make him hurt as much as she did.

Just as she reached for the decorative bowl she used to store her fruit, Devon was on her, one hand gripping her outstretched wrist and the other wrapping around her back, pinning her free arm to her side. "*Janie.* Will you let me get a fucking word in?"

"I don't want to hear any more of your words." She sniffled, throat aching, but she'd be damned if he got to see her cry. "They're all bullshit."

She'd been here before. Thought things were finally going to be different. But just like all those times before, she was wrong.

"Not a single word I've said to you is bullshit." Devon's tone was suddenly sharp. Angry. "And I think you know that. I think you're looking for reasons to believe this isn't what it is, because you're scared."

She scoffed. "So you not telling me I'm living in your wife's old house is just me being scared? You're a real—"

"You're right. I should have told you." He didn't shy away from it the way she thought he would. "I fucked up and I'm sorry. But I can promise you I'm going to fuck up again one day, so we need to figure out how we're going to get through that shit. What's going on with us is real, J, and real relationships are messy sometimes." He shifted his hold on her, pulling her a little closer. "You were less than sober the night I found out where you lived, and then I got sidetracked." His lips curved. "Distracted by horseback rides and football games and fire pits."

A little of her anger bled away at his apology. At his claim of what was between them. He wasn't walking away or shutting down. He wasn't yelling or swinging low blows. "You should have told me."

"I should have." He dropped his forehead down to rest against hers the way he had the night before. "I'm sure there's a lot more shit I should tell you, but it will take time."

The reminder was sobering. "That's not really something available to either of us."

She wanted to believe him. Wanted to think Devon would have told her the next time it came up. But would it matter if he did? He still had three daughters to take care of. She still had two jobs—three, counting cleaning his house—to work.

And then there was the debt lingering between them. It hadn't seemed like a big deal at first, but if she did what he was suggesting and let this be more, it would become a big deal.

Sorta like his mother-in-law owning her rental.

"That's why we have to make time." Devon's body pressed into hers, urging her backward. "Like me coming over here after work instead of going to the gym because I'd rather see you than sweat my ass off and you'll like me even if I get soft."

Someone making a sacrifice to spend time with her wasn't something she was used to. Normally she was the one bending over backwards to make it happen. "You're putting words in my mouth."

"Mmm." Devon hummed, the sound a low rumble through his chest. "Are we already talking about where we want to put our mouths?" He continued using his body to direct her, leading her down the short hall and into her bedroom. "Because that's actually the reason I came here."

She was supposed to be mad. Outraged that he kept something so relevant from her. Instead, her stomach and thighs were clenching in anticipation. "You should have come here to tell me your mother-in-law owned my house."

"I should have." His arm tightened at her back and her feet left the floor. "For the record, I probably would have remembered to tell you tonight." He hauled her body against his, pinning her to him as he walked over her mattress on his knees. "But probably not until I was done putting my mouth in various places. Telling you before probably would have ruined the mood."

"Probably." She grabbed onto him as Devon leaned forward, dropping her back to the bed. "Then again, I wouldn't be questioning just about everything."

"That's fair." Devon didn't back away at her bluntness. He stayed close, his nose running alongside hers. "But we have plenty of time for you to figure it all out."

Did they though? Because she sure as hell didn't. Especially not now that she knew Sharon was planning to sell her home out from under her, adding 'find a new place to live' to her already full schedule. "How exactly am I going to do that?"

"You don't have to do anything." Devon hooked one hand behind her knee, bending it alongside his hip in a move that settled his body between her thighs. "I'll show you everything you need to see."

It sounded so good. So simple.

But things like this were never simple. Not for her.

"What do you think, J?" Devon's lips brushed hers. "Can I show you how good this can be between us?"

She should say no. Kick him out and make him clean his own house.

But...

"You don't know that it would be good between us. It could be a whole train wreck." Was she looking for reassurance? Agreement? Denial?

No. None of those. She wanted proof. She wanted to see what he claimed to see. Feel what he claimed to feel.

Devon's lips curved against hers, lifting into a heart-stopping smile. "I'm up for the challenge." Those sinful lips slid along her jaw, teasing down her neck. "But you have to be the one to pull the trigger."

Was that something she wanted to do? To face down the reality of what could be?

If Devon was wrong, this would all be over and she could go back to the way she was. The life she had.

Minus the little trailer she called home and plus the weight of another broken heart.

But if Devon was right...

She honestly didn't know what would come after that, and if she thought about it too long, she might shove him out of her house. Out of her life.

And—in spite of her better sense—she wasn't ready for him to go. Not yet. He'd somehow managed to establish himself as a fixture in her world. Someone she could talk to. Laugh with.

Count on.

So, before she could talk herself out of it, Janie slid one hand between them, gripping the solid line of his cock through the dark blue fabric of his uniform pants. "Bang."

CHAPTER EIGHTEEN
DEVON

JANIE WAS IN her head. He could practically see the conflicting thoughts flying around as she fought with herself over him. What he'd inadvertently done.

Or not done, in this case.

He fucked up. Did probably one of the worst things he could do to her without realizing it. Without meaning to. It would be easy to fall into the same line of thinking she had. To tell himself he forgot because he didn't have the time or bandwidth for a relationship, going down the same doubt filled road Janie was on.

But he could make time for her. He could find the bandwidth to be what she deserved. What she needed. Because Janie was what he needed, and the past few minutes only made him more positive of it. She hadn't pretended everything was fine when he pissed her off. She didn't smile in his face and let her anger fester inside until it poisoned what was between them.

Would some people see her behavior as an

overreaction? Maybe. But they didn't know her the way he did. They didn't understand what she'd been through. The way she saw the world.

The way she saw herself.

"What do you think, J?" He brushed a kiss over her lips, the motion already familiar. "Can I show you how good this can be between us?"

Her eyes moved over his face. "You don't know that it would be good between us. It could be a whole train wreck."

He smiled, because she was wrong. He did know, and couldn't wait for her to see it too. "I'm up for the challenge." He trailed his mouth along her jaw, skimming down the soft skin of her neck. "But you have to be the one to pull the trigger."

The ball was in her court. Janie decided how fast or slow they went. He'd unwittingly sent them a few steps back, so if she wanted to spend the hour he had talking, that's what they'd do.

And for a second, as she stared up at him, jaw set, expression resolute, he thought that might be where things were headed.

But then one sneaky hand had him hissing out a breath, her grip on his cock both welcome and unexpected. Her eyes locked onto his as a single word passed through her lips. "Bang."

This woman. Holy hell was she a handful. She was loud and stubborn and determined and unflinching.

And it had him concerned about his ability to keep his shit together. To keep from rushing this. To keep from stripping her naked and burying his body in hers so he would finally know how it felt to have her around him.

His mouth crashed over hers as he ground against her, needing more friction. More of her against more of him.

He'd already removed his vest on the way over, feeling optimistic about how the evening would go. Even then, his optimism was limited to spending a little time with his mouth between her thighs, wringing a couple orgasms out of her before heading home.

But those plans had changed. Drastically.

Janie didn't need to know how good he was—though he'd love nothing more than to show her—she needed to see how good *they* were. To feel how in sync they really were. How perfectly they fit.

And she seemed to realize it too.

He fought with his shirt, her hands frantic as they came to help, fingers working the buttons as he yanked at the fabric, trying to get loose. Her teeth bumped his lip, making it sting as he tugged his undershirt free of his pants, barely breaking contact to peel it off before claiming her mouth again.

Grabbing her own shirt, Janie wiggled under him as she worked it higher, grunting when it tangled at her armpits.

Pushing up to his knees, Devon snagged her by the arms, bringing her along with him before relieving her of the long-sleeved T-shirt she wore to work at The Baking Rack. Keeping her upright, he took advantage of her exposed back, reaching behind her for the clasp of her bra. When his hand met smooth fabric, he leaned to peer over her shoulder. "How do you get this thing off?"

Janie laughed, her head tipping back on the light sound. "It's a sports bra, nerd." She hooked her fingers into the elastic band at the bottom. "It goes over my head."

He frowned at the tight fit. "It's a fucking straitjacket is what it is."

"Only when I'm sweaty." She contorted her arms as she wiggled the stretchy garment up, making it about halfway before he dipped his head to pull the dark bud of one nipple into his mouth.

Janie moaned, her movements going still as he sucked in a steady pulse, pausing to flick at the tight pucker before drawing against it again.

He reached up to find the stretchy bra, picking up where she left off as he moved to the other nipple, teasing it as he worked the difficult to remove undergarment free. Once it was off, he pushed her back to the mattress, palms coming to cup the small mounds of her tits, pressing them together so he could move between them more easily. When her hands tangled in his hair, pulling tight, he groaned against her spit-slicked skin. He could spend all night on her tits, sucking and pinching and licking to see if he could make her come from that alone.

And one day he would. Not today though. He had an agenda and he needed to stick to it.

Lifting his head, he moved back to her lips, tongue sliding against hers as he worked the fly of her jeans open, pushing them down her hips, taking the panties underneath along with them. His reach ran out when they were in the middle of her thighs, forcing him to lean back on his heels to get them all the way off. Once they were on the floor, he let his eyes roam over her, taking in every inch of her. She was long and lean. Narrow hips. Willowy limbs. Slim thighs. Almost delicate. A stark contrast to the personality packed into the body.

A body that had clearly been through some things.

He reached out to trace along a scar low on one side of her abdomen. "What happened here?"

"Appendix." Her eyes went to where he followed the path of silvery skin. "It ruptured when I was sixteen. I almost died."

The possibility hit close to home and brought on a storm of conflicting emotions. He moved away from the spot, needing to put it out of his mind, and found another, smaller scar just above the dark hair of her pubic line. "And this one?"

"Surgery to remove endometrial tissue a few years ago." She traced across a matching scar to the left of the one he noticed. "They did it laparoscopically."

It was evidence of one facet of her suffering. One point of her pain. He leaned down, tracing the small line with his lips. Repeating the process with the one under Janie's finger. Lifting his eyes to her face, he asked, "Any more?"

She slid her finger to another small, barely noticeable line. "There."

He pressed a kiss to the scar, keeping his lips on her skin as he met her eyes again. "More?"

She shook her head. "No more."

As much as he loved the feel of her skin under his lips, he was relieved there were no more scars. None that could be seen, anyway. He suspected Janie had still been broken many times, doing her best to reassemble the pieces. But there was no missing the cracks that remained, sometimes splitting wider when they were stressed. No amount of kisses would fix those. Only time. Time and patience.

Devon slid lower, hands curving under the backs of her thighs, spreading her legs wide. He kept his eyes on her face as he dragged the flat of his tongue up her seam, stifling a groan at how slick she was.

When he was younger and most of his friends were obsessed with fucking, he was obsessed with this. His mouth buried in the wet heat of a willing pussy, licking and sucking as a pair of soft thighs clenched around his ears.

Unfortunately, the single partner he'd had in his life up to this point hadn't been quite as interested in it. It was another sign he ignored. Pretended didn't matter. But it was another thing that sat between them. Slowly growing. Widening the gap he didn't see until it was too late.

It didn't appear he'd have that sort of issue with Janie. When his tongue settled on her clit, one hand came to fist in his hair while the other grabbed at the blanket beneath her back. The narrow line of her hips worked in small, rolling movements, chasing everything he gave.

His dick was so hard it was throbbing, the urge to thrust against the mattress nearly overwhelming. Next time. Next time he could come like this, the hard bud of her clit against his tongue, drowning in the taste of her.

He doubled down his efforts, the need to make her come overwhelming. The muscles of her thighs jerked and he lifted his eyes to her face, wanting to watch every expression as she came. But Janie didn't just lay there and take what he gave her. She pushed up on one elbow, her other hand still gripped in his hair, gaze locked on to where his mouth met her body. Watching with parted lips, her hips bucked, a low, ragged moan filling the air as her fingers tightened against his scalp.

She held him in place, both with her hand and with her stare, as her orgasm dragged out. When it was done, she fell back against the mattress, knees falling open, one arm slung across her eyes. "That was..."

"Not all." Taking advantage of her need for a break, Devon stood at the foot of the bed, shucking the rest of his clothes before retrieving the condom he brought just in case and crawling over her. He nosed along her neck. "Unless you want it to be."

Janie's lips curved, her expression soft and sweet. "You set a pretty high precedent. You sure you want to try to follow that up?"

"Positive." He didn't hesitate.

Her dark brows lifted. "Someone's confident in themselves."

Devon shook his head. "I'm confident in us. That's different." Sex wasn't just one person performing for another. It wasn't a one-sided sort of thing.

Shouldn't be anyway.

"Your confidence in my half of the equation is wrong, because so far I've just laid here." Janie's hands skimmed down his chest, their destination clear.

He caught them before she could get past his waist. "And that's all you're going to be doing this round." He lifted her fingers to his lips, nipping the tip of her pointer. "It's been a while, and I'd like to make it through the night with my pride intact."

"Full disclosure," Janie wiggled, fighting his grip, "that makes me want to behave even less."

"Shocker." He tightened his hold on her just in case, bringing both arms over her head. "Janie wants to be a pain in the ass. Never saw that one coming."

The sound of her laugh filled the room, changing the moment into something new. Something so much more than he could have planned or hoped for. Something that wasn't just about need or desire or sex.

It was about connection. Real and raw and true.

"I have kind of lost the element of surprise with you, haven't I?" She continued squirming, her body brushing his, and he gritted his teeth against this new side of her. This new side of intimacy.

He came here with a goal in mind. Focused. Determined. Ready to do whatever it took to show her what he wanted her to see. Instead he was the one having his eyes opened.

Devon traced her lips with his. "You are full of surprises, J." Keeping her wrists in place with one hand, he collected the condom with the other, bringing it to his mouth so he could pinch one corner with his teeth, carefully tearing it open.

It wasn't the preferred method, but desperate times.

Sliding the rubber free, he let the foil fall and went to work sliding the protective layer into place.

"I can't get pregnant." Janie's hushed words lifted his eyes to her face. "Just so you know." Sadness lined the explanation and flooded her expression.

A little of the fire licking through his veins cooled. Releasing her hands he traced along her cheek, leaning close. "I'm sorry."

Janie lifted one shoulder in a small shrug, her freed hands sliding over his chest. "It is what it is, right?" Her lips twisted into a wry smile. "It's not like I had anyone banging down my door to knock me up." Her expression fell even more. "And it's not like I could have done it on my own."

Devon rested his forehead to hers, hand curved along the side of her head. "I don't believe that for a second. You are the most stubborn, determined woman I've ever met. You make shit happen, J. You would have made that happen too."

Janie's eyes searched his face, brows tipped up in the middle. "You think?"

He smiled. "I know."

She blinked a few times, eyes soft. Then she leaned up, hooking one arm around his neck, dragging his

233

mouth to hers. Her legs wrapped around his back, pulling his hips into the cradle of her thighs, the hard line of his cock sliding against her slick slit.

Her nails scratched at his skin. Her teeth raked his lip. Her heels dug into his ass, urging him closer.

Again, the mood turned on a dime, and all he could do was ride the wave, just like he'd promised to do.

Shifting to make room between their bodies, he angled his hips, notching the head of his dick into place, then slowly pressed, sinking into her heat at a painfully slow pace. He was about three quarters of the way in when she sucked in a sharp breath, body stiffening. He went still, stopping in his tracks. "J?"

"It's fine." Her voice was tight. Strained.

"No." He waited for her to look at him. "It's not fine. What's wrong?"

"I just..." She looked everywhere but at his face. "I'm a little tender down there right now since my period starts tomorrow."

He looked down at where their bodies were joined. "I have an idea." He angled one brow in question. "You want to try it?"

Janie pressed her lips together and gave him a quick nod.

Shifting around, he unhooked her legs from around his waist, bringing them flat to the mattress before tucking them between his, locking them tight together with his knees. In this position, he couldn't come close to bottoming out since the V of her thighs was in his way, making it much less likely he'd get deep enough to cause her discomfort.

His next thrust was slow. He watched her face as his front flattened against hers, his entry stopped short by her pelvis. He was still squeezed tight all the way to the root thanks to the press of her thighs, and it nearly had his eyes rolling back in his head.

He blinked a few times, finding his focus and putting it on Janie. There was no sign of pain on her face so he stroked into her again. This time Janie's eyes widened, her lips circling on a surprised sounding, "Oh."

"That a good, *oh*?" He pressed into her again, watching as his sheathed dick slid free before sinking back in.

"A very good, *oh*." Janie's fingers dug into his biceps, nails pinching his skin as he moved a little faster. "Don't stop."

He couldn't feel how wet she was, but he could hear it, and the sound was driving him fucking crazy. Pushing him closer and closer to spilling.

But he wasn't going alone.

Bringing one hand to tease a nipple, he changed his angle, dragging the length of his cock along her clit with each thrust.

"Holy shit, Devon." Janie's body jerked beneath his, twitching each time he passed across the tiny collection of nerve endings he was counting on to help her get where he wanted her to go. "I'm going to come again."

He'd have to warn her about saying shit like that, because the words had barely cleared her lips before his balls were pulling tight, egged on by knowing she was about to milk the cum right out of him.

Luckily Janie was right behind him, wailing as he groaned, her orgasm and the flex of her pussy amplifying his own climax until he was sure he might black out.

Lose both his hearing and his sight.

To be fair, he'd lost just about everything else to the woman under him. What were a couple more things?

CHAPTER NINETEEN

JANIE

"WHY DOES YOUR face look so weird?" Mariah tipped her head, eyes squinting as Janie pulled on the chef's jacket she wore while working at The Inn. "Did you get Botox?"

Janie snorted, buttoning up the front of the double-breasted white coat. "Yeah. Because I have so much extra money to throw around."

Mariah winced. "Sorry."

As one of the closest friends she'd ever had, Janie had told Maria all kinds of things she'd never shared with anyone else. She knew about her money struggles. Her man struggles. Her period issues.

Well... She hadn't shared those things with anyone else until Devon managed to worm his way under her cold, hard shell.

And also her panties.

Mariah gasped, pointing at her. "You just smiled.

That's why your face looks funny. You don't look like you want to stab someone."

Was that really how she looked in the morning? Grumpy, sure. But stabby?

"I had extra coffee this morning." She went to the sink to wash up, scrubbing her forearms and hands before drying off and reaching for a pair of the disposable gloves they wore when prepping. "But if you keep giving me shit, all the caffeine in the world won't keep me from looking like I want to stab somebody again."

Coffee was not the most likely culprit behind her improved morning mood, but that wasn't information she was ready to unload on her friend. Not yet. What happened between her and Devon the night before still felt too fresh. Too new. Too raw.

And it felt private. Which was weird. She and Mariah had shared plenty about their sexual conquests, but last night wasn't a conquest. And if she thought about it too hard, she'd start to panic over what it actually was.

"Touchy, touchy." Mariah's face split into a wide smile. "That's the Janie I know and love."

Mariah was one of the few people unfazed by her temperament. The younger woman didn't take shit personally. She didn't expect Janie to be something she wasn't. That's part of why Janie moved to Moss Creek when Mariah told her about the job at The Inn. If there was anyone in this world she didn't mind being around, it was Mariah.

As luck would have it, she accidentally crossed paths with Dianna—the owner of The Baking Rack—soon after her arrival, finding another person who took her as she was. They'd had a little bit of a tumultuous start, but once they were over the hump, Dianna moved into the second place spot of people she didn't mind being around.

But now that podium was starting to get a little crowded, and Mariah had a little competition for her first place spot.

"At any rate, I'm glad you didn't come in looking miserable this morning. I know the beginning of your period is always tough for you." Mariah started cracking eggs into a huge stainless-steel bowl. "I'm glad this one isn't hitting you as hard."

Her periods were infamous among the people she knew and worked with. There was no hiding the way they affected her—and ultimately, everyone around her. "Me too. Hopefully last month was just a fluke and things won't go back to the way they used to be."

"I hope so." Mariah shot her a sympathetic look as she continued cracking eggs. "I hated seeing you suffer and not being able to do anything to help."

"There's not much that can be done." She'd tried just about everything over the years. Spent more than a few nights in the ER over the pain and sympathetic reactions from the organs unlucky enough to be in the same area code as her misbehaving uterus. "I'm just glad I haven't had bladder spasms again." They were the final straw that led to the surgery Devon saw evidence of the night before.

Her stomach clenched, belly flipping at the memory

of how he brushed his lips over her scars. Had a man ever been so sweet to her? Had anyone?

No. They hadn't. And part of that was probably her fault. She didn't give off sweet vibes. Just bitter, cynical ones.

"I know you tried just about everything there is, but I read an article the other day about how orgasms are actually great at helping to relieve cramps." Mariah paused. "I know your cramps aren't normal cramps, but every little bit might help."

"Interesting." It was something she'd actually heard before, but the thought of letting anyone near her lower half this time of the month had her vagina sealing itself off. Usually.

Normally she would never attempt to have sex the day before her period was set to start. Everything from her belly button down was gearing up to be a complete bitch, and having some guy cram his dick up in there didn't feel the tiniest bit pleasurable.

But she'd wanted so much to be close to Devon last night. To share something intimate. And thank goodness she had. Because, holy cow. Not only had Devon gone down on her like a champ, but he didn't just think about himself when it came time to actually fuck. He genuinely wanted her to enjoy herself too, and was willing to think outside the box to make it happen.

Technically, he was also thinking inside the box.

And she'd gotten off twice because of it.

Was that why she didn't have a uterus shaped

monster trying to claw its way out of her body this morning? The theory was worth considering.

"Speaking of orgasms." Collecting one of the day-old loaves of bread from the counter, she used a serrated knife to begin cutting it into bite-size pieces for the savory egg casserole Mariah had planned for breakfast. "How are things going with the baby cowboy?"

"Okay, I guess." Mariah dropped a whisk into the bowl of eggs and began stirring them together. "He's been kind of busy this week, so I haven't gotten the chance to talk with him much." There was something off in her tone. An edge that made it seem like there was more to this story.

Janie scowled down at the bread as she sawed through it. "What in the hell does he have to do that's keeping him so busy?"

Mariah shrugged.

"Does he have kids?" Janie's good mood was starting to dissipate. "A house to maintain? Is he taking college classes? Has he started volunteering at a homeless shelter?" All would be reasonable explanations for why a man might not have a ton of spare time. But even then they'd still be excuses. The same kind of excuses she'd accepted for years. "If a man wants to see you, he makes it happen." Devon had all kinds of things eating up his time, and he still found room to see her.

Mariah was silent beside her, jaw tense as she chopped through a pile of mushrooms.

Janie didn't want to upset her friend further, but for the first time in her life, she had useful advice to offer. "If he wanted to, he would." She'd faced down enough men who didn't want to be in her life, and if she could save her friend from the same fate, she would. "If you're important, he'll find a way to spend time with you."

Mariah's next chop is a little more aggressive. "So what you're telling me is, I haven't been important to any of the guys I've ever been with." She hacked through another mushroom cap. "Because if that's true, it would suck a bag of dicks."

She'd had a similar sort of revelation before coming to Moss Creek. With one difference. "I'm sure there were some who wanted to be up your crack." Janie blew out a breath. "But if your luck is anything like mine, they were probably asshats."

Mariah snorted. "Even the asshats don't want to spend time with me, I guess." She swiped the pile of mushrooms into a waiting pan, the sizzling scent of them browning filling the kitchen in just a few seconds. "I just thought that was how men are now. They expected us to chase them."

"You shouldn't have to chase anyone. You are fucking awesome." Janie turned to her friend. "If a man can't see that, he's too stupid to waste your time on anyway."

Mariah gave her a sad smile. "Thanks."

It was a hard lesson to learn, but if she could spare Mariah the years of frustration and broken hearts she'd suffered through, it would be worth the pain she saw in her friend's eyes now. "I'm not trying to shit on your show. I just want you to be with someone who treats you like the fucking queen you are."

Mariah barked out a single, sharp laugh. "Right. I'm pretty sure I'm more like a decently paid Cinderella."

Janie leaned into Mariah's side, giving her a grin. "Don't forget that Cinderella ended up with Prince Charming."

"Who couldn't even remember what she looked like so he had to rely on a freaking shoe to identify her." Mariah shook her head. "I feel like that's worse than a man not making me a priority."

"Good point." Janie went back to cutting chunks of bread. "What was the guy from Snow White's name?"

Mariah lifted a brow. "The one who found a dead chick in a glass casket in the woods and his first thought was to kiss her?"

Janie cringed. "Someone at Disney is really into dead moms and toxic men."

"I wouldn't have any of them." Mariah wiggled her brows, perking up a little. "Maybe The Beast. But only if he stayed a beast."

"He did have a pretty nice library." Janie pursed her lips. "You'd have to overlook an awful lot of kidnapping though."

Maria laughed, still looking a little bummed, but better than she was. "I think I just like grumpy, growly men." She thought for a second. "Maybe that's the problem with this guy. He's not sour enough."

"The problem with this guy is he's too stupid to know a good thing when he sees it." Janie blew out a breath. "To be fair, that's the problem with about ninety-nine percent of the men I've come across."

Mariah turned to her, brows lifted. "Not one hundred percent?"

Janie turned away, going back to her task, hoping Mariah didn't catch the heat creeping across her cheeks. "I figured I'd leave room for error."

She hadn't planned to tell Mariah about what was happening between her and Devon before, but she sure as hell couldn't tell her now. It would be a dick move. Especially since Devon was so different from the asshole ranch hand Mariah should have never fucked with.

Luckily it seemed like Mariah was done with the conversation and she changed the subject. They spent the rest of the morning in idle chat, making breakfast for The Inn's visitors. Once everything was assembled, Janie packed up and headed out, going home to eat a quick lunch before her shift at The Baking Rack.

She was piled up on her sofa, a heating pad on her belly and an ice pack on her back, watching episode three of a crime documentary while a bowlful of leftover spaghetti heated in the microwave. The appliance beeped, signaling the end of the process right as someone knocked on her door.

It took a second to unwind the blanket covering her lap and detangle from the heating pad cord. She was barely halfway across the small room when the door cracked open.

"J?"

Janie smiled, quickly pressing down the expression as she closed the distance to her door, swinging it wide to reveal Devon standing on her porch looking damn delectable in jeans and a thick, plaid flannel layered over a Henley. She lifted a brow at him. "Now you're just coming into my house?"

"I didn't come in." He crossed the threshold, negating his statement. "And do I need to remind you that you have a key to my place?"

"Is that your way of asking for a key to mine?" The question brought an odd feeling to her gut. One that didn't sit right and had nothing to do with the cramps beginning to rev their engines.

The reason behind the uncomfortable twinge had to do with knowing any key she might give him wouldn't be useful long. It didn't sound like she'd be living there much longer since Sharon planned to sell the place out from under her.

And she hadn't told him. If it was simply a thing between her and her landlord, maybe it wouldn't feel as bad, but Devon's connection to Sharon meant the information would affect him.

His girls.

And she was keeping it from him. Just like he'd kept Sharon's identity as his mother-in-law from her.

No. Not just like. If she believed him—and maybe she did—he'd forgotten to bring it up.

She wasn't forgetting.

"It is not." Devon looped one arm around her waist, pulling her close. "It *is* my way of letting you know you can use your key whenever you want."

It was the kind of thing she'd always wanted. A man to invite her into his world. Make her a part of it without prompting or negotiations. She'd chased this for years and now that it was happening, all she wanted was to pretend it wasn't.

"What are you doing here?" Thinking of letting herself into Devon's house for any reason other than the cleaning he'd basically hired her to do made her chest tight, and the last thing she needed was body parts seizing up. "I thought you had to help your dad get his snow blower running?"

When he'd told her he'd be busy today a little part of her was relieved. She needed time to figure out what was going on between them. What was going on inside her. If they were as real as she wanted to think they were.

The conversation with Mariah took her already lifting hopes and sent them soaring. Had her thinking she'd finally found someone different. Someone who wanted her the way she wanted him.

But was that really true? Or was she once again seeing what she wanted to see?

It was what she needed to figure out, but thinking when Devon was around could be damn near impossible.

Like it was now.

He bumped the door shut, keeping her close as he kicked off his work boots. "I wanted to make sure you were feeling okay. See if you needed my magical cramp cure." He dug into one pocket, pulling out a bag of M&Ms. "And I thought you might need some chocolate."

She nearly groaned at the thoughtfulness he brought with him. "You really know the way to a girl's heart."

"Not true." A smile curved his lips as he brushed

them across hers in an almost kiss. "I know the way to *your* heart." His big hands slid to rest against her lower back, their heat sinking through her clothes, warming the ice-chilled skin beneath it. "Hmmm. Feels like you've been implementing part of my cramp cure already."

"I will grudgingly admit the ice and heat combination helps quite a bit." She looped one arm around his neck, letting herself relax into his embrace. "The chocolate won't hurt either."

She wanted this to be real. Wanted Devon to be all he appeared. More than that, she wanted to be who she was when he was around. He made her feel less like a failure. Less like the mess she'd done her best to embrace. Like maybe she was done fucking up. Like maybe she was done ruining everything she touched. Like maybe she was worth his time. Worth his effort.

Worth being loved.

CHAPTER TWENTY
DEVON

DEVON WALKED THROUGH his front door, ready to change clothes and tackle the garage Janie had been on him about clearing out before the weather turned. He'd barely made it off the welcome mat before Riley was there, brows lifted. "Where's Janie?"

He knew his girls liked Janie and expected them to notice she wasn't there for her Sunday cleaning. What he didn't expect was the way his daughter glared at him, arms crossed over her chest, as if he'd done something wrong.

After closing the door, he bent to unlace his boots. "She's at home. Taking a day to relax."

Riley studied him with a wary gaze. "Are you sure that's why she's not here?"

He was very sure that's why she wasn't there. In fact, he was the one who told her to stay home and rest when he stopped by her place that morning on his way into work. Luckily this period hadn't been as bad as the last one—the one that first brought him into her home—but she still looked tired and drained. Cleaning his house was the last thing she needed to be doing when she felt bad.

It was the last thing she needed to be doing regardless. And that was a conversation they'd be having just as soon as he figured out how to negotiate the situation without ruffling her feathers.

"I'm positive that's why she's not here." He wasn't about to tell Riley Janie's personal medical business, so he left it at that, passing his oldest daughter on his way into the kitchen.

She followed, staying right on his heels. "Are you sure you didn't upset her?"

That stopped him short and had him turning to face her. "What are you talking about?"

Riley lifted her chin. "I just want to be sure you didn't do something that hurt her feelings." Her lips pursed, the skin around them turning white from the pressure before she continued. "I know you have a habit of doing that."

That sent his brows climbing his forehead. "I have a habit of doing things that hurt people's feelings?" He shifted on his feet, bringing himself face to face with the young girl who was more adult than he might have given her credit for. "Have I hurt your feelings?"

Riley's expression changed, turning almost sad. "I'm not talking about me." Her voice grew softer. "I'm talking about mom."

That almost sent him stepping back. "About me doing things that hurt your mom?"

She nodded, the movement jerky.

Where was this coming from? Could his daughters have figured out something was going on between Janie and him and mistakenly thought Maggie would be upset over him being with someone else? "What did I do that hurt your mom?"

Riley shifted on her feet, eyes dropping his. "Before she died, I heard her talking on the phone sometimes." She paused, the fingers of one hand picking at the pointer on the other. "About how she wasn't happy. How you didn't even notice."

Shit.

He scrubbed one hand down his face, bringing it to rub the back of his neck as he tried to find the right words for his daughter. "Riley honey, I..." That was it. That was all he had.

"I know mom wanted to divorce you." She blurted out the admission. "I know she didn't love you anymore."

There was little she could have said that would have stunned him more. Except she kept going, breaking his heart as she stole the belief he'd clung to—that his daughters would never know the truth about their parents' marriage. That they would never know their mother lost even more than her life and the chance to see them grow up.

"I couldn't sleep one night. She'd been going to a lot of doctors and I was worried. I got out of bed because I wanted to see her, and I heard her voice in the kitchen." She blinked against the shimmer of tears lining her eyes.

"I didn't make it all the way down the stairs. I stood there listening. I heard everything."

He remembered that night. Well. It had changed not only his future, but also his past.

And now he knew it had done the same for his daughter. Tainted the way she saw her mother. Saw him. Saw them.

Riley sniffed. "And you didn't get mad or anything." A tear slid free. "You didn't try to tell her why she should love you."

"Come here." He pulled her in for a hug, tucking her close so he could rest his chin on top of her head. "You can't tell someone to love you, sweetheart. They either do, or they don't. And your mom hadn't been in love with me for a long time."

"But she should have loved you." Riley's words were edged with anger he'd felt himself. "You took such good care of her when she was sick. Even though you knew she didn't want you anymore."

"Just because your mom didn't love me the way a wife loves a husband, doesn't mean she didn't love me at all." His chest ached at the thought of his daughter carrying this around all these years. Trying to come to terms with something she didn't fully understand. "Your mother was a great mom. She was an amazing person. The way she felt about me doesn't take away from any of that."

Riley wiped at her eyes, sniffing against his chest. "It's hard to separate it all out."

"I know." It was what he'd been struggling with for years. "But she wasn't wrong." He took a deep breath, revealing a truth he was still sorting through. "We were very different people. We'd been together since we were fifteen. After we graduated college, it was just a given we'd get married. Neither of us really thought about whether it was the right decision or not. If we fit together as adults." He'd always thought he was lucky for finding the love of his life so early. For seamlessly moving from being a kid to being a man and a husband and father. It might have been willful blindness, but it worked for him. Right up until Maggie shined a light on all that was missing. "And it turns out we didn't fit so well."

Riley was quiet for a beat, but her next question wasn't about her mother. "What about Janie? Do you fit with her?"

He opened his mouth to tell her it wasn't like that, but Riley deserved the truth. Likely needed it. "Seems like we do."

A slow smile worked across her lips, and her expression brightened for the first time since he'd walked in the door. "We knew it."

Another surprise. "We?"

The smile on her face turned sly as she peeked up at him. "Olivia, Gwen, and I knew you guys liked each other." She wiggled her brows. "And you're welcome for us making sure you got alone time with her whenever she came over."

Devon's jaw went slack as he stared at his sneaky,

meddling, conniving, brilliant daughter. "You know I'm capable of getting a woman on my own, right?"

Riley's face scrunched up. "Are you though?" She lifted her brows, looking around. "Because it looks to me like you might have made Janie think you didn't want to see her tonight."

He'd worried plenty about his daughters and the relationships in their future. Turns out they'd been doing the same thing.

And it looked like they were worried he was going to fuck it all up.

"For your information, I've already seen Janie today." He smirked, giving her a final squeeze before releasing her to turn toward the kitchen. "I went past her place before work."

Riley followed him in, trailing along as he went to the fridge and pulled out the stuff to get dinner started. "Did you bring her flowers?"

He was starting to regret telling her the truth. "I did not bring her flowers at five in the morning, no." He lined the preformed pie crust, carton of eggs, and container of ham onto the counter before washing his hands in the sink. "I did bring her candy on Tuesday when I went to see her." He dried off, slinging the towel over his shoulder before starting to crack eggs into a bowl.

Riley watched him work, her brows pinched together. "What are you doing?"

"Making dinner." He tipped his head to the oven. "Can you set that to three hundred and seventy-five?"

"I see that you're making dinner." Riley punched in

the numbers before returning to his side as he chopped through the ham. "But what in the hell are you making?"

"We're cussing in front of each other now?" He dropped the ham into the bowl with the eggs. "It's quiche. I asked Janie for a few easy meal ideas I could make you meddlers for dinner."

"And quiche was one of her ideas?" Riley snorted. "I guess she did go to culinary school for a while."

"She's done a lot of things." He'd managed to eke a little time out each day to see her, usually at her place, occasionally at The Baking Rack, and was starting to learn more about the life Janie led before coming to Moss Creek.

"She started school to be an accountant when she was my age." Riley fiddled with the discarded ham container. "But realized it wasn't right for her and dropped out."

"That doesn't surprise me." Janie was always on the move. Even when she was at home, her ass didn't sit for long. She was up and turning over laundry. Running the vacuum. Going through her closet to bring her winter clothes to the front and send her warm weather items to the back. No way would she be happy sitting behind a desk all day. "Careers are kind of like relationships. What you want when you're young might not be what you want as you get older. You can keep pushing through and end up with a degree in something you hate, or you can cut your losses and move on."

It was one more thing he liked about Janie. She didn't settle. She didn't keep going down the wrong path just because it was the one she'd picked. Like the different careers she'd started and left behind. Like the twat she ditched in Tukwila.

On the flipside, when Janie wanted something, nothing got in her way. When she enjoyed what she was doing she was a fucking machine. He'd seen her in action at The Baking Rack and attacking the clusterfuck of his house. He had to assume she was the same way with relationships. When she thought it was right, she went all in. Possibly to a fault. One that left her devastated when things didn't work out the way she planned.

That's why he had to be careful. Had to take his time. Work up to where he wanted them to be slowly so he didn't scare her off. Things had gone wrong for her too many times, and at any sort of blip, she would jump to the conclusion that it was wrong once again.

But it wasn't. He was even more sure now that he knew his girls saw the same thing he did.

He'd just finished pouring the egg, cheese, and ham combination into the pie crust and was in the process of sliding it into the oven when the doorbell rang. Riley's excited gaze met his, and he knew who she was expecting on the other side of the door.

If she was right, it meant Janie still wasn't comfortable using her key unless no one else was home, and that dampened his spirits a little.

But, as he made his way down the hall, it wasn't Janie he found in the entryway.

"It's my favorite people." Sharon came in, giving

Riley a long squeeze before coming to offer him the same.

His mother-in-law came into town a few times a year and always went out of her way to spend as much time with his girls as possible, even though he could see how difficult it was for her. Especially with Riley. Riley was the most like Maggie, both in looks and temperament. While he imagined it was great for Sharon to see a piece of her daughter living on, it was likely equally painful.

"I just put dinner in the oven." He tipped his head, hollering up the stairs. "Girls. Nana's here."

Olivia and Gwen hurried down the stairs. They'd been close with Sharon before she moved to Florida, and it was nice to see they still held the same amount of affection for her.

"I'm going to go shower and change real quick." If his daughters heard him, they didn't acknowledge it. They were all focused on Sharon, much like they were when Janie came over.

A realization hit him like a punch to the gut. Their reaction was likely due to the loss of Maggie. When they had a motherly figure around, they soaked it up.

While she hadn't been able to have any children of her own, Janie was certainly motherly. She didn't just have fun with his girls—though they did spend time learning how to do hairstyles, practicing backflips, and watching movies—she made sure they did the things they should. Things he'd slacked on because of guilt and exhaustion.

It felt wrong to give his daughters shit about cleaning

their rooms or taking out the trash after they'd gone through so much, ultimately losing their mom. It was also exhausting to argue and continuously remind. But Janie stepped in to do that without blinking. Seamlessly picking up the ball he'd dropped.

Riley had asked if he and Janie fit, and everywhere he looked he could see how her edges aligned with his.

After jumping in the shower and scrubbing down, he pulled on jeans and a long-sleeved shirt, padding down the steps to find his girls and Sharon in the living room, piled up on the sofas much the way they did with Janie. He gave them a glance on his way to the kitchen. After checking on the quiche, giving it a little shake to test for doneness like Janie had instructed, he pulled a bag of shredded potatoes from the freezer and started heating a pan to fry them up.

"Look at you being all fancy." Sharon sidled up to the counter beside him as he dumped the frozen potatoes into the screaming hot oil. "The girls said you're making quiche?"

"A friend of mine told me it would be a good simple dinner to try." He didn't want to keep what was going on between him and Janie from Sharon, but it didn't feel right to come out and say it either. He knew Sharon wouldn't begrudge him finding happiness, especially since—after talking to Riley—he was suspicious she might have also known what happened between him and Maggie. Even so, Maggie was her daughter, and telling Sharon he'd found someone was like throwing the fact that her daughter was gone in her face.

"That's good." Sharon gave him a smile. "The friend part, not the quiche part." She looked him over. "You could use some friends." Her head tipped to one side as she continued studying him. "You know it's okay to have a social life, right? Those girls are going to grow up and move away. If they're the only people in your life, you're going to be real lonely."

He'd always gotten along with Sharon. She was a good mom. Both to him and Maggie. He appreciated it then, and he appreciated it now. "I know, and I've been working on it."

"Good." Sharon slid one hand across the counter, eyes wandering around the kitchen. "I'm glad you're starting to get back in the swing of things. I worried about you for a while, but it looks like you're getting it all sorted out." Her eyes continued roaming. "The house looks great. The girls are happy." Her eyes came back to his face. "And supposedly you have friends."

"They're not even imaginary." He gave her a wink, turning back to shift around his cooking potatoes.

"That's extra good, because I've got something I need to tell you." Sharon took a deep breath, blowing it back out. "I know I kept the trailer because I thought I'd move back after a few years when it got easier, but I've decided to stay in Florida, so I'll be selling it."

Devon's head snapped her way. "You're selling the trailer?"

Sharon nodded. "It's time. I can't come back here to live full-time. It's too hard."

He understood. He'd honestly never expected Sharon

to move back to Moss Creek, in spite of her claims. He also hadn't expected her to sell the trailer. "But I thought you were making money renting the trailer out."

Sharon shrugged. "I am. But sooner or later I'm going to have to start replacing things, and Janie's not going to live there forever. Who knows what kind of renter I'll end up with when she's gone."

"Do you already have a buyer lined up?"

Moss Creek's housing market was a tough one. Even more so now that Brett Pace and his wife Nora were flipping houses left and right. Even a trailer like Sharon's would be easy to move because the pickings were slim. Moss Creek also wasn't exactly brimming with apartments. Finding a place to rent in town was just as difficult as finding one to buy. If Sharon yanked the rug out from under Janie like that—

"I'm hoping Janie will buy it. I told her what was going on, and she said she needed a few days to think on it." Sharon leaned close, reaching in to pull a chunk of browned hash browns free and popping them into her mouth. "I'm pretty sure she'll buy it. She loves that little place."

Devon stared at Sharon, his stomach bottoming out. Because, while Sharon was right about Janie loving her trailer, she was wrong about the rest. Janie wasn't going to buy it.

Because she couldn't.

CHAPTER TWENTY-ONE
JANIE

THE KNOCK AT her door had her entire body reacting. She might as well be one of Pavlov's dogs at this point, because the sound was now connected with Devon. It had her heart racing and her stomach doing somersaults, anticipation biting at her heels as she rushed across the floor.

She'd come to Moss Creek thinking it would be easy to swear off relationships. And honestly, for a while, it had been. Not anymore. Now she was caught in this giddy, terrifying, aggravating place where a full-on relationship with Devon was all she wanted. But it was also the last thing she needed.

So far, he hadn't distracted her from her goal of paying off all her bills. But how long would that last? Not long considering she practically ran across her trailer to get to the door, flinging it open with a dumbass smile on her face before whispering a breathy, "Hey."

She'd busted her ass to finish up as early as possible

at The Baking Rack so she could get home, take a shower, and be ready for his visit. And it was worth every iota of effort as she basked in the warmth of his smile.

"Hey." He stepped in, leaving his boots by the door before gathering her in his arms, pulling her close and breathing against her skin. "You smell really good."

She giggled.

Fucking.

Giggled.

This idiocy couldn't continue. Unfortunately, she couldn't seem to stop it.

"I got home a little early, so I took a quick shower."

She also might have sprung for an order of scented body wash and lotion. Spent a little extra time shaving her legs and making sure her skin was soft and her hair looked extra good—as good as it could considering the regrowth giving away her age.

"That's pretty impressive. I thought you'd whittled down every second you could off the cinnamon roll making process." Devon straightened, gaze warm as it moved over her face. "I should know better than to doubt you."

Janie toyed with the fabric of his coat. "You really should."

He nuzzled her once more before stepping away, working his coat free before hanging it over the back of one of her two dining chairs. "It's pretty cold out there." He paused, turning to face her, straightening to his full height. "And, while I know this is going to go over real fucking bad, we need to have another conversation about your tires."

The topic used to make her want to scream. It hit her like nails on a fucking chalkboard and had her ready to throw things. Heavy things. Right at Devon Peter's head.

Now?

Now she was a salivating dog. "Fine. We can talk about tires."

Devon's brows lifted, expression skeptical. "Really?"

"Really." Tires were still not at the top of her list of priorities, but he was probably right. They should be a little higher than they were. Especially with the impending snow. "I'm sure it won't surprise you to discover I threw away the name and number of that guy you know."

Devon laughed, the sound low and deep. "Not even a little surprised." He moved closer. "Also irrelevant because we're going to switch keys before I go. I don't want you on the road at four in the morning, going all the way out to the Pace ranch on bald tires in three inches of fresh snow."

Janie forced in a breath. Made herself relax instead of allowing her knee to jerk the way it wanted to. After years of being let down by the people she'd wanted to love her—to take care of her—it'd become easier to reject any and all attempts. Then she wasn't let down. Then she wasn't hurt.

Allowing Devon to do this would be setting herself up for the possibility of being hurt again. But fuck if it wasn't starting to feel good to have someone she could rely on.

So even though it made her want to both throw up and cry a little, she nodded. "Okay."

Devon's brows lifted higher as he stared at her like she'd grown two heads. "Really."

Janie nodded once more, confirming either the best decision she'd ever made or the worst. "Really."

"Well," Devon spoke slowly, "in that case, I'm going to press my luck and say we have something else we need to talk about."

"Oh?" Her stomach dropped, falling straight to her feet. Devon wouldn't want to trade cars if he was about to tell her this wasn't working, would he?

No. She was overreacting. Letting that damn knee get in her way again.

"Sharon told me she was selling this place."

All the air rushed from her lungs. "Oh." She struggled to breath, watching his face for any sign of the anger she knew was there.

Hadn't she just lost her mind on him a few days ago for not telling her his mother-in-law was her landlady? And then she'd turned around and done the same thing, holding back something he should know just because she was afraid to let him too far into her life.

Because of that fucking knee.

"I was going to tell you." The words rushed out. "I just—"

Devon's brows came together. "You don't have to tell

me everything, J. You're an adult. You have a life, and parts of it don't involve me right now."

She didn't miss that qualifier he put on the end. "But she's your mother-in-law, and selling this place cuts all ties she has to Moss Creek. It means she might not come back as often—"

"Sharon was never coming back to live in Moss Creek." Devon moved close, snagging her by the arm and reeling her in. "She was done with Moss Creek the day Maggie died. I knew it. She knew it. My girls knew it."

Janie pressed her lips together, eyes on his face. "You're not mad that I didn't tell you?"

Devon shook his head. "I'm not mad you didn't tell me."

She sat on that a minute before asking, "Is that just so I can feel like an ass for being mad at you over not telling me Sharon was your mother-in-law?"

Devon's lips curved into a small smile. "Maybe a little."

"Ugh." Janie's head dropped back on a groan. "And here I was about to tell you my period's done."

"Done, you say?" Devon pressed against her, moving her toward the bedroom. "I feel like that's information you should have shared the minute I opened the door." He suddenly bent his knees, hooking both hands around her thighs to pull her body up his, legs circling his hips. "I might be mad you didn't tell me about *that* sooner."

Janie held onto his shoulders, eyes on Devon's face as he made his way to her bedroom. "I'm sorry about getting so upset with you over not telling me about Sharon being your mother-in-law." She chewed her lower lip, struggling to make her next admission even though Devon already knew. "Sometimes I jump to the worst-case scenario and occasionally it makes me overreact."

He angled a brow. "You don't say."

This was why she wanted to apologize. She knew Devon wouldn't gloat. Wouldn't revel in her acceptance of fault. That wasn't the kind of man he was.

"I messed up. I'm probably gonna mess up again." She repeated the words he'd given to her before, but the next ones would be different. "It's probably a good thing you know how to deal with it."

She didn't want to think too hard on the fact that dealing with criminals as a cop was what prepared him for dealing with her. Whatever the reason, he had never batted an eye at anything she'd said or done. He'd made it clear that while she could feel a certain way, act a certain way, they would be figuring it out. Because, no matter what, Devon wouldn't run away. He wouldn't back down from her outbursts or that damn knee always trying to get in the middle of everything.

"It is a good thing." Devon flexed, letting out the smallest of grunts a second before her body went flying.

By the time she realized what was going on, her back hit the mattress and she bounced, bringing out a laugh instead of a scream. "Did you really just throw me onto the bed?"

Devon shrugged as he started to crawl over her. "It was easy. You don't have any body fat, remember?"

Janie rolled her eyes. "Whatever." She poked him in the stomach. "I just think you're trying to show off."

Devon's big body settled over hers. "Maybe. Is it working?"

"Meh."

"Meh?" He looked shocked, and not in a completely fake way. "My powers of seduction are better than just *meh*."

Janie groaned. "Your powers of seduction are a little better when you show up in your uniform."

Devon's expression turned serious. Mostly. One corner of his mouth twitched like he was holding back a smile. "The truth finally comes out. It's all about the uniform for you."

Janie laughed. "Right. Because I'm clearly such a fan of authority figures." She hooked her legs around his hips, feet sliding between his thighs. Before he could anticipate it, she latched tight and rolled, taking the controlling position. "I respond so well to being told what to do."

"So what you're saying is, it's actually the dad jeans that do it for you." He ran his hands up her thighs, palming them through the soft fabric of her leggings. "Noted."

She smoothed her hands over his chest and the waffle weave Henley covering it. "I don't hate these shirts either."

"I think you just don't hate me." Devon's palms followed the line of her hips upward, curving around her waist on their way to her ribcage. "You accidentally started to like me."

Gathering the fabric of his shirt, she worked the tail free of his jeans. "It's a little annoying how you wormed your way under my skin."

"Yeah?" Devon's wandering hands hit the band of her bra and his brows pinched together. Without warning, he pushed the hem of her T-shirt up and out of his way, revealing the lacy cups of her front clasp bra. "Well, this is different."

"You seemed to struggle with the sports bra. I figured I'd make it easy on you since you're so out of practice." Making it even easier, she shucked her shirt, tossing it away before going back to Devon's, pushing it up his chest. "Don't want you pulling one of these big muscles trying to get me out of my clothes."

"Is that why you wore these?" He snapped the waistband of her leggings. "Ease of access?"

She went to work on his belt, unfastening the buckle as a smile worked across her face. "Maybe."

"So, all those times you wore leggings to my house..."

She scoffed. "I told you already. It was because they're comfortable to clean in."

"Likely story." He watched as she flipped the button on his waistband loose and dragged down the zipper. "I don't think I believe it."

She spread the fabric of his jeans wide before tugging down the elastic of his boxers to reveal the hard line of his straining cock. It flexed under her attention, a drip of wetness collecting at the tip.

"Fuck, J. You can't lick your lips like that when you look at it." Devon reached for her. "Why don't you take those leggings off and come up here and sit on my face." His voice grew strained at the end and his cock flexed again, like the thought of that scenario genuinely did it for him.

And while she liked the sound of that plan, it would have to wait. "This time it's your turn to just lay there." She hadn't minded Devon taking charge last time, but she wasn't the kind of woman who liked to just take what she was given.

She preferred to be an active participant.

"I don't think so, J." Devon started to sit up, ready to hit the brakes on her control.

Wasn't going to happen. She ran her life, messy or not, and she was never going to let a man—even one like Devon—be completely in charge of any part of it.

So she did the thing that would stop him right in his tracks and leaned down to wrap her lips around the thick head of him, pulling his length deep into the well of her mouth.

As expected, his brain shorted out on a garbled swear, body falling back to the mattress as she swirled her tongue around his leaking tip, lips curving at the heady swell of female power his reaction created.

When she sank over him again, Devon's hand tangled in her hair, fingers fisting at her nape as she hollowed her cheeks and lifted her eyes, watching his face as his eyes locked onto the slow glide of her mouth. His lips parted, pupils dilating as she sank over him again, the flex of his cock against her tongue almost as arousing as the expression on his face. Like it was taking everything he had to—

His hand tightened in her hair, pulling her off him. "That's enough."

She scoffed, wiping at the corner of her mouth. "Already?"

Devon's eyes trailed down her front, pausing on the swell of her tits peeking out of the top of her bra. "Like you said, I'm out of practice." He met her gaze. "Guess we'll just have to keep at it until I get back in the swing of things." He jerked his chin at her lower half. "Why don't you get naked."

Janie lifted a brow. "That sounds dangerously close to an order, Officer Peters."

"All right." Devon lifted up, reaching behind his head to pull his shirt off, back to front. "Why don't you get naked... now."

God he was a pain in the ass. And he did that shit on purpose.

"Ugh." Janie slid off the edge of the bed, shucking her leggings, panties, and bra with a roll of her eyes. "I'm not doing this because you told me to. I'm doing it because I want to get laid."

Devon kicked away his own clothes before stretching back out down the center of her bed. "Reasons don't matter, J. Only results." He lifted one hand, a condom pinched between his first and middle finger. "Don't get lazy on me now. You said all I had to do was lay here, and I'm going to hold you to it."

She snatched away the rubber, still fucking smiling because somehow sex with Devon wasn't just hot, it was also fun. "Watch it. I might have all my fun and then get off the ride." She tore open the foil packet and started rolling the condom into place. "Leave you to fend for yourself."

"We've already established that I'm well-versed in the art of fending for myself." He gripped her hips as she settled over him. "And you never know, you might like watching."

She leaned forward, the thought of one of Devon's big fists working his cock circling through her mind as she aligned their bodies and slowly sank down. "Is that an offer?"

Devon's nostrils flared as he watched her body engulf his. "I'm sure we could work something out." He let out a low groan as she seated herself completely, the backs of her thighs meeting his hips. "Fuck that's good."

"Yeah?" Janie braced both hands on his chest, using it for leverage as she moved, rocking her body onto his.

"Yeah." One of Devon's hands gripped her hip as the other flattened across her lower belly, pressing in just a little on the soft flesh above her pubic bone as his thumb settled over her clit.

The next time she sank down had her pussy clenching as sensation swirled both inside and outside. Her eyes flew open on a gasp to find Devon smirking up at her. "Told you it was good."

She rocked again and again, his dick hitting something inside that had her toes curling and the threat of an impending orgasm barreling toward the finish line. When his palm pressed a little more, she discovered the pressure he put on her belly was creating the star-seeing sensation.

If she hadn't already been dangerously close to falling in love with him, that move would have done the trick. Between his hand and his thumb, there was no stopping her. She barely made it another minute before she started to lose her rhythm, unable to maintain her stride as her pussy clenched.

Devon picked up where she left off, thrusting up into her, sending her flying over the edge, his cock swelling as he came along with her.

When it was over, she collapsed on top of him, breathing heavy, that stupid smile still on her face.

Because Devon was right. They did fit. She could deny it all she wanted. Spend every day waiting for the other shoe to drop, sure it would all fall apart. Or she could embrace it. Embrace him. No pressure. No fear. If things didn't work out, she was the only one who would get hurt, and it's not like she hadn't been through that before.

Devon rolled them to their sides, grabbing the throw she draped across the bottom of the bed and pulling it up over their naked bodies. "By the way," he pulled her closer, sliding one of his legs between hers, "the girls know we're together."

CHAPTER TWENTY-TWO
DEVON

SHARON FLIPPED ON the oven light, bending at the waist to peer through the window at her cooking turkey. "It's looking good." She straightened, wiping her hands on the apron tied at her waist. "What time did you say your parents were going to get here?"

"They'll be here at two." He continued scrubbing through the large pots and pans that didn't fit in the dishwasher. "And I made sure my mom is only bringing her sweet potato casserole." He'd tried to convince her to bring nothing at all, but failed.

"Well that is very nice of her." Sharon grabbed the large bowl she used to mix up the stuffing as he rinsed it and she went to work drying it off. "That's just our generation. We don't feel right showing up somewhere without bringing food."

It wasn't just her generation that felt that way, which is why he hadn't been completely forthcoming with Janie about what was going on this afternoon.

Or who all would be there.

Janie had a tendency to get in her own head and overthink. Knowing she'd be spending the day with not just his parents but also his dead wife's mother would have had her climbing the walls. She wasn't going to be happy, but he'd take her wrath over knowing she'd spent the past few days stressing herself out over this.

But Janie wasn't the only one he'd been holding back on.

Taking a deep breath, he braced for Sharon's reaction. "I invited a friend of mine to join us today."

Sharon continued drying the bowl in her hands. "Oh?" She wasn't looking at him, but her spine barely stiffened and her head tipped his way.

"It's actually someone you know."

He knew Sharon wouldn't fault him for having a relationship. Knew she wouldn't be angry or offended. But she would be sad, and his mother-in-law had already spent so much of her time sad, he hated to add any more minutes to her tally.

After putting the bowl away, she turned to meet his eyes. "Janie?"

Part of him was a little surprised at the accuracy of her guess. She had caught him coming to Janie's place, but the differences between Janie and Maggie were vast enough he thought she might not put it all together.

Offering a nod, he confirmed her suspicions. "Janie."

Sharon took a deep breath, blowing it back out before slowly smiling. "I think she's a good match for you."

Again, he was surprised. "You do?"

She nodded, collecting the next bowl after he rinsed it, working her dish towel around the edge. "I do. She's a good girl and a hard worker who doesn't hold back." Sharon spared him a glance. "And you need that, because sometimes you're not the most observant." Her brows lifted. "Not when it comes to the emotional side of things."

That answered any lingering questions he had about whether or not Sharon knew where he and Maggie stood when she passed. He'd held up his end of their promise to keep the status of their marriage between them. And while he wasn't upset with Maggie for sharing, he really fucking wished he'd been in the loop about how many people knew the truth.

Especially his daughter.

He was, however, a little irked at Sharon for her comment. It was a low blow. *Especially* if she knew what happened between him and her daughter.

And how the whole thing played out.

"No one's perfect, Sharon. You know that." He didn't want to rock the boat today, but keeping feelings inside was what led to the problems of his past. They weren't going to taint his future the same way. "I sure never claimed to be."

To her credit, his mother-in-law looked regretful. "I'm sorry." She lifted her chin on an inhale, a sad smile on her lips. "I just wish Maggie had gotten the chance to find happiness too."

"I know." He wished the same thing. Carried an immense amount of guilt because of it.

Sharon sucked in a deep breath, spine straightening. "As long as she's good to the girls, that's all I care about." A sly smile spread across her lips. "I suppose it will be nice if she's good to you too."

He finished scrubbing down the last bowl and passed it off, changing the subject so his mother-in-law's thoughts didn't linger and put a damper on her day. "What about you? Anyone special in your life?"

Sharon's smile turned devilish. "I don't kiss and tell." She gave him a wink. "But don't worry about me spending my nights lonely."

He tried not to think about how his mother-in-law spent her nights at all. Especially when he was getting ready to eat. "Good to know." He dried off his hands and turned his attention to the other side of the room, just in case she changed her mind about not kissing and telling. "I should get the extra leaves in the table."

He spent the next hour setting up the eating area. Bringing in additional chairs. Lining up place mats and giving the floor a quick sweep. Since she'd stayed home to rest the week before, Janie hadn't cleaned his place in two weeks. He and the girls had done a decent job of maintaining all her hard work, so there wasn't much he had to do to get the house presentable.

Normally he and the girls would be scrambling to shove everything they could into hidden spaces so they wouldn't have to listen to Sharon and his mother give them shit about the state of the house. Thanks to Janie, his home was clean and comfortable and guest-ready.

But he went ahead and ran the vacuum in the living room anyway.

His parents showed up fifteen minutes early and the volume in the place went up substantially as his daughters and their grandmothers clustered the kitchen.

It wasn't only the noise that increased, but also the temperature. After turning down the thermostat, he cracked a couple windows to get a little of the air moving.

The snow from earlier in the week was still on the ground, reflecting the sun, leaving the outside looking bright and cheery. Hopefully it was a good sign. He needed today to go well. Needed Janie to feel welcomed and wanted. Accepted and embraced.

He needed her to see that there was space for her in his life so she would make space for him in hers.

When the bell rang, his stomach tightened. Smoothing down the front of his shirt as he went down the hall, he braced for what was coming. Even simply thinking she was coming to hang out with him and the girls had her a little wound up, so there was no telling how she'd react when she saw the collection of people filling his kitchen.

He opened the front door to find Janie frowning at him from where she stood on the porch. She pursed her lips. "I don't want to do this."

"I know." He reached out to pull her inside. "But it has to happen."

She stood in place as he unbuttoned her coat, eyes

darting between his face and the kitchen doorway. "Maybe we should wait."

"For?" Devon slid the heavy layer down her arms.

Janie's frown deepened. "For me to not feel weird about this."

"The only way for you to get used to it is for you to face it." He hung her coat up in the closet she'd convinced his daughters to clean out. "And you've been around the girls lots of times already. This isn't anything new."

She scoffed. "That was before *I* knew that *they* knew I was fuc—" Her words cut off, eyes widening on the kitchen doorway as a fake smile smacked onto her face. "Your parents are here." She lowered her voice, forced smile still in place. "I'm going to kill you."

"Wait until you find out Sharon's here too." He hooked one arm around her shoulders, pulling her along with him as he went down the hall and into the kitchen where his family was milling around, dishing out food and drink.

Riley was the first to notice her. She deposited her plate onto the counter and raced their way, grabbing Janie in a hug. "You're here. I was worried you might not come." She leaned into Janie's ear, whispering something he couldn't hear before letting her go and giving her an exaggerated wink.

Devon lifted a brow. "What was that about?"

Janie's weird smile was still on her face, like she was afraid to let it go. "Nothing."

His mother turned around, gasping when she saw

Janie at his side. "There you are." She grabbed a plate from the stack and brought it to the woman sticking to him like glue. "Get started filling that up. Can't have you freezing to death this winter." She took Janie by the shoulders, directing her toward the line of food arranged down the counter. "Make sure you get some of that sweet potato casserole. It's my specialty."

"Great." Janie's eyes drifted to where Riley sat at the table.

"Give her some space to breathe." Devon tossed out the reminder his mother would likely need for the foreseeable future. Smothering was her love language and she spoke it fluently. "You've got all night to invade her personal bubble."

"Oh, pshh." His mother waved him off. "She's fine." Even as she argued, his mother backed off, giving him a pointed look as she went to take her place at the table. "Make sure she gets enough to eat. Can't have anyone going hungry."

Janie turned toward the counter, shooting him a scowl from the corner of her eyes. "Why didn't you tell me this was a Thanksgiving thing? I should have brought something."

"I didn't tell you because you cook all week and the last thing you need to do on your day off is make more food." He followed behind her, watching with interest as she skipped right over his mother's casserole. "And I knew there would be plenty here. Sharon loves to cook and she always goes overboard."

"He's not lying." Sharon sidled up to them.

285

"Thanksgiving is my favorite and I always make a big dinner here before I go back to Florida. Then I make one for all my friends down there." She added a scoop of stuffing to a bare spot on her plate. "Don't know how I missed that the first time." She leaned back, practically yelling over one shoulder. "Frank was probably trying to hog it all."

His dad's head popped up, eyes swinging around the kitchen. "What?"

Reaching across the table, his mother patted her husband's hand. "Nothing, dear."

He glanced over to find Janie watching them with a genuine smile on her face. When she noticed him looking, her lips flattened.

"I saw that." He bumped her shoulder with his as she grabbed a roll and added it next to the collection of mashed potatoes, stuffing, turkey, and green bean casserole. "See? It's not bad."

"It's still strange." She glanced back over one shoulder. "They've never seen you with anyone but Maggie." Her eyes found where Sharon sat between Gwen and Olivia. "And it's got to be hard for her."

"She knows life has to go on, J. That's why she's selling the trailer." Devon rested his hand on her lower back, adding a little more pressure when she jumped at the touch. "She's moving forward the best way she can and knows I'll do the same." He leaned into her ear. "Plus, she's probably a little happy to have someone else around who can cook."

Janie's eyes jumped to his.

He grinned. "Riley told you not to eat my mom's casserole, didn't she?"

Janie pressed her lips together, rolling them inward with a little nod.

"If that doesn't prove she likes you, I don't know what does."

His mother had never been a good cook. The worst part was her complete oblivion when it came to her lack of skills. She either didn't have taste buds or they'd all gone numb out of self-preservation.

He led her to their chairs, putting Janie between him and Riley, and resting his forearm on the table to block his mother's view of her plate, just in case. Janie sat silently beside him, taking in the conversations happening around them, looking a little like a deer in the headlights as Sharon talked about her adventures in Florida. They sounded just this side of bullshit.

Also occasionally just this side of legal.

"You dumped chickens into a construction trailer?" Gwen's eyes were wide. "Did they get hurt?"

"Nah." Sharon waved off Gwen's concern. "They got to sit in the air-conditioning for a while. They were fine."

Janie started to choke beside him, likely surprised to discover just how wild her landlady could be. "You okay?" He stood, dragging Janie along with him. "She probably needs some air. It's pretty warm in here." He grabbed Janie's drink before leading her down the hall and out the front door, passing off her glass and waiting while she swallowed it down.

"I probably should have warned you that Sharon

seems normal, but she's actually a little unhinged." He took her glass and set it on the porch before pulling her close, wrapping his arms around her to keep her warm. "And it's only getting worse the longer she's in Florida. I think all those people she lives around are a bad influence on her."

"I don't know. It sounds like she's having a great time." Janie cuddled close to him. "So maybe they're a good influence."

Sharon was having fun, and she deserved it after the hell she went through losing her daughter, but fun had limits. "As long as I don't get a call in the middle of night that she's been arrested."

Janie laughed, the sound loud and hearty. "I'm gonna go ahead and let you know you will never have to worry about that. I'm pretty positive you are *not* Sharon's bail money bitch."

He lifted his brows. "Bail money bitch?"

"Don't act like you're not picking up what I'm putting down. It's pretty self-explanatory." Janie seemed to relax a little as she grinned up at him. "Every girl has one."

"It seems like I might be yours." He leaned in to whisper his lips across hers. "We need to talk about that whole thing too." There was no room for a debt between them. Not now. "I think you've more than held up your end of the bargain."

Janie's brows lowered. "The deal was that I would clean your house for six months."

"If you remember, the deal we made left out a lot of

important information." *He'd* left out a lot of important information. "If you'd known then what you know now, would you have made the same deal?"

Janie snorted. "Hell no."

"That's what I thought." He pulled her a little closer. "Would you be mad at me if I said I'd make the same deal all over again?"

Janie's mouth twisted to one side before working into a slow smile. "Only a little."

Today was about moving forward—bringing Janie deeper into his life—and he had one more place he wanted to bring her. "Well, since I'm the only one who would make it again, then I get to be the one who says when it's over." Janie scoffed, but he kept going. "I still want you to come over on Sundays, but only to spend time with me and the girls." He leaned close, lowering his voice as he added on the last bit he wanted her to think over. "And maybe sometimes you can pack an overnight bag to bring with you."

CHAPTER TWENTY-THREE
JANIE

"WELL IF IT isn't the latest victim of the Moss Creek rumor mill." Dianna grinned at her as she walked in the back door of The Baking Rack. "You are a hot topic around town today, ma'am."

It wasn't an unexpected development. She knew it was only a matter of time before someone said something and her private life suddenly became everyone else's business. "Well that's just fucking great."

The Thanksgiving dinner she'd had at Devon's house the day before had gone well, all things considered. She managed to get away without having to eat any of his mother's sweet potato casserole—which apparently was basically a bland concoction of mashed up sweet potatoes topped with marshmallow fluff that was then baked, turning the fluff into a rock-hard layer of tooth-breaking taffy.

She'd gotten to spend time with his girls. Gwen told her all about the project she had planned for the science fair. Olivia asked for a few pointers on perfecting her back handsprings. She commiserated with Riley over the difficulties of college math courses.

She even got to hear a little more about Sharon's shenanigans. It made her regret not knowing her landlady was off the chain sooner. They probably could've had a lot of fun together. Not now, though. Now things were weird. Because she was dating Sharon's dead daughter's husband. And that changed everything.

"So, is it true?" Dianna spaced the words out, pronouncing each one carefully. "Are you dating Devon Peters?"

Janie tied on one of the aprons lined down the wall, trying to decide how to explain the situation to her friend. "I don't know that I would say *dating*."

The word didn't sit right. Not because it felt too serious, but because it didn't feel serious enough. And that was fucking terrifying. Since coming to Moss Creek, she'd been avoiding having any sort of connection with a man, and without even realizing it, she'd accidentally skipped right over a lot of the relationship steps and...

Fucking fallen in love.

And not just with Devon.

That was one of her more difficult revelations at Thanksgiving. Even harder than accepting her presence would always be a stark reminder of someone else's loss.

"We've been spending time together and getting to know each other." Again, the description felt wrong, but it was as much as she was willing to admit. The only confession she was currently prepared to make.

It was enough for her friend, whose mouth dropped open as her eyes widened. "Holy shit." She continued to stare at Janie, mouth agape. "I told everyone there was no way it was true because you hated his guts."

"I didn't hate him." The denial jumped right out, unbidden and unstoppable.

Had she hated him? At one point the thought of Officer Devon Peters made her blood boil, so maybe. It was difficult to imagine now though. Hating Devon seemed ridiculous. He was the kindest, most generous man she'd ever met. He was a good dad. Responsible and hard-working and really fucking good in bed and...

And she loved him.

Fucking hell.

The bell on the door rang and she jumped at the opportunity to get a little space from the conversation. "I got it." She hurried out of the back room, feet moving so fast her sneakers squeaked against the tile floor as she came to a sudden stop at the sight of the man standing at the counter.

He gave her a slow smile that made her want to pick up the closest heavy object and smack him upside the head with it. "Hello, Janie."

"What in the hell are you doing here?" The question hissed through her lips, low and hinting at the violence she was just considering.

Aiden held both hands out at his sides. "No hello?" He clicked his tongue. "That's not a very nice way to greet someone you used to—"

"If you finish that sentence I swear to God..."

Like the manipulative ass he was, Aiden lifted his brows in feigned surprise. "No need to get upset, Janie. I just wanted to come by and see how you were doing."

She scoffed. "No you didn't. You came here to piss me off." She pointed at the door. "Mission accomplished. Now go home."

"Why would me coming here piss you off?" He made no move to leave. "You managed to pay off that balance you owed Tukwila, so I figured you must be doing great out here in..." He paused, looking through the front windows at the street outside. "Podunk, Montana."

"You breathing pisses me off, Aiden." She moved closer, glaring at a man she actually did hate. "And there's no way you're here because you thought I was doing great."

Aiden's smile slipped. "That's because there is no way you're doing great." He narrowed his eyes. "I'm not sure who you conned into giving you that money, but I'm sure they'll be interested to know a little about your financial situation and how unlikely it is that you'll be paying them back anytime soon."

She laughed. At him. At herself. How had this fucker managed to convince her to date him for almost half a year? "Then I guess it's a good thing I already paid them back." It wasn't Aiden's business who gave her the money or where the debt stood, but she wanted him to leave. Wanted him the hell out of Moss Creek.

"I don't believe that for a second." Aiden's eyes traveled around The Baking Rack. "Not when you're still working basic jobs, driving your basic car, and living in someone else's rented trailer." He leaned closer, gaze icy. "You are still exactly what you'll always be, Janie. A fucking failure who never finishes anything. You've got no career. No family. No money. No friends."

Janie lifted her chin, keeping her expression as neutral as she could manage. "Get out before I call the cops and have you trespassed."

Aiden's slow smile came back. "Still the same bitch you've always been, aren't you?" He straightened away from the counter, rocking his jaw from side to side as he backed toward the door. "I'm glad I came. Glad to see I was right about you. Getting rid of you was the best thing I ever did."

The bell on the door rang, drawing her attention to the entrance and sending her stomach into her shoes.

Aiden had a similar reaction, sidestepping the uniformed man taking up the bulk of the doorway as he darted out onto the sidewalk, likely worried she'd make good on her threat and endanger his precious position of power.

Devon watched Aiden go, one brow angled as the smaller man glanced back over his shoulder, stepping faster and faster until he was out of sight.

Devon turned his questioning brow to her. "Who in the hell was that?"

She opened her mouth, but the truth wouldn't come out. "Some guy who didn't know he needed to be here about four hours ago if he wanted anything good." She forced on a smile and attempted to change the subject. "How are you?"

Devon gave Aiden one more glance, twisting her stomach with fear. What if Devon figured out who he really was and tried to talk to him? Would he listen to all the bullshit Aiden spewed?

Was it really bullshit?

She did have friends, but other than that, he was right. She had no career. No family. No money.

Devon finally turned to face her. "I'm good." He came to lean against the same counter Aiden just tainted. "Glad *I* can come in for a cinnamon roll whenever I want." He gave her a wink. "It pays to have connections."

She kept smiling, the expression starting to ache on her face. "It does." She went to the case holding special orders and the peach cinnamon roll she reserved for Devon knowing they were his favorite. "Want me to warm it up?"

He shook his head. "Nah. I'm going to save it for dessert tonight." He followed her down the counter as she went to pack it up. "You can share it with me." He leaned closer. "That's my way of asking if you want to come over for dinner tonight."

She closed the roll into one of the small-sized bakery boxes that got very little use since most people ordered more than a few things at a time. "What's for dinner?"

"The girls have requested quiche again." He grinned as she passed over the roll. "It was a big hit."

A little of the tightness in her chest eased. "I'm glad." She scrambled to think of something else that might be an easy meal for Devon to put together after work. "Do the girls like enchiladas? I can teach you an

296

easy way to layer all the stuff into a casserole and bake it."

"They love enchiladas." He gripped the box in one hand, resting the other on the case between them. "Maybe you can come over later this week and show me how."

Her shoulders ratcheted down from where they were nearly anchored to her ears. "Perfect."

She wasn't a failure. She might not have skills everyone would find useful, but they were perfect for Devon and his girls. She could show him great things to cook. Olivia's back flips were getting better and better with her pointers and Gwen had the cutest hairstyles around while she curled up with a book in her clean room.

Devon gave the case a pat. "Then I'll see you tonight."

She was still smiling when he walked out of sight. His visit might not have completely negated the fallout from Aiden's, but it sure took the edge off. Hanging out with him and the girls tonight would smooth it the rest of the way over. By tomorrow her ex's appearance would barely be a blip on the screen of her future.

"THERE YOU ARE." Devon reached through the open door, snagging her hand and pulling her inside. "I was starting to wonder."

She laughed, rolling her eyes even though she loved

it. "I am here exactly when you told me to be here." Looping her arms around his neck, she tipped her head back to look up at him. "Actually I'm five minutes early."

Devon tucked his chin, meeting her gaze. "Maybe I thought you'd put that house key I gave you to good use and would be here waiting for me when I got home."

A day ago, she might have blown off the suggestion, but in the hours since Aiden had shown up, she'd had time to really think about everything he said and came to a conclusion.

Fuck him.

Fuck all his stupid assumptions and what he thought he knew. Fuck him saying she would never have a career or money or family.

That's what she was *trying* to conclude. The accuracy of his words still rang a little too true for her liking, but she would feel better after tonight. Better because all the things she'd done in her life were useful to the people around her.

People who might someday be the family he said she'd never have.

Devon's brows pinched together as he looked down at her. "Are you okay?"

Janie nodded, forcing a smile. "I'm fine." She took a deep breath, finally registering the scent of baking pastry and egg. "Smells like quiche in here."

"That's good news, because I'm pretty sure I made quiche." Devon pulled her deeper into the house, tipping his head toward the living room. "Why don't you sit down. I'm gonna run upstairs and jump in the shower. I'll be right back."

"Okay." She wandered into the empty living room, feeling a little strange since she'd never been there by herself before. Not like this. Any alone time she'd had in Devon's house was while she was attacking it with cleaning products and scrub brushes, not making herself at home.

Lowering onto one of the couch cushions, she tried to relax, but struggled to get comfortable.

Maybe she should go see if there was anything that needed to be done. Surely he and the girls hadn't been able to completely keep up with all the cleaning she'd done. Then that would be one more thing she offered them. One more reason Aiden was wrong.

Going into the kitchen, she discovered some granola bars and a few other snacks hadn't made it into the cabinets, so she went to work organizing everything, condensing and breaking down extra boxes. She was scrubbing the kitchen sink when the door to the garage opened and Riley came in, a wide smile on her face. It wasn't usually how she looked on Mondays. Normally, by the time she got home from school on Monday, she was exhausted from spending the whole day on campus.

Janie set down her scrub brush and started to rinse away the layer of soap she'd worked into every nook and cranny. "Looks like you had a good day."

Riley slung her bag onto the table, letting out a long sigh as her smile widened even more. "I did."

Janie finished rinsing away the soap and wormed the

sprayer back into its slot. "That's fantastic. Sounds like you're getting into your groove with school."

"Actually, I quit."

Janie turned from where she was drying the edges of the stainless steel basin, sure she wasn't understanding what Riley was trying to tell her. "Quit, what?" Stressing? Waiting until the last minute to work on assignments? Putting pressure on herself to be perfect?

Riley's eyes were bright as she rocked up on her toes. "School. I dropped out. I went to my counselor today and told her I was done. That I didn't want to do it anymore."

Janie opened her mouth, then clamped it shut again. After taking a few more seconds to let her brain wrap itself around everything, she asked, "Why would you do that?"

Riley came toward her, continuing to beam. "Because of you." She grabbed Janie's hands, gripping them tight. "I don't want to spend my life doing something that will make me miserable. I want to figure out what's going to make me happy, just like you did."

"You quit because of me?" The words were nearly impossible to push through her lips.

Because of what they meant. What she'd caused.

She could pretend everything she'd done all worked out in the end, but now that it was Riley starting down that same path? Now she had to face the truth.

Her life had amounted to a whole lot of nothing. And it all started when she dropped out of college. She quit one thing after another. Maybe because she knew it drove her mother nuts because she had nothing to brag about. Maybe she was just too picky. Or—more likely—maybe she thought she couldn't fail if she didn't finish. Failing had always been the worst thing she could do, and not completing anything was a way around the humiliation.

Only it wasn't. Not really.

Riley gripped her in a tight hug, not noticing Janie's stiff posture as she continued cutting deeper and deeper. "Without you, I would have gone all the way through school and spent the rest of my life sitting behind a desk." She released her, stepping back to grab her bag. "You saved me." She practically skipped out of the kitchen, leaving Janie standing alone, all her pretend hopes and imaginary dreams crashing down around her.

"J?" Devon's voice was hesitant. "You good?"

She sucked in a breath, knowing what she had to do. Hopefully it wasn't too late.

Turning to Devon, eyes on his chin because she couldn't meet his gaze, she forced out the words she had to say. The words that would make sure he didn't chase her or ask her to come back. "I can't do this." She swallowed, trying to smooth over the wobble of her chin. "I don't want to be with you. It's not working for me." The second she finished cutting into his old wound, she pushed past him, practically running for the door, kicking herself for always taking her shoes off.

"J." Devon was right behind her, voice getting sharper and louder each time he called for her, so all she could do was grab her coat and boots, not pausing to put either on as she flung open the door and rushed out into the cold. The snow soaked into her socks as she ran to her car, refusing to look back as Devon continued calling her name.

There could be no looking back. No second guessing.

Once again her heart was broken. Once again it was time to move on.

And once again, it was all her fault.

"HEY, MAMA." DEVON crouched down to scratch the black cat, who now resided in his barn, behind one ear. "How are you doing today?"

She meowed up at him, leaning into his touch, purr loud as it rattled around her chest.

"Sounds like you're doing good." He smoothed down her spine before standing. "Glad one of us is."

It'd been almost three weeks since Janie walked out of his kitchen and out of his life. He thought at some point the ache in his chest would begin to ease, but so far every day it only got worse.

He was fucking miserable. Back to only having his horses to talk to. At least now he also had a collection of barn cats to round out his friend group.

"It'll get better. It has to." He continued talking to the black cat as he grabbed her food bin and popped the lid open. "I guess I should just be glad she told me she didn't want to be with me right out of the gate instead of powering through for years."

He wanted to be glad. Wanted to be happy Janie would be able to go find someone she did want, but it turned out she may have been right from the beginning. He might actually be an asshole, because his brain simply couldn't come to terms with the possibility that some other man could make her happier than he could. He couldn't accept she would be better off without him.

She'd been happy with him. He knew it. He thought he did.

He thought he could take Janie at face value. That she said exactly how she was feeling, would put it all out there when something was wrong. But obviously that wasn't true. No one decided they were done with a relationship in the blink of an eye. Once again, he'd been blind. Missed the signs that had to have been there. And this time, he was actually looking.

He finished filling the cat dishes, giving a couple of the less feral kittens some attention before moving on to the horses.

Taking care of them was both a blessing and a curse, just like it had always been. Only now, instead of simply reminding him of the good times he genuinely shared with Maggie, they also carried memories of the good times he shared with Janie. And those were what had him dangerously close to calling up Brody Pace to see if they had room on their ranch for Winston and Winnie.

The first week hadn't been so bad. The horses had been a welcome distraction. Something to eat up all the spare minutes he used to share with her. Now they just made him think of her. The way she was so excited to get close to them that first night. The sight of her clinging to Winnifred's side when she tried to get in the saddle.

The kiss they shared down by the creek.

He raked one hand through his hair before scrubbing his palm over his face. "Fuck."

The sound of the barn door sliding open sent the cats scattering. He dropped his hand, straightening at the sight of his oldest daughter. "You're home."

"I'm home." Riley gave him a small smile. "And you just dropped the F-bomb."

"I forgot to pick up more horse feed." The lie slid right out, just like so many others had over the past few weeks. "I didn't get the chance to talk with you last night. How was your first week of school?"

Riley's smile widened. "Great." The joy on her face was evident as she scooped up one of the kittens. "I think we get to start practicing cutting in a couple weeks."

"Fantastic." He rounded the corner to collect a bucket of pellets for Winston. "I'm glad you're enjoying it."

"I love it." Riley watched as he went into Winston's stall, her smile slipping. "Where's Janie been?" She tucked the kitten in her arms against her chest. "Honestly."

He'd given his girls excuse after excuse, thinking maybe Janie would change her mind. That she'd simply run away the same way she did the night by the creek. Or the way she tried to when she discovered Sharon was his mother-in-law. And that once she took a breath and remembered what they had, she'd be back.

No such luck.

He also hadn't wanted to burden his daughters, especially this one, with his own misery. She'd carried the weight of knowledge that should never have been hers for too long already. "I told you. She's been busy with work."

Riley stared him down as the silence stretched between them. Finally she lifted her chin. "Fine. I guess I'll just go down to The Baking Rack and ask her myself." She started to put the kitten down, giving him no choice but to fess up.

"It just didn't work out, sweetheart." And he still wasn't completely sure why. Didn't know what had sent her racing from his house that night. What revelation pushed her over the edge.

And that in itself was a sign.

"I think she's looking for something else, and honestly so am I." He wanted—needed— someone transparent. "I want someone who isn't going to walk away without telling me why. Not someone who comes at me out of left field with—" He stopped short, pressing his lips together to stop himself from unloading on his teenage daughter.

Riley lifted her brows. "You really have no idea why she didn't want to be with you anymore?"

"I'm not discussing this with you." He turned back to the horses, filling Winnie's bucket with feed before taking it into her stall.

"So your plan is to just stay out here in the barn

forever?" Riley barked out a laugh. "Because I'm pretty sure no one out here is going to offer you decent advice."

"And you are?" He wasn't trying to be an ass, but his daughter was barely an adult. She had no idea how complicated things could get.

"I'm sure as hell a better option than a horse with no balls and a herd of feral cats." Riley lifted her chin, staring him down. "Did you *ask* Janie why she didn't want to be with you?"

Clenching his jaw, he turned away to get hay.

"You're kidding, right?" Riley followed him. "You didn't even ask what upset her?"

"I shouldn't have to beg for someone to tell me how they're feeling." There was bitterness in his words. Bitterness in his soul. "And I shouldn't be blamed when they don't."

Riley's expression softened. "I'm not blaming you, but you can't expect Janie to spew her feelings at you twenty-four hours a day so you don't have to put any effort into understanding how she feels."

"I put in effort. I probably understood her better than anyone." He fought to keep his tone from sharpening. "But I'm not going to try to make someone be with me. I've been with a woman who didn't want me once. If she doesn't want me, then that's fine."

"Do you really think that?" Riley's voice was soft. "That she doesn't want you?" She tipped her head. "And do you really think Janie would walk away from all of us without saying goodbye to Olivia, Gwen, and me?"

"No." He straightened. "But as we both know I've been wrong about things like this before."

He took a deep breath. This conversation needed to end. Shouldn't have happened in the first place. Riley was a kid. She didn't need to deal with his shit.

"It is what it is, Ri. One minute she was all smiles and then she walked out before the fucking quiche was even out of the oven." He knew this would be rough on his daughters. That's part of the reason he'd avoided telling them the full truth. "And honestly, we don't need someone who can do that in our lives."

Riley's lips pursed, moving from side to side, a sad expression on her face. "But I liked having her in our lives." She blinked a few times. "Without her I never would have quit college." She huffed out a little laugh. "I would still be crying over math every night." Her next breath was shaky. "I didn't even get to tell her I enrolled in cosmetology school." The line of her lips lifted into a small smile. "At least I was able to thank her for being the one who made me realize I didn't want to get a stupid accounting degree."

That made him pause. "You told Janie you dropped out of school?"

Riley nodded. "That night you said she had an emergency at..." Her shoulders slumped. "That was a lie, wasn't it? That was the night she walked out."

He ignored her question, stepping closer. "That's the same night you told her you dropped out?"

"Yeah." Riley's brow creased. "Why?"

A combination of dread and hope swirled in his gut. "And you told her she was the reason you did it?"

Riley nodded. "She was. Janie didn't stay where she was miserable just because she was worried what other people would think and it made me see that's all I was doing. Forcing myself to do something I hated because I didn't want someone else to think I was a quitter."

Devon wiped one hand over his face, lifting his eyes to the rafters. "I'm a fucking asshole."

He'd been so blinded by his own hangups and fears. So wrapped up in what he wanted and his own past pain. Instead of doing what Riley was doing now—trying to figure out what went wrong—he got in his own way. Let old wounds infect new flesh.

"I didn't trust myself to know what was real and what wasn't." He'd been wrong before and it only made sense that he'd be wrong again.

And he had been. He'd gone and been as fucking wrong as it could get. The way Janie felt for him was very real. Just as real as the way she felt for his girls. That's why she was willing to walk away from something so good.

Something so right.

"We should go talk to her." Riley was already turning toward the door. "She's still at The Baking Rack, right?"

Devon checked his watch. "She should be there another half hour." He practically ran out of the barn and around the treeline, needing to get to her as fast as he could so he could try to explain.

Try to apologize.

Try to make her understand she was exactly the kind of person who should be influencing his daughters, regardless of what she thought.

"*Olivia. Gwen.*" Riley's voice echoed through the house as he fished his keys from their hook. "We've gotta go."

"What?" Gwen poked her head around the corner of the upstairs hall. "Where are we going?"

"To get Janie." Riley was at his side. She smiled wide. "Dad's gonna propose to her."

His head snapped toward his oldest daughter. "What?"

Gwen asked the same question at the same time. "*What?*"

Riley's brows pinched. "You weren't going to?"

"I don't have a ring." He patted his pockets like one would magically appear.

"That's not a no." Riley gave him a grin.

It wasn't, was it. "And I'm not sure you girls should go. Janie can be kind of—"

"Reactive?" Riley lifted her brows. "It's not great that you acknowledge that but still let her run out of here without asking any questions, you know that right?"

He stared at her for a second, a little taken aback. "Are you lecturing me?"

She snorted. "Someone needs to." Her retort felt so familiar. So close to the many that were slung his way by the curly headed woman he couldn't live without.

He started to laugh, head tipping back. How in the hell could Janie think she was anything but the best kind of influence on his girls? "Fair enough." He turned to the stairs. "You girls are staying here."

Good influence or not, this was between him and Janie. If she wanted to scream at him, he didn't want her holding back because his daughters were playing peanut gallery.

As he reached for the door, his three daughters arguing his decision behind him, the doorbell rang. Maybe—

"This place is a tundra." Sharon strode in, shaking icy flakes off her heavy coat. "It's not even Christmas and there's already a foot of snow on the ground."

"I was just about to walk out the door." He was itching to get on the road and his mother-in-law's unexpected visit—

His brow creased. "What are you doing back in town?"

She turned to him, face a mask of confusion. "Well to put the trailer on the market, of course." She smoothed down her brown bob, giving him a wink. "I can't say I wasn't hoping Janie would buy the place off me, but I guess I won't be too sour since she makes you so happy." Her eyes traveled around the main floor. "Where is she? Did you two get everything moved out or should I wait another day to have the realtor come over?"

He stared at her a beat as what she was saying sank in. And once it did, his heart stopped. "I've got to go." He turned and raced out the door without looking back, hoping to catch Janie before she did something stupid.

Like leave Moss Creek.

He needed to fix what he'd fucked up. Needed to prove he was better than he used to be. Because it was never just Maggie's fault that things went the way they did. In all the years they were together he'd never pushed her to open up to him. Never dug in his heels when he thought things were off. If she said she was fine, he believed her. Even when all the signs pointed a different direction.

Just like he did with Janie. And with Janie he hadn't just believed she was telling him the full scope of her feelings. He expected it. Thought it would keep him from making the same mistake he'd made before.

Wrong.

Falling into his truck, he turned over the engine and set the wiper blades on high, slinging the morning snowfall away as he backed out of the driveway, kicking himself for not finishing the task of clearing out the garage like Janie told him he should.

It would be the first thing he did once all this was straightened out.

No. That was wrong.

It would be the second thing he did.

The first thing he was going to do was buy a fucking ring.

CHAPTER TWENTY-FIVE
JANIE

"ARE YOU REALLY sure you want to do this?" Mariah sat next to her on the floor of the bedroom, helping pack the clothes from her dresser into a moving box. "I know Moss Creek is small, but it's not that small. You've been able to avoid him for almost three weeks. I bet you could avoid him forever if you really wanted to."

She didn't want to avoid Devon. Quite the opposite actually. It was a concentrated effort on her part not to run right back to him. To bury her face in his chest and take a deep inhale of that damn scent she'd never been able to fully identify.

But it would be a mistake.

Not for her—Devon was the best thing that had ever happened to her. It would be a mistake for him. For his daughters.

"I have to go." She folded up a stack of the long-sleeved T-shirts she used to wear at The Baking Rack. "It'll be easier." She forced on a smile so her friend wouldn't worry. "And I'll be able to pay my shit off in record time."

Mariah frowned, looking even more worried than she did before. "You don't think it's a little suspicious that they're paying that much for a private chef?" She wrinkled her nose. "I've never seen anyone offer that much."

"Different parts of the country have different pay scales." Janie repeated the same explanation she'd offered Dianna when she brought up the shockingly high salary. "Things are way more expensive in some places. Food. Gas. Housing—"

"That's another thing." Mariah wasn't helping pack at all now. She was just back to trying to talk her out of this move. "Are you sure you want to commit to living on-site? These people could be serial killers. Or worse." Her eyes widened. "They might not take their shoes off at the door."

"If they can afford a private chef, I'm sure they also spring for a housekeeper." She finished adding the shirts to the box Mariah was supposed to be working on and stood, folding in the top flaps before writing across one corner with the Sharpie in her pocket. "And if not, then I'll just Bird Box my way around the place." She could survive a year. That's all it would take to pay off everything she owed. The school loans. The credit cards. The medical bills.

It was the same goal she came to Moss Creek to achieve. Shocker—she'd failed. At least this time it was for a good reason.

One she would never regret.

Mariah's sour expression lingered. "I don't like this. At all."

Janie scooted closer to her friend, wrapping one arm around the younger woman's shoulders. "I can't stay here. You know that."

Mariah was the only person who came close to knowing the full story of what happened. She'd told her friend just enough for Mariah to understand her decision to find a new job in a new state, but kept a lot of what went on between her and Devon close. Something she could hold close now that she'd lost the heart and soul she'd clung to for so long.

Things might not have gone the way she wanted, but that didn't mean she hadn't finally found what she was looking for. She had. And then she'd learned the hard way that you can never really escape your mistakes. No matter how hard you try.

And she'd made a shit ton of them.

But loving Devon—and his daughters—with her whole heart and soul would never be one of them.

Neither would leaving them.

"Ugh." Mariah's head fell back. "I hate this." She sniffed. "Who am I gonna talk to in the mornings?" She rolled her face Janie's way. "And don't say Maryann. That woman has the best 'I'm disappointed in you' face, and if she knew half the shit I did, she'd never stop giving it to me."

She squeezed Mariah tighter. "You are under thirty with a career, great tits, and you've never been arrested."

She rested her head against Mariah's. "You are fucking killing it." She straightened, crouching down to collect the box. "And what does she expect? You're a single, childless woman. You should be out having the time of your life."

A shadow of something flickered across Mariah's face before being replaced by a smile. "Who am I going to have the time of my life with now that you're not going to be here to be my wingwoman?" She let out another groan as she stood, lifting one of the flattened boxes off the stack. "I'm going to end up the new babysitter for the Bridge Bitches, aren't I?"

"I think you're in the clear. I heard Gertrude talking about how sweet Evelyn Haynes' new assistant was the other day when she came into The Baking Rack to pick up a cake." The smile the memory brought on slipped when she remembered that would be the last bit of gossip she heard here.

"I kinda feel bad for her. She probably has no idea what she's getting into." Mariah expanded the box and started sticking packing tape along the seams. "Not bad enough to drive the old birds around myself, though."

"How long do you think it will be before they get her in trouble with the PD?" Another stab of sadness cut into her gut, but she'd done it to herself. Bringing up the Moss Creek PD sent her brain jumping straight to the officer who was almost hers.

To be fair, just about everything sent her brain jumping to the officer who was almost hers.

Cinnamon rolls. Aprons. Horses. Henleys. Period cramps. The list was never-ending.

And inescapable.

"I give her two weeks before she ends up in one of the cruisers." Mariah's eyes squinted as she considered. "Front seat though. They'll feel too bad to put her in the back." Her face split into a grin. "That's where they'll put Gertrude and the rest of the girls."

Right on time, her brain settled onto the day Devon was waiting for her behind The Baking Rack. Not to lecture her on tire wear or brake lights, but—thanks to Aiden the asshole—to take her in.

Her throat got tight and tears bit at her eyes. She couldn't start crying. If she did, she'd never stop. "I'm going to carry this out to the truck."

Leaving Mariah in the bedroom she'd never sleep in again, Janie cut through the trailer, stepping into her boots but leaving them unlaced, the large box balanced in her hands as she stepped out into the frigid air. Closing her eyes and tipping her head toward the sky, she pulled in a deep breath, willing the surge of emotion to get its shit together. There was no time for breakdowns. No time for broken hearts. No time for—

"You shouldn't leave that door open. Your heating bill will be astronomical."

Her head snapped down, eyes flying open to fix on where Devon stood at the base of the stairs leading to her porch. "What are you doing here?"

"Right now?" He took the first step. "Lecturing you on the importance of proper home care and the effects it can have on your energy usage." He took another step. "Later, I'm thinking I'll drive that truck to my place and unload everything inside it into my house. Where it belongs."

She swallowed hard, struggling to keep herself upright. A moment like this had been both her dream and her nightmare. "I don't belong there, Devon." She said it with as much conviction as she could muster up, hoping it was enough to send him away before she lost the last bit of self-sacrifice she was clinging to.

"I know you think that." He kept coming closer, taking the box in her arms and setting it onto the wood planks before stealing the last bit of distance between them. "But you're wrong, J. You absolutely belong there."

Sucking in a breath, she blinked hard, fighting the tears that had been trying to break free for weeks. "No." She shook her head. "I don't want to be with you." The lie was just as sour today as it was the last time she said it. Hurt just as much coming out.

But this time, Devon didn't flinch when she said it. He actually smiled, the corners of his eyes crinkling as he stared down at her. "That's why you belong there, J. With me. With my girls." He smoothed his hands down her arms, rubbing away the cold sinking into her cotton shirt. "I know what happened. I know why you left."

She swallowed hard, keeping her mouth shut because she didn't trust herself to keep saying what she needed to say.

"And I want to ask you something?" His hands rested on her shoulders, eyes pinning her in place. "Do you really think I would ever want one of my daughters to keep doing something that made them miserable?"

It was easy to see where he was going with this and she had to shut it down before he talked her into believing him. "I'm not the kind of person your daughters should be listening to. I'm—"

"You are exactly the type of person I want my daughters to listen to." His hands slid up her neck to curve around her face. "You are hardworking and independent and determined and you fight for what you want." His lips quirked. "Usually."

"But Riley—"

"But Riley pumped the brakes on something she knew was wrong because someone she respected and cared for gave her the courage to do it." His eyes fixed on hers as he leaned down. "And now she's in hair school and if she hates that, I'll tell her to quit that too. Life's too short to be somewhere you don't want to be, J." His thumbs moved over her cheeks. "No one knows that better than me." He tipped his head toward the small moving truck she'd rented. "That's why that truck is coming to my house instead of wherever you thought you were taking it. Because the only place you should be is with me."

"I'm a mess, Devon. Your girls—"

"My girls will be lucky to have someone who is willing to sacrifice so much for them." His eyes moved over her face. "And I don't give a shit if they go through five hundred different careers and a million different jobs. As long as they're happy." He dropped his forehead to hers. "And I want the same thing for you, J. So if you can tell me, honestly, that you won't be happy with me, then I'll leave and you can go on whatever little adventure you had planned." He lifted his head, gaze intense. "It's up to you." His hands dropped from her face and she nearly stumbled at the loss. He backed toward the steps. "If I don't see you again, good luck. I hope you find what you're looking for."

She watched as he turned and went to his truck, backing away, leaving her to face everything he dropped at her feet.

"What's taking so lo—" Mariah came out the still open front door as Devon drove out of sight, her eyes widening. "Was that..."

Janie nodded because she couldn't do much else. She couldn't speak. She couldn't blink. She could barely breathe.

"Did he come here to ask you to stay?" Mariah asked the question carefully.

Janie nodded again.

"Wow." Mariah blew out a breath. "I did not have 'Devon shows up at the eleventh hour' on my BINGO card." She looked from the moving truck to the trailer to where Janie still stood frozen in place. "What are you going to do?"

That was a very good question. One she was not prepared to answer. "I'm going to finish packing." Crouching down, she hefted up the box Devon took, carrying it down the steps he was just on, flinching a little when his scent hung in the air.

Once the box was in place, she marched back inside, putting all her attention on the task at hand. She was moving. She had a new job in a new place all lined up. The pay was excellent. So were the benefits.

And if she didn't go she would be quitting before she even started. A new record. Even for her.

Since most of her stuff was already packed, it only took another hour for her and Mariah to load everything into the truck. When it was done and her friend was gone, Janie stood at the front door, giving her little home one last look. "Bye, house."

It was never this hard to move on. She was well-versed in leaving things behind. Hell. She'd practically made a career out of it.

Guess she had one after all.

After locking up the door, she slipped the key into the lock box Sharon's realtor had secured over the knob. She turned to face the box truck and the trailer hauling her car behind it, hooked up and ready to carry her straight into her new life.

Taking a deep breath and straightening her shoulders, she lifted her chin, ready to tackle what was in front of her. "Here goes nothing."

CHAPTER TWENTY-SIX
DEVON

WALKING INTO A silent house did nothing for the anxiety making him restless and edgy. Leaving Janie standing there on her porch was one of the hardest things he'd ever done. All he wanted was to bring her home. Bring her back where she belonged.

But it had to be her choice. He could show her the truth, but he'd meant it when he told Riley he wouldn't convince a woman to be with him. No matter how much he wanted to.

Pulling out his phone, he paced down the hall as he swiped across the screen, finding the text from Sharon letting him know she was taking the girls to a movie so he could have a little time to himself.

He didn't know whether to thank her or throttle her. If Janie had run into his arms the way he was hoping she would, having the house to themselves would have been perfect. But she hadn't jumped like he'd wanted, and it left him with too much silence. Too much room to doubt what he was trying so hard to believe would happen.

She had to pick him. Had to. She just needed to see herself the way he did.

The way his girls did.

But expecting someone to change their whole way of thinking after so many years was a big ask.

"Fuck." Raking one hand through his hair he went for the garage, choosing not to get caught up in that way of thinking.

He was going to clean out the garage. So she would have room for anything that didn't fit in the house. So she would have somewhere to park.

Swinging the door open, he stared down the half organized pile of shit he'd abandoned when Janie walked out of his life. He went straight for the biggest items, hanging bicycles from ceiling hooks screwed into the rafters, lining tools onto the bank of steel shelving running along the back wall. Folding up tarps and stacking unused bags of potting soil left from a school project Gwen did comparing GMO and non-GMO seeds.

He stopped every half hour to check his watch and his phone, jaw clenching tighter and tighter as more and more time passed.

She wasn't coming. She was going to listen to all the dumbfucks in her past who told her she was a failure. That she was wrong for refusing to stay where she didn't want to be.

All the motivation seeped out of his veins, replaced by a bone-deep exhaustion he'd probably feel for a long time. Pushing the last of the debris scattered across the floor to the edge of the space, he leaned the wooden handle of the broom against the unfinished drywall. Just as he flipped off the lights, a car pulled up on the other side of the door, engine shutting off.

Sharon and the girls were back. And now he had to explain to his daughters that Janie was gone.

He would never tell them her reasons for leaving. That would be another secret he kept, and this time there was no one else to leak the truth.

Closing the door, he walked through the kitchen, dread building in his gut as they unlocked the front door. He reached it just as it opened, girding his loins for the upset that was coming.

But it wasn't his daughters staring at him with wide eyes.

Janie licked her lips, shifting on her feet. "Hey." She cleared her throat. "I hope it's okay that I used the key you gave me."

He'd all but given up on seeing her here, and having her on his porch had stunned him into silence. Rendered him unable to string words together. All he could do was stare, a little worried he was hallucinating. That one of the gas cans in the garage was leaking and the fumes shorted out his brain.

She took a shaky breath, turning toward the driveway to motion at where the box truck was parked. "I just pulled in. I can try to back it—"

Her words cut off on a little yelp as he grabbed her by the front of her coat and dragged her inside, pulling her tight to him as he pulled in deep breaths against her hair, letting the rich, deep scent fill his lungs the same way it would soon fill his house.

"You scared the shit out of me, J." His hold on her tightened. "I thought you weren't coming."

Her arms slowly came to circle his back. After a few beats, she finally started to relax against him. "I tried to talk myself out of it." She tipped her head back, eyes lifting to his. "Your girls—"

He sealed his lips over hers to shut her up. Keeping one arm around her waist, the other came to the side of her face, fingers sliding into the dark curls of her hair as he dropped his forehead to hers. "My girls are lucky as hell to have you in their lives." He kissed her again, needing the contact. The feel of her skin on his. "And they know it." He met her searching gaze. "They love you, J." He didn't pause. There was no need. "I love you." Stroking the pad of his thumb across her lower lip, he pulled in another breath, trying to settle the unrest he'd been living with for weeks. "I'm sorry I didn't figure out what happened sooner."

She gave him a small smile. "You're not a mind reader."

"No, but I should have thought shit through instead of getting hung up on my own shit." He kissed her again. "I can't expect you to spell it out for me all the time."

Janie's brows lifted. "Are you sure?" Her eyes drifted to the still open front door. "Because it looks like you're going to heat the outside." Her gaze dropped to his feet. "And you're wearing your barn boots in the house."

He smiled, the expression real and genuine for the first time in weeks. "I did clean out the garage, if that changes anything."

"It does change things a little." Her smile matched his as both arms lifted to drape around his neck. She took a deep breath, her eyes widening. "Bergamot!"

He waited a minute, expecting her to explain, but she just continued grinning up at him. "What?"

Janie shook her head. "Nothing. Never mind."

He chuckled, shaking his head. "We can circle back to that later." Keeping her against him, he leaned to close the door then pulled her along as he moved toward the stairs. "Would you like a tour of your new home?"

She laughed, the sound light and easy as it filled his house. "I've been here before, nerd."

"But you haven't been upstairs." She'd had plenty to keep her busy on the bottom two floors, and she'd managed to get his girls to handle their own rooms, so there hadn't been a reason for her to explore the top floor. "Full disclosure, I'm primarily interested in showing you one room in particular."

One dark brow angled. "I bet I can guess which one." Her eyes drifted down his body. "And I think I'd like a very thorough tour."

She didn't have to tell him twice. In the blink of an eye, he had her up over his shoulder, ready to make up for all the time they'd lost.

But his boot had barely hit the first step when the front door banged open and loud voices filled the entry, firing off three questions simultaneously.

"What's that truck in the driveway?"

"What's for dinner?"

"Why's Janie over your shoulder?"

He stopped in his tracks, looking around for a reason to explain the last one. "Uhh."

"He's practicing for work." Janie wiggled around, letting out a little grunt as he put her down. Once she was on her feet, she turned to face the girls. "It's a requirement that he has to be able to carry an adult up a flight of stairs." Her expression was deadpan. "For safety purposes."

"Ohhh." His two younger daughters seemed to buy the explanation.

Riley and Sharon, not so much.

"I thought that was a fireman thing?" Riley crossed her arms, one brow angling.

"Nope." Janie didn't miss a beat as she matched Riley's crossed arm stance. "Cops too."

They stared at each other for a second. Then his daughter launched herself at Janie, nearly knocking them both to the floor in the process.

In quick succession his other two daughters joined in, pinning Janie into the middle of their group for a few silent seconds. Then, as usual, they all started to talk at once.

"I started hair school and I freaking love it."

"They bumped me up to the varsity basketball cheer team."

"I scored a twenty-four on my practice ACT."

Janie leaned back, her eyes wide as they bounced

around the girls surrounding her. "No shit?"

They all nodded.

"Well," she took a deep breath, "I was offered a crap ton of money for a job in a different state." She glanced at him. "But then I remembered I never taught your dad how to make layered enchiladas, so I decided to pass on it."

"So you're staying?" Riley's question was soft. Hesitant.

Janie nodded, reaching out to stroke down his daughter's hair. "I'm staying."

"Here with us?" Olivia rocked up on her toes, eyes bright. "Is that your moving truck in the driveway?"

Janie nodded again, though this one was a little slower. "If that's okay." She glanced Devon's way. "If you girls don't want—"

"We do." Gwen leaned closer, dropping her voice like he wouldn't still be able to hear her. "Our dad is kind of a downer when you're not around."

"Downer, huh?" She lifted her brows, turning his way. "I guess I'll have to stay then."

He wasn't naive enough to think this was how it would always be. That his daughters would never have moments where they were frustrated or even mad at the woman beside him. But right now, this moment, was fucking perfect. For Janie. It was what she needed more than anything. To know these girls loved her with their whole hearts. That no matter what, they wanted— needed—her around.

Even if they blamed it on him.

He clapped his hands. "Since everyone is so excited that Janie's staying with us, then I'm sure everyone will be happy to help get her truck unloaded."

His girls went quiet.

"That's what I thought." He crossed to the door where Sharon was lingering. She caught him as he passed, his daughters back to chatting excitedly with Janie about all she'd missed.

Her hand gripped his, holding tight. A sad smile curved her lips. "I'm happy for you, Devon. You deserve someone who loves the hell out of you."

His chest tightened as he struggled to find words that might ease Sharon's pain.

There weren't any.

No matter what, her daughter would never have the chance to find someone she could love the hell out of. She would never have the chance to watch her girls grow up.

But hopefully, wherever she was, Mags would be happy to know the woman picking up where she had to leave off would make sure her daughters were loved and appreciated. Understood and encouraged. That they never settled.

And never stayed anywhere but exactly where they wanted to be.

EPILOGUE
JANIE

"ARE YOU SURE you're okay with this?" Riley asked for the tenth time.

"I'm positive." Janie adjusted the towel at her neck. "It can't be any worse than the box color I've been using for the past year and a half."

Riley took a deep breath, squaring her shoulders. "Okay."

She was barely halfway through the first of the four sections she'd parted her curly hair into when her cell phone started to ring.

"You can get it." Janie grinned. "I won't dock your tip."

Riley hesitated for a second before grabbing her cell from the table with her ungloved hand, swiping across the screen to answer the call. Her eyes widened a second later. "I totally forgot. I'm so sorry." She chewed her lower lip, looking a little panicked. "Let me see what I can do."

Janie didn't wait for her to hang up before waving one hand at the door. "Go. I can handle this."

Riley shifted from foot to foot. "But I promised I would color your hair."

"And you did." Janie pointed at the right side of her head. "This whole part of it." She took the brush from Riley's gloved hand. "Go. Have fun with your friends."

Riley's worried expression lingered, but a smile slid into place. "Thank you." She leaned down to give Janie a tight squeeze. "You're the best."

"That's what I tell your dad all the time." Janie tipped her head to the door. "I'll let him know you agree with me."

Riley nodded. "You should." She ran to grab her keys, coat, and shoes, carrying them along as she raced back through the kitchen for the door leading to the garage. "Thanks again, J."

"Be careful and have fun." She waved as Riley ducked out the door, then turned to the bowlful of mixed color, picking it up just as Devon came down the stairs, fresh from the shower after a day of keeping Moss Creek in line.

"Where'd Riley go?"

"It sounded like she might have forgotten she made plans with her friends tonight." Janie pointed at her head with the pick end of the brush. "I'm gonna go put the rest of this on. I'll be back."

Devon's eyes skimmed her head then landed on the bowl. "You need help?"

She lifted her brows at him. "You want to play hairdresser?"

"I mean," he snagged away the bowl, "role play might be a little fun."

Her head tipped on a laugh. "You are such a nerd."

"And you picked me, so what does that say about you?" He reached for the brush, taking it and dropping it into the bowl.

"So many things." Janie went back to the kitchen chair and lowered into the seat, crossing her legs and tucking her feet into the seat. "But it's nothing that hasn't been said a million times before."

"Who said them?" Devon took his spot behind her, setting the bowl onto the towel Riley spread across the table's surface. "I'll hunt them down and make them regret it."

She wasn't going to name any names. He hadn't reacted well when he found out Aiden was part of the catalyst that led to her walking out of his life three months ago. "Right. Because it's such a good idea for cops to turn into vigilantes." She tipped her head back to look up at him. "How about you focus on your new profession and make my gray hair regret its appearance in my life."

Devon leaned down to brush one of his whispers of a kiss across her lips. He barely pulled back, mouth hovering over hers. "I could do both."

Janie leaned up to press a firmer kiss to his upside-down face. "You don't have enough time to do both, Peters. We have a game to be at in two hours."

"Shit." He checked his watch. "That's right." Straightening, he looked over the task in front of him. "What's the plan of attack here?"

Janie explained how to work in rows down each section, painting color on both the front and back side of each slice, then he went to work. The man wasn't fast by any means, but he was thorough.

Not surprising. That was kind of his MO.

Once her regrowth was well-coated, she straightened, wincing a little with the movement.

And Devon didn't miss it.

His brows pinched together in concern. "Are they getting bad?"

She shrugged. "Meh."

The non-answer earned her a frown. "Have you taken anything?"

"Everything except whiskey." She shot him a mock scowl. "But last time I did that I never heard the end of it."

Devon's frown deepened. "Last time you did that, a strange man had to take you home and make sure you didn't die in your sleep."

"At least you admit you're strange." Janie turned for the front living room. "I'm going to go vacuum while this cooks."

"No fucking way." Devon hooked an arm around her waist, pinning her to his side as he pulled open the freezer to fish out an ice pack. "You're going to relax so those cramps don't get any worse." He pressed against her, urging her down the hall. "You know what happens when you try to push through."

"Are you lecturing me, Peters?" She tipped her head back, careful not to drag color across the shoulder of his Henley. "Because I don't like being lectured."

"If you didn't like being lectured you wouldn't have agreed to marry me." They reached the couch and he pointed to the cushions. "Sit. I'm going to get the heating pad from our room."

She sighed, rolling her eyes even though he was right. Deep down she loved this. Loved his lectures. His forced care.

Actually, it probably wasn't down that deep anymore. Her love of Devon's dad ways was pretty much right at the surface.

He was back less than a minute later, plugging in the pad before holding it up, one brow lifted in question. "Front or back?"

They'd discovered rotating the heat and ice actually helped more than just delegating one an official position. It must have kept her rage-filled nerve endings confused, because the past few months her cramps had been remarkably manageable. Still a complete bitch to deal with, but they weren't debilitating like they'd been in the past.

"Front." Janie leaned forward so he could tuck the wide ice pack at her lower back, then straightened, resting the heating pad on her front. Letting out a sigh, she relaxed knowing relief was on its way.

"Better?" Devon settled beside her, one wide palm

coming to rest on the heating pad, the steady pressure helping the warmth sink in faster.

"I hope so." She pursed her lips. "I don't really want to sit on bleachers miserable."

"You can stay home." Devon used his free hand to collect the throw from the end of the couch, releasing her stomach just long enough to spread it over her lower half before putting his palm back in place. "Olivia will understand."

"No freaking way." She forced her muscles not to tense. "This is the last game of the season. I'm not missing it."

Olivia had worked so hard. She would never let the teenager think she was anything but ridiculously proud of her.

Devon studied her face. "I'm assuming that means you won't consider taking the day off tomorrow either?" He checked the temperature of the pad, cranking it up a degree. "No matter how you're feeling?"

"Life doesn't stop for cramps." She almost let her head fall back against the couch, but caught herself at the last minute. "And with Mariah gone, Maryann Pace is in panic mode. She would have a heart attack if I couldn't come in."

"Maryann Pace would get over it." Devon carefully moved a piece of hair back from her face. "Have you heard from Mariah?"

She nodded, emotion clogging her throat. It made her feel awful about when she almost left. Now she knew how Mariah felt.

And it sucked.

"She said it's not at all what she expected." Janie had tried to get more information out of her friend, but Mariah was being oddly closed-lipped about the whole thing.

Which was weird considering she ended up taking the job Janie backed out of.

"I'm sure she's just really busy." Devon reassured her the way he had countless times before. "I bet she'll get it all figured out soon and you'll get all the gossip."

Janie blew out a breath. "I hope so."

Devon's phone went off, the alarm signaling the end of her processing time.

Janie pushed up with a groan, being careful not to flex too much or move too fast. "I'll be back."

She made her way to the second floor and the small bathroom off the bedroom she shared with Devon. Instead of trying to hang her head over the side of the tub, she decided to take a full shower, hoping the heat would knock out any lingering muscle cramps trying to ruin her night.

Once her hair was washed and conditioned and her body was scrubbed clean, she dried off and went to pick an outfit. Going through her jeans, she frowned at the options, dreading the way they would pinch her bloated stomach. Leggings would be comfortable, but not super cute, and she wanted to look a little cool since she'd be spending the evening surrounded by teenagers.

Then an idea came to her and she grabbed a slouchy sweater, a pair of loafers, and a belt.

Ten minutes later, she was dressed, hair slicked with curl cream, and a coat of mascara on her eyes. She checked the clock, then hustled down the stairs, shoes hooked over her fingers.

Gwen was there waiting, ready to go. She gave Janie an up and down look. "You look really cute."

"Thanks." Janie grinned as Devon came in, wiggling her brows at him. "Dad jeans for the win, I guess."

Made in United States
Troutdale, OR
07/07/2025